Novel Crimes

Fact and Fiction Lines Blur in Four Stories of Aspiring Mystery Writers

SUSAN K. DOWNS
PAMELA GRIFFIN
DIANN HUNT
SUSAN MAY WARREN

BARBOUR
PUBLISHING

Published by Barbour Publishing, Inc., P.O. Box 719, Uhrichsville, Ohio 44683,
www.barbourbooks.com

> *Our mission is to publish and distribute inspirational products offering
> exceptional value and biblical encouragement to the masses.*

 Member of the
Evangelical Christian
Publishers Association

Printed in the United States of America.
5 4 3 2

INTRODUCTION

Love's Pros and Cons by Susan K. Downs

Tina Frank envisions Miguel when she tries to picture a real-life model for her mystery's hero. Just one glance at her Hispanic neighbor, with his sultry looks, adventurous job, and thundering motorcycle sends chills tingling through her. But when a drug-related murder occurs in their quiet community and an undercover federal agent moves in across the street, Tina suspects her neighbor's link to a life of crime may go beyond fictitious imaginings. Is she flirting with danger by befriending Miguel Villarreal?

Suspect of My Heart by Pamela Griffin

Raine E. Wells has no problem sketching a group of suspicious characters for her mystery-writing exercise, but on her return to her hometown, she's shocked to encounter them in the flesh. Mysterious incidents make her think that one—or more—of her five acquaintances is after her newly inherited art collection. As much as she hates to admit it, the prime suspect is her new friend Lance. Is he simply a kind maintenance man with a strong love of art—or is he a thief with hidden motives?

Love's Greatest Peril by Susan May Warren

Justine Proof is certain she is being stalked. Mysterious "accidents" have her looking over her shoulder and jumping at shadows. Everyone seems suspect, including handsome Patrick Bells, local coffee shop owner. What Justine doesn't know is that Patrick is indeed on her tail—hoping to keep her from making the worst mistake of her life. But Patrick isn't the only one after her. Can her "hero shadow" save her from her greatest peril?

'Til Death Do Us Part by Diann Hunt

With every chapter of her mystery that author Cassie Jordan writes, her life takes another frightening twist or turn. Her fictional sleuth finds dried bridal bouquets in the grasp of several murder victims weeks before this same scenario begins to occur in real life. Only the handsome bookstore owner, Ethan Hamil, knows about this detail of Cassie's mystery novella. Will Ethan prove to be Cassie's gumshoe hero as they work together to complete this maze of suspense? Or is Cassie falling hard for a prime murder suspect?

Novel Crimes

Prologue

And So the Mysteries Begin...

N ow, there's a terrorist if I ever saw one!" exclaimed a male voice coming from behind Drake Axelrod.

Drake craned his neck in search of the subject of the conversation taking place in the next booth. The padded seat back Drake shared with the unseen speaker wobbled as the man punctuated his words with a snort of laughter.

"If you ask me, when they start searching for weapons on the likes of her, they've taken this passenger-screening business one step too far."

Drake looked past the coffee shop's glassless window into the security area that portaled the terminal. An airport security screener was running his detection wand over the soles of a well-worn pair of black boots. Drake thought he could even detect a faint earthy odor wafting his way. A woman, dressed in the monochrome garb of a conservative Mennonite with a doily perched atop her tightly braided bun, sat beside the uniformed guard. The way she rubbed her stockinged feet together hinted at her embarrassment over her podiatric nakedness. She held what appeared to be a blanket-wrapped baby in her lap.

Looks like the perfect disguise for a murderer to me. Drake pulled out his bifocals and a Pocket PC from his sports coat. At the top of the miniature screen, he scribbled "Mennonite Assassin" with a stylus pen. *She's ideal for my next villain.* Underneath the heading, he scrawled a string of adjectives. He wanted to jot down every detail of this rogue in spiritual camouflage before security finished their search and sent her on her way down the concourse.

"Yoo-hoo! Mr. Axelrod!"

He froze, his stylus in midstroke, and turned in his seat to track the voice that paged him. Four women sat at a nearby table in the center of the restaurant. Carry-on bags littered the floor around their feet. Immediately, Drake recognized the diverse female quartet as his students from the mystery writer's workshop he'd just finished teaching.

A casual observer might assume the chummy foursome had been fast friends for life. But Drake knew otherwise. He had watched their relationship develop from strangers to acquaintances to writer-compadres over the course of the six-day writer's conference that had brought them together—each woman so different from the other, yet bound by a common love of writing and a determination to hone their skills.

"Can you join us?" The group's lone blond cranked her hand in small circles as though reeling him toward them. If memory served him correctly, her name was Justine. Justine Proof. And her pearly white smile, classy persona, and fashion-plate wardrobe oozed a confidence that suited well her broadcast journalist "day job."

He glanced at his watch before he nodded his response, working hard to swallow a grin. While he removed his bifocals, then returned his stylus to its leather sheath and the electronic notepad to his pocket, he repeated the mantra he'd rehearsed all week: *Don't make a fool of yourself. You're thirty years their senior. Aloof. Stay aloof.* Although he was a widower and technically an eligible bachelor, none of these single young women would ever consider a crusty old wordsmith as a candidate for romance.

Drake plunked down a fistful of change from his pocket sufficient to cover his coffee and a tip. Then, telescoping the handle on his roller bag to its full height, he weaseled through the maze of empty tables and chairs toward the women. They had already scooted their seats closer together and wedged a fifth chair up to their circular table.

"Well, if it isn't the Sleuth Sisters!" All four women smiled at his salutation. He'd dubbed them with the moniker earlier in the week. "It's an unexpected pleasure to see you all one last time." He took his seat, leaving his roller bag within arm's reach.

The serious and, of late, unemployed Raine E. Wells stopped pumping the straw through the lid of her disposable cup. She shook her sleek, dark hair away from her face in one quick tic. "Can we get you a cup of coffee? Oh, are you hungry?" Her forehead crinkled when she paused. Concern shadowed her tortoiseshell eyes. "Can we order you something to eat?"

Drake shook his head before she even finished her offer. "No, no," he said. "Thank you, but no. I really don't have much time before I need to head to my gate. I just couldn't pass up one last chance to visit with my star pupils and favorite gumshoe protégées."

Admiration oozed from their responding glances. His ears

rang with the heady rush of their hero worship. He hated to go home and leave behind this aura of high regard. No one in New York seemed too impressed with his publishing credits or mystery-writing skill, but these novice writers made him feel like Tom Clancy, Jerry Jenkins, and Sir Arthur Conan Doyle rolled into one. He would miss their adulation.

"Professor Axelrod, do you have any parting advice before we head our separate ways?" The question came from Tina Frank, the pixie-sized woman whom her colleagues called by the less-than-creative nickname of "Tiny." Drake watched as she raked her fingers through her spiky, short-cropped tomato red hair. Although longer on top, the style reminded him of the butch cut he wore during the early '60s.

This pint-sized dynamo from Ohio made him recall the days of his youth for more reasons than one. He watched her give a habitual tug to the gaudy earring that dangled from her left ear. With her free hand, she strummed her manicured nails across the dust jacket of the how-to book that bore Drake Axelrod's name.

"If you'll take the time to work through the exercises that accompany each chapter of my book, you'll be well on your way to success. I poured the sum total of my mystery-writing knowledge into that one little volume." He nodded to the hardback, which Tiny Tina continued to drum.

Cassie Jordan reached out and stilled Tiny's hand. "What I've learned from you this week was well worth the cost of the entire conference, Sir."

The compliment left him uneasy and at a loss for words. Of the foursome, Drake felt the strongest affinity for Cassie. Maybe the connection came from the fact that she shared his deceased wife's love for all things purple. Every day she showed up for class attired in a variation of the same color scheme. Even her notebook paper had a lavender hue. The pen she'd handed him to autograph a book for her had been a fluorescent grape shade. The turtleneck she wore now reminded him of eggplant and left him craving Italian food.

"You're too kind, Miss Jordan." Drake held her gaze before a wash of embarrassment forced him to look away. "Believe me, I'm honored to think I might play even a small part in aiding writers with such potential as the four of you show. The future of inspirational fiction is in great hands." He chuckled to himself when he caught an exchange of shrugs and smiles between Raine and Tina.

"While I don't have much to add by way of instruction, I might offer a word of caution and then put forth a challenge to you gals."

In unison, the four leaned toward him. He found their anticipation contagious. He, too, inched forward in his seat.

"First, the caution." Drake paused. "When you write in the mystery genre, you delve into the dark side. . .the underbelly of humanity." He couldn't hold back a sigh. This quartet of novice authors seemed so sweet and innocent. He wondered if they had a clue what they were getting themselves into.

"We talked a lot about the nuts and bolts of mystery writing this week, but we spoke little of the spiritual challenges particular to this genre." Drake allowed his gaze to linger on each of the four. He studied their solemn expressions as he spoke. "I've learned from our interaction that you are all women of faith. Don't allow the evil and darkness you write about to invade your spirit. Remind yourself of this when you feel tempted to despair—even though evil is pervasive, as it says in 1 John 4:4 (KJV), 'Greater is he that is in you, than he that is in the world.'" He fell silent to let the full effect of his words take hold.

"There's another verse of Scripture I keep posted over my computer on a sticky note. From Romans 12:21, I believe. It says, 'Do not be overcome by evil, but overcome evil with good.' Ladies, I expect to see a lot of good coming from you as far as your writing is concerned." Drake brought himself up straight and took a deep breath.

"Which brings me to my note of challenge." The air crackled with the Sleuth Sisters' palpable suspense. He resisted the urge to string them along, taking them down some rabbit trail, as he would if he were plotting a story.

"I wanted to propose this at the conference but never found an appropriate opportunity to pull you aside. I've seen the esprit de corps of your team. You are all talented and compatible in your writing styles, yet through the samples of your work, I could tell each of you possesses a unique and distinct voice. I think you ought to join forces and write a mystery novella collection. The road to publication is hard, but I believe you all stand a good chance of success."

He smiled at the sudden glow on their faces and Tiny's audible surprise.

"What a great idea!" Justine said. Tiny and Raine echoed her sentiment as Drake looked down at his watch.

"Ladies, I've let the time get away from me. I've got to run if I'm going to catch my plane." He pushed back from the table and stood. "I'll leave you Sleuth Sisters to discuss my proposal, but I expect an invitation to your first book-signing event one day soon." He retrieved his luggage and took his leave amid a chorus of thank-yous and good-byes. Then, as Drake Axelrod made his way down the concourse, the whodunit author scanned the sea of travelers in search of a murder suspect in Mennonite garb. . . .

Love's Pros and Cons

by Susan K. Downs

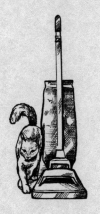

Dedication

To David, the tall, dark, and handsome hero
who swept me off my feet.

The Makings of a Great Mystery
by Drake Axelrod

Chapter One
The Battle Between Good and Evil

Rule: Thou shalt make your villains believable and your heroes unstoppable.

Exercise: Create a realistic villain and list the motivations that drive him/her to their unscrupulous ways. Dream up a corresponding superhero and describe what makes him/her tick.

Chapter 1

Somewhere in the skies over Middle America, Tina Frank looked evil square in the face.

She couldn't fathom how this snarling carcass across the aisle slipped by her unnoticed. Some mystery writer she was going to be, when she failed to see until now the epitome of wickedness in seat 13D.

Tina looked away before Mr. Creepy could lock her in a death stare, but she copped another peek from the corner of her eye. The glance confirmed he was, indeed, real and not just a figment of her overactive imagination. No mistake about it, the steel-eyed, hairy mass of tattooed flesh with a concrete scowl was a living, breathing thing—although Tina couldn't say for sure he was human.

She caught the strap of her canvas book bag with the toe of her shoe. Then, taking great pains not to make any sudden moves that might call the hulk's attention to her, she eased the bag out from under her seat and filched her notebook and pen. She figured she ought to take notes, although she felt confident his terrifying image would be forever emblazoned in her memory. He presented her with the perfect prototype she needed for a three-dimensional antagonist in the mystery novella she planned to write.

She thumbed past those pages already filled with descriptions of villains and heroes. When inclement weather over northeastern Ohio delayed her return flight home from the writer's conference, she appeared to be the only passenger in the gate area who didn't grumble and moan over the three-hour wait. In fact, she relished the chance to stay in civilization a little longer to conduct further research. She used the time to make note of the facial features, attire, and body language of the intriguing characters who crossed her path in the airport terminal. Once she returned home to Canal Pass, her available options for role models of all but "good ol' boys" dropped to a slim few.

Her thoughts wandered toward home, and she began to tap the armrest's metal plate with her ink pen. She wondered if her neighbor, Miguel, had gotten her postcard yet. . .if he'd had to clean up any of Mr. Poe's hairballs. . .if he remembered to set out her trash for collection on Friday. . . .

Tina's reverie shattered when a toddler dashed down the aisle, his mother hot on his tail. The little guy bumped Tina's elbow as he passed and knocked her pen out of her hand. It landed at the foot of the beast on her right.

Tina gulped. Ever so slowly, she allowed her gaze to travel from the guy's size-sixteen boot to his face.

The lines of his meaty chops crinkled as he broke into a smile. "Here, let me get that for you." With an oomph, he bent and retrieved her ballpoint and offered it to her.

"Thank you," Tina squeaked. The gentle giant smiled again, nodded, and looked away.

She stared at the vile description she'd jotted down of the man in 13D. *Shame on you.* She felt her cheeks flame. She'd always taken pride in her ability to find something good in everyone. She made an effort never to jump to conclusions based on looks alone. Yet here she sat, deeming a man evil because of his girth and misfortune in the looks' department.

Drake Axelrod's workshop must have affected her more than she thought. If writing mysteries meant she had to take a jaundiced view of the world, maybe this genre wasn't right for her. She slid her pen into the notebook's spiral binding and returned the items to her book bag.

Tina figured she was getting home none too soon. She needed a good dose of Canal Pass's salt-of-the-earth folks. The other three members of her newly formed writer's group, the Sleuth Sisters, teased her about being so naive, but she wasn't ready to give up the trait that came from living a sheltered life in the suburbs. Unlocked doors and open windows appealed to her too much. If she wanted the rat race, she could have moved to Florida last year with her folks. Small-town, Ohio, might be dull and predictable, but she never needed to fear coming face-to-face with real wickedness. She preferred her adventures come from the tales she concocted rather than from life experience. In Canal Pass, the only foul play to which she risked falling prey sprang from her overactive imagination. Such an arrangement suited her just fine—if she could rein in this recent bent toward vilifying innocent strangers.

To heap coals of fire on her already burning guilt, when they prepared to disembark the plane, Mr. 13D first helped her retrieve her jacket from the overhead bin, then he insisted that she step ahead of him into the aisle. She muttered another round of thank-yous before falling into line behind a woman in the plain dress of a Mennonite, who held a sleeping baby in her arms.

Once inside the terminal, Tina stepped out of the flow of arriving passengers. She slid her book bag off her shoulder and rifled through it for her cell phone. The handlers needed a few minutes to unload the luggage and transport it to the baggage claim area. She might as well make good use of the time. She hadn't checked her messages all day. Tina finally found the miniature device and flipped it open. The phone emitted a series of beeps and clicks as it powered up and searched for a signal.

"You have seven new messages," a computerized female voice announced.

Tina flinched. Who. . . ? What. . . ? She tried not to let her fearful thoughts run ahead of the voice-mail playback, but she hadn't received this many calls the whole time she'd been gone. She relaxed a bit when the first message began and she recognized the voice of Widow Grigsby, Tina's longtime tenant in one of the duplex properties on Maple Street.

"Miz Frank," she warbled, "this is Ruth Grigsby over to your place at 254 Maple."

The elderly woman had lived in the same Frank Family Properties rental since her husband died some two decades ago and left her with no more to live on than a Social Security pension. She called every week to request another "urgent" household repair. Tina hardly needed to be told the widow's name or address.

"Yesterday, I tried to call Lenny like you told me to before you left town, but I couldn't get no answer. My bathroom sink's started in a drippin' and the racket kept me up half the night. When you get home, can you send him over straight away? I know you always say he can hear me, even though he can't talk back, but I'm just not so sure—"

Tina knew the senior citizen would twitter on for another ten minutes, so she hit the "3" key and fast-forwarded to the next message. She could only imagine where her maintenance man, Lenny Sanders, had disappeared to this time or into what kind of mess he'd gotten himself tangled.

In message number two, Tina could hear someone breathing into the phone before the caller hung up. She shrugged it off as a misdialed number, then erased it and moved on to the next.

"Hey, Mi Pequeña—" Tina broke into an instant smile at the sound of Miguel Villarreal's Tex-Mex drawl. His voice reminded Tina of warm praline syrup, smooth and rich and sweet. He'd jokingly dubbed her with the Spanish nickname for "my little one" on the day he moved in next door. He was the first person of Mexican descent she'd ever met face-to-face, and she thought she would impress him by greeting him in his native tongue. She'd bombarded him with the full extent of her high school Spanish 101 vocabulary, only to learn his command of English put hers to shame.

"I just got a call from flight operations. One of the Canton steel plant bigwigs needs to make a quick trip to Houston, and our other pilot is en route from California, so I'm pegged to make the flight. I know you're due to land in fifteen minutes or so, but just in case something happens and you don't make it home tonight, I left Mr. Poe with enough food and water to last him a couple of days. If my plans go according to schedule, I should be home early the day after tomorrow, so don't worry yourself over ol' Sophie or bother bringing in my mail. Again, I'm really sorry to be running out on you like this. I can't wait to hear all about your conference. . . ."

Regardless of what he said, the two of them had a reciprocal agreement, and Tina still planned to check on Miguel's tabby cat, Sophie. Whenever one of them had to leave town, the other looked after the absent party's household necessities such as feeding the cat, taking out the trash, watering the plants, and carrying in the mail.

The fact that Miguel traveled for a living and was gone as often as he was home didn't bother Tina in the least. She felt blessed to have someone as kind and considerate as Miguel Villarreal living next door, even if he refused to let down his guard and talk about himself or his past. His tall, dark, and oh-so-handsome looks didn't bother Tina one iota either.

Her Hispanic neighbor brought a refreshing contrast to an otherwise graying community. He was also one of a select few new residents under the age of forty to move into town rather than away. Most of the younger generation left Canal Pass for college or a job in the city, never to return. Miguel said he saw enough of the big cities through his work, and he preferred to come home to the slower pace of a small town.

"Oh, say, Mi Pequeña, listen."

Tina jerked her attention back to Miguel's recorded message.

"If I leave now, I might have time to swing by the commercial passenger terminal and say hi before I head out. Look for me at baggage claim. If we don't connect, I'll give you a ring when I get home."

Tina hiked her book bag onto her shoulder and prepared to dash down the concourse to baggage claim. She stopped short when she realized Miguel had placed the call hours earlier, just before her flight was originally scheduled to land.

He would be long gone by now.

She breathed out a deflated sigh and forwarded to her next voice-mail message. Another hang-up. Tina replayed the recording two more times and listened closely for any background noises or voices that might provide clues as to who the caller might be. She heard nothing, no one.

Caller number five left no doubt as to his identity. At the booming voice of Canal Pass's local sheriff, Tina yanked the phone away from her ear.

"Tina? Jed Yocum."

Yocum the Yokel Cop, all the high schoolers called him behind his back. If the truth be told, most of the other townsfolk did too. They just bandied the term about with a bit more discretion.

"I'm afraid we've got ourselves what you might call a situation here," the sheriff bellowed with foghorn intensity. "I need to speak with you when you get back to town. If you'll give me a call soon as you pull in, I'll swing by your place. Number's 9-1-1. Better yet, since you're already out and about, why don't you just drop by the station and save me makin' the trip?"

A groan percolated up from Tina's chest. For Sheriff Yocum to track her down and call her on her cell phone could only mean one thing. Lenny had fallen off the wagon again and landed himself in the drunk tank.

She had first hired Lenny almost two years ago as an act

of Christian charity. She felt sorry for the disabled Vietnam veteran who had been rendered mute when hit in the throat by shrapnel. Tina's pity waned quickly, however, in light of Lenny's lackadaisical work habits and mysterious midday disappearances.

If her suspicions were confirmed and Lenny was the reason behind Sheriff Yocum's call, this time Tina refused to post his bail. She'd counted on Lenny to help her out. She'd trusted him to keep things running smoothly at her rental properties while she was gone. He'd obviously let her down. Again.

She mashed the buttons on her phone to take her to the next message

"Miss Frank, my name is Hal Princeton, and my company is temporarily relocating me to Canal Pass. I'm interested in a short-term lease on one of your properties. Let's see, I know I wrote that address down somewhere. . . ." The stranger's bass voice trailed, and Tina could hear the shuffling of papers. "Ah, here it is. Yes. Eight-Six-One Towpath Road."

Tina repeated the address in her head: *861 Towpath.* Her own home was 860. That would make 861 the old Gaynor place across the street. No one in his right mind would want to live there. The place had sat empty for years. He must be mistaken. He probably transposed a number when he wrote it down. Tina cradled the phone to her ear and dug in her bag for paper and pen. Once she had the necessary tools in hand, she replayed the last part of Mr. Princeton's message and jotted down his cell phone number, then saved the message to voice-mail archives should she need to refer to it again.

The flight crew from the plane on which Tina had just flown emerged from the jet way. They passed by her, chattering amongst themselves, and left her as the lone straggler in the gate area.

A wave of fatigue flooded over her. And she had yet to make it home. She hesitated to play the final voice mail, but the combination of curiosity and a sense of duty won out over dread.

"This is Eli Crow, over at the *Courier.*"

The newspaper publisher had given Tina the cold shoulder ever since she'd chosen to hire a virtual stranger to do the maintenance on her rentals over his sister's boy, Vernon Peck. She couldn't begin to guess why Eli might be calling her now.

"I'm wondering—" His voice cracked.

He paused and cleared his throat and began again.

"Yes, I'm wondering if you'd be willing to issue a statement concerning the murder of Lenny Sanders, your handyman?"

🎕

"Yoh, Boss, gotta run. Looks like our Intel source has finally arrived. I'll call tomorrow." He snapped his cell phone shut without bothering to say good-bye and clipped the device to his belt. After the weekend he'd endured, topped off with a three-hour wait for Tina Frank's delayed flight to arrive, he had little use for civilities. Even toward his superiors.

The saucy little hoyden with blood red hair pushed her way through the other arriving passengers in the baggage claim area and positioned herself alongside the revolving carousel. By the looks of her, all sweet and innocent, she saw no need to blend in with the crowd. She seemed devoid of all suspicion and mistrust. Stupid broad.

With Miss Frank's help, he should be able to wrap up loose ends and blow the one-horse town of Canal Pass before winter set in. Surely, with this latest assignment he had proven himself to the big dogs. They owed him a stint in warmer, more stimulating climes. He'd paid his dues.

He watched the subject of his surveillance grapple to free her bag from the pool of circulating luggage before it bobbed past her reach. A person Tina's size could have ridden inside her suitcase and saved on airfare. He snorted a silent chuckle. If she didn't cooperate, she might just find herself packed in that very bag and traveling in the cargo hold of a doomed plane.

When she left the terminal, he stepped from behind the concrete pillar where he'd been hiding. With a suitcase prop in tow, he followed her at a safe distance in the direction of the long-term parking lot.

Halfway up Row G, Tina stopped and glanced over her shoulder. She seemed nervous. Jittery. Or was she upset? From this distance, it was hard to tell. He grunted. Who could figure the mind of a woman? Either way, he couldn't risk her catching sight of him. He stopped beside a minivan and pretended to search for something inside his coat. Had she flown into Cleveland Hopkins instead of the smaller and less populated Canton/Akron Regional Airport, tailing her without detection would have been a whole lot easier. On the other hand, if this naive front of hers was just an act and she was on to him, she stood less of a chance of losing him in traffic out here in the suburbs and then tipping off a contact or the local authorities.

No one had asked his opinion. If they had, he would have told them he found her alibi for leaving town the very same week everything "hit the fan" a bit too far-fetched to be believed.

Did she really fancy herself becoming a mystery writer? Or was it all an elaborate plot to substantiate her feigned innocence—a ruse to cover her involvement in Lenny's profit-skimming deals?

The pretty little Miss Frank better hope her virtue wasn't an act. She was dealing with the major leagues now, not some backwoods farm team. If she didn't play by their rules, she was liable to get hurt.

Just ask Lenny. The dead mute.

Chapter 2

Residue from the afternoon's thunderstorms glistened on the parking-lot pavement. The effect reminded Tina of the chintzy, mood-enhancing ploy used in every scary B-movie she'd watched on late-night TV. Gray and heavy with moisture, the dusky sky seemed to close in on her. She caught herself snatching quick, shallow breaths.

An eerie feeling snaked up Tina's spine as she loaded her suitcase into the trunk of her black Saturn. She hurried around the car, jumped behind the wheel, and started the engine.

On her way to the tollbooth, she drove past the private hanger for the executive jet service where Miguel worked as a pilot. She spied his faded red clunker parked outside, and she imagined how he must have groused about the rain keeping him from riding his new Harley to work.

Miguel and Lenny used to spend hours tinkering with Miguel's old bike before he traded it in for his new one.

Tina wondered if Miguel had heard the report of Lenny's death. Surely, he would have told her had he known. . .unless he didn't want to break such horrible news over the phone. Replaying his message in her mind, she dismissed the possibility that Miguel knew about Lenny's murder. Miguel's voice and manner of speaking sounded quite normal in his message, with no undertones of withheld news. She liked to think she knew him well enough that she could pick up on such betraying subtleties.

Poor Lenny.

Murdered.

Perspiration glazed Tina's palms as she pulled out of long-term parking. She tightened her already white-knuckle grip on the steering wheel.

No matter how irritating Lenny could be, he didn't deserve to meet such a horrible end. Tears filled her eyes and made the task of driving all but impossible. Yet, no matter how fast she blinked her tears away, others sprang up and took their place. She managed to pull her car into the parking lot of a country church until she could gain a tighter rein on her emotions, but the sight of the house of worship only added to her grief and pricked her heart with guilt.

She hoped and prayed Lenny made his peace with God before he died. The few times she'd invited Lenny to church, he'd firmly rebuffed her offers. *Not interested,* he would type into his portable keyboard, then turn the small screen toward her so she could read. She hated to judge another person's spiritual condition, but Lenny never once showed a lick of interest in matters of the soul.

When Tina exhausted her wellspring of tears, she eased her car back onto the county highway and pressed toward home. Although her eyes were dry for the present, she could not assuage her guilt. If only she had looked for more opportunities to share her faith, maybe things would have turned out differently for Lenny. Maybe he'd still be alive. Now, it was too late.

Poor Lenny.

Murdered.

An involuntary shudder launched a mesh of chills down Tina's back and through her extremities. Who would do such a thing? Why? She couldn't imagine a premeditated homicide occurring in their peaceful little hamlet. There hadn't been a murder in Canal Pass since the Ohio and Erie Canal barges floated into permanent dry dock some hundred and fifty years ago. With their demise, all the area saloons and other establishments of vice dried up as well.

The idea of a killer loose in her neighborhood triggered a fresh wash of gooseflesh over Tina's arms.

She cast another glance at her rearview mirror. The road stretched empty behind her as far as she could see in the waning daylight. It had to be a bad case of nerves, but try as she might, throughout the thirty-minute drive from Canton to Canal Pass, Tina hadn't been able to shake the sense that someone was following her. . .watching her. Maybe she could convince Sheriff Yocum to see her home after she stopped by the station as he'd asked.

The thought occurred to her this might be some cruel practical joke cooked up by the sheriff and Eli Crow—that good-for-nothing newspaper-editor buddy of his—to give them a belly laugh at her expense. They both had more time on their hands than was good for a soul.

For all she knew, Lenny could be in on the scam too. As soon as they heard the reason for her trip to Kansas City, all the good ol' boys who hung out at Pearl's Café began to rib and goad her mercilessly. Tina could hear them now, hootin' and hollerin' over the scare they planned to give her—the mystery writer wanna-be. If such were the case, she refused to play along. She'd keep a cool head when she breezed back into town and dropped in on Sheriff Yocum. Then, someway, somehow, she'd figure out a scheme and turn the joke on them.

⚜

Sheriff, are you here?" Tina stepped into the old storefront police station on Barge Boulevard, Canal Pass's main drag. The small-town operation served a dual role as police department and village jail.

"Be right out," the lawman's voice bellowed from the back room. An immense shadow darkened the painted-gray floor a moment before his form passed through the double leaves. In one hand, Sheriff Yocum held a half-eaten, chocolate-coated éclair and in the other a half-gallon milk jug. He took a swig, then wiped his mouth with the back of his hand. His girth lobbed over the waistband of his beige uniform like yeast dough that, left too long unattended, oozes over the rim of its bowl.

"Hey, little lady, welcome home."

"For the millionth time, name's Tina," she muttered under her breath. She had been forced to accept long ago that she would always be referred to in diminutive terms, regardless of her age. That she stood a towering five-feet-two wearing two-inch heels didn't help matters. Miguel alone could make reference to her size in such a way so as not to rile her.

"Thank you," she said, pasting on a smile. "Glad to be home."

"Can I get you a donut?" He looked back over his shoulder into the break room.

Tina wondered if he was tipping off his cohorts as to her arrival. "No, thanks, Sheriff," she said, shaking her head. "I can't stay. I'm worn out and ready to be home. Did you want to see me, Sir?"

She tamped down the urge to snap at him. If he and his pals were out to get her goat, she wouldn't give them the pleasure of seeing her mad.

"Um, yep. Sure did." The sheriff lumbered over to his desk and wedged his form into a swivel chair. After adding his snack to the pile of papers on his desk, he dusted the pastry crumbs from his hands.

"Take a seat." He nodded toward the straight-backed chair opposite his desk. "You might need to be sittin' when you hear what I'm about to say." He paused to suck in a draught of air through his teeth. "Yep, seems as though you no sooner go off to the big city lookin' for excitement, than excitement comes ridin' right into our own little town. First murder in these parts in all my born days."

"Murder, you say?" Tina steeled her features to portray a look of mild curiosity while she analyzed the sheriff's reaction. To her surprise, no glint of mischief twinkled in his eyes. She listened for whispers or any sign of movement from the back room that might betray the presence of his cronies, but she heard nothing but the sheriff's wheezy breath.

"I suppose the best way to break the news is to just be out with it."

He locked his hands together and leaned across his desk. His chair protested the shift of weight with a grating squeak.

"Little miss, I'm afraid your maintenance man has met with an untimely end." Sheriff Yocum's jowls wobbled as he shook his head. "Yesterday evenin', Wendell Strand down at the canoe livery was finishin' the winterizing of the canal barge exhibit and getting ready to lock it up till next tourist season. He found Lenny Sanders's beaten body stuffed in a lower deck storage closet."

The sheriff plowed his fingernails across his chin's stubble.

"Me, I thought it was just a fight between two drunks that went way too far. But somehow, word of the incident got out to the Feds."

"The Feds?" Tina peeped. "You mean the FBI?"

"Um, yep." The lawman eased back in his seat but kept his gaze fixed on Tina. "One of their fellas called me even before the rigor mortis had set in on poor ol' Lenny. They seemed to think there's more to the story than meets the eye, so they sent in an agent to conduct a full inquiry. Can't say as I mind the help. This kind of crime is way outta my league. They did ask me to assist them in their investigation, though."

The sheriff's chest swelled with apparent pride until he resembled a saltwater puffer fish. Tina wondered if he'd gone to the trouble of taking a lesson in method acting from Mr. Braley, the high school drama coach.

"That's part of the reason I asked to speak with you." He paused, and she met his gaze. Judging by his response, he must have read her expression as one of bewilderment or shock. The sheriff's chair screeched again as he shifted his weight.

"Right off the bat, I want you to know I told this FBI agent, and he seemed to agree, that we have no reason to view you as one of the primary suspects in this crime. So, don't you go worrying your pretty little head about that, even if some of my questions might lead you to believe otherwise."

Tina fought the urge to roll her eyes. How absurd. She, a murder suspect. Now she knew this must be some kind of a joke.

"Anyway, as I was starting to say, the agent assigned to this case is working undercover, so he wants me to serve as what he calls 'a conduit of information.' A 'go-between,' you could say. A well-versed writer such as yourself might use the term liaison." He looked at her as if to make sure she'd been duly impressed by his extensive vocabulary.

Tina seized the moment to try and get a word in edgewise.

"Sheriff, maybe you can tell me—"

"Now, now. Before you start in asking a bunch of questions, let me share with you a sayin' we have in my business. Goes something like this. 'If I told you what I know, I'd have to shoot you.'" He offered an exaggerated wink. "I'd be much obliged though, little lady, if you could answer me this one thing." He steepled his two index fingers and pointed them toward her. "Were you aware Lenny might have had a. . .how shall I say it. . .what one might call a second line of work?"

"A second line of work? Do you mean a side job?"

While she forced herself to remain calm, Tina vowed payback once she exposed this little escapade as a hoax.

"Sir, I hate to speak ill of the deceased, but Lenny didn't have the energy to fulfill the few demands I placed on him, much less work another job." In the unlikely event the sheriff was being truthful and sincere, she offered an honest answer, but she couldn't keep a note of irritation from creeping into her voice.

"Yes, well, while that may be true, the agent assigned to this investigation believes Lenny's murder bears the markings of someone who was snuffed out after double-crossing a certain drug kingpin from over in Youngstown by the name of Zambezi or Zamboni. Maybe he said Stromboli. . .one of those foreign-sounding names." He rubbed the arms of his chair while he rocked. "The FBI wants to keep this investigation undercover as much as possible in hopes of nailing not only Lenny's killer, but fingering the thugs at the top of this little crime family as well. They suspect Lenny may have been an entry-level henchman who had the guts, or stupidity, to skim more than his fair share from his supplier's drug sales. According to what they call a reliable source, for the past year or two, your employee contributed to the delinquency of our county's youth by supplying them with methamphetamines."

Tina tugged on her left earlobe and fidgeted with her earring. She didn't find Sheriff Yocum the least bit amusing anymore. If this proved to be an elaborate setup to a prank, one thing was for certain. Either the sheriff had pushed his imagination beyond its limited borders or he'd had a good deal of help in creating such a farfetched scenario. The second option seemed much more likely.

The sheriff hoisted himself from his chair and moved around his desk to tower over Tina. "There I go, rambling on like the Widow Grigsby—and after our FBI boy warned me to keep a tight lid on these details 'til he can wrap up his investigation. Well, the way I figure it, you have a right to know some of this inside information—being Lenny's boss lady and all." He pinched his lips in a thin line, then puckered them and pursed them together again.

"All joking aside, let's just keep all this between you and me for the time being, shall we? I've told you more than I should have, but I'd hate to have to shoot ya now." He snuffled a snort of laughter. "What do ya say, little miss? Is it a deal?"

"Deal." She rose from her chair and, without bothering to look behind her, backed away from the sheriff.

"You're lookin' mighty green around the gills. You'd better get yourself on home and fix yourself a headache powder before I have to carry you there." He crossed the room and started to open the door, but paused with his hand on the knob. "Let me add this one note of instruction as you leave. I'm sure it goes without saying for one as bright as you, but don't be snooping around upstairs in Lenny's apartment until I give you the all-clear."

"Sure. Yes, Sir. I understand. I'll cooperate however I can." Tina licked her lips and tried to swallow around the wad of cotton that seemed to be forming in her throat.

"In the meantime, if you see anything suspicious, anything at all, you let me know ASAP, you hear? I'll send Vince over in the squad car pronto to check things out. We can't let anything bad happen to Paul and Margie Frank's little girl, now can we?"

She answered with a silent shake of her head.

The sheriff pushed open the door and held it for her. A blast of cool air swooshed across Tina's flaming cheeks.

Practical joke or no, Sheriff Yocum had succeeded in scaring her. She was ready for his little game to end.

She slid past the sheriff and out the door, all the while expecting the sheriff's merry band to jump out from their hiding places and yell, "Gotcha!"

No one did.

Chapter 3

With night settling over Canal Pass, Tina could virtually claim the downtown street and sidewalk as her own. Even so, she kept glancing back over her shoulder. She fully expected to see Sheriff Yocum chasing after her to confess the macabre joke he'd played at her expense.

But the longer she waited, the lower her hopes dwindled... and the larger her fears grew that this was no joke. The sheriff just may have been telling the truth.

As much as she hated to admit the idea, she could picture Lenny Sanders as a drug dealer. She had always felt rather uncomfortable around him. Creepy, in fact.

Of course, who wouldn't feel unsettled in the presence of a guy who wore a threadbare black satin jacket bearing an intricately stitched eagle and an embroidered inscription across the back that read:

Vietnam 1967–69
47 Confirmed Kills.

She stood under the police station's canvas awning and

looked across the street and four doors down to her own office storefront. The corner streetlight at Barge Boulevard and Towpath Road illuminated the plate-glass window's decorative gold lettering: Frank Family Properties Management. The business had been in her family for three generations, starting with Tina's grandfather Frank and then passing down from him to her father and from her father to her.

Tina let her gaze drift to the two second-story windows above her office. They opened into the furnished apartment where Lenny had lived, rent-free, in exchange for work. The small stipend she'd paid in addition to his use of the apartment made Lenny's total salary package a more-than-generous one, particularly in light of the work she'd gotten out of him.

Since Lenny moved in, Tina never had cause to step inside his place, but she wouldn't be surprised to find the whole apartment trashed if Lenny's housekeeping proved half as bad as his reputation.

The living-room window on the south end of the apartment had been raised about six inches and left open. The hem of the hand-sewn curtains Tina had made prior to Lenny's move-in now fluttered from the screenless opening, no doubt ruined by the rain.

She winced to think that she would need to call her father in Florida and inform him of this latest, and most tragic, news concerning Lenny. The last time the two of them had discussed her employee, the main debate revolved around Lenny's drinking habits. Her father let her know in no uncertain terms that he would have terminated Lenny Sanders long ago. "Didn't I advise you to fire that good-for-nothing the last time he landed in the drunk tank?" His words rattled and rankled in her memory. She still heard the I-told-you-so tone in his voice. If she had listened to him then, she might have saved their company this scandal.

While her father never came right out and said as much, she knew this matter would give him one more chance to express his disappointment that she—the only child born to her parents and the last in the Frank family line—had not been born a boy. A son would have surely run the family business with a firmer hand. In the world according to Paul Frank, women thought with their hearts, not their heads. In Lenny's case, she feared her father was right.

A golden flicker pulled Tina's focus back to the open window. For a nanosecond, another pinprick of light jabbed the darkness that leached from Lenny's apartment. Tina scrunched her eyes and stared, willing the light to shine again, to no avail. Afraid to blink lest she miss a third flash, she moved toward her car, keeping her eyes trained on the window.

For another long moment, Tina stood in the middle of the brick-lined street. The music of a bullfrog and cricket choir wafted from the canal and kept her company.

She kept her eyes focused on the window as she fumbled in her jacket pocket for her key fob. Without looking down, she felt for the button to release the door locks. Tina eased into the driver's seat. Started her engine. Pulled away from the curb. She intentionally switched off her headlights before steering, ever so slowly, down the deserted block to the corner four-way stop.

In the middle of the empty intersection, Tina debated as to whether or not she should explore the source of the mysterious beam. Even if she found the courage to go in search of answers, she reasoned, Sheriff Yocum had made Lenny's apartment off-limits to her.

She looked into the plate-glass window of her office building. The streetlight illuminated a radius that took in the waiting area in front of her desk. Nothing appeared disturbed there. *My eyes must be playing tricks on me,* she reasoned. *The travel and excitement and shock of the day are taking their toll.* She turned on her right blinker, intending to head for home. But before she could change her mind again, she flipped on the signal in the opposite direction and drove toward the canal bridge instead. Just a quick swing by the entrance to Lenny's apartment should put her mind at ease.

Tina passed the brick exterior of her office's north wall and approached the bridge. She eased up on the accelerator until the speedometer failed to register.

From this vantage point, she could survey the length of the boardwalk that spanned the canal's left bank. The footpath traveled past her building's rear entrance and served the landing for the stairs leading to the apartment she provided for her maintenance man. On the canal's starboard side, moored in front of the museum, floated Canal Pass's main tourist attraction—the refurbished barge on which Lenny's body had been found.

The landscape appeared exactly as she remembered it, like the sleepy little canal town she'd left a week ago. Yet an oppressive cloud seemed to hover in the humid night air. She felt a need to pray, but for whom or what or how, she didn't know for sure, so she mouthed a prayer asking the Lord to answer her plea before she even knew enough to speak the need.

When a quick but careful scan of the area failed to solve

the riddle of the light, Tina convinced herself that her imagination had merely been working overtime. She drove across the bridge, made a U-turn in the canoe rental parking lot, and started to pull back onto the street to head for home.

She reached to turn her headlights on again, but before she could complete the task, Tina looked across the canal to see the shadowy form of a man. The figure appeared to dart from the bottom tread of the steps leading to Lenny's place. He raced across the boardwalk to a short span of sidewalk leading to the pedestrian underpass, then vanished beneath the bridge.

Tina choked down a swelling cry when her heart lurched to her throat. The familiar shape of the fleeing man usually made her pulse rate soar for reasons much different than the fear coursing through her now. She would recognize that lean frame and long gait anywhere, even in the ethereal glow of the distant streetlight.

Miguel!

⚜

A cyclone of dead leaves swirled past Tina. Though the orange-and-red canopy overhead had not reached its peak brilliance, winter's precursor was evident in the few trees already sloughing off dry foliage.

"No one in his right mind would live in this decaying Victorian," Tina groused as she crossed the street from her house to the old Gaynor place. "What a waste of my time and that of this Mr. Princeton."

At least the sun had decided to shine. Tina didn't think she could handle one of Ohio's infamous overcast days in her present anxious and tired and grumpy state.

She had spent a sleepless night with her bedroom TV on,

her hand clutched tightly around a baseball bat. She jumped at every sound outside her window. She tensed each time her fat black cat, Mr. Poe, shifted at the end of her bed.

Should she need to fend off an intruder intent on doing her harm, her neighbors to the right presented her next-best option for swift aid. But neither Marvin Banks nor his wife, Willa Mae, could hear a sonic boom without their hearing aids, much less Tina's screams for help.

Sometime around 2:00 A.M., in hopes of taking her mind off her present miseries, Tina logged online and set up a special E-mail loop to allow quick and easy communication between their new Sleuth Sisters group members. Then she sent out a test message to the other three gals, announcing she'd arrived home safe and sound. She didn't have the wherewithal just yet to divulge the gruesome details of her homecoming to her newfound mystery-writer friends.

Visions of Lenny filled what snatches of sleep Tina did manage to catch, each nightmare the same. A look of evil—or was it desperation—flashed in Lenny's eyes as he raced toward her. He waved his keyboard and motioned for her to read what he'd typed on the screen as he approached, but he never came quite close enough for her to make out the words before he and his keyboard dissolved into the blackness of her dream.

A tormenting tug of war plagued her thoughts of Miguel. Any other time, she would have reveled in the fragrance from the "Welcome Home" bouquet Miguel had left on her kitchen counter. The gesture represented, by far, his most romantic overture to date. Yet the arrangement of fall flowers served only to remind Tina of last night's mysterious sighting of her strong-armed neighbor's look-alike.

Every time she passed by a window with a view of his house, she'd pause and watch for any signs of life next door. Not once did she see anything that would arouse suspicion.

She debated whether or not she should have reported to Sheriff Yocum what—and whom—she thought she'd seen. But her heart wouldn't let her make such traitorous claims against Miguel. Not without real proof and hard evidence. He deserved the benefit of her every doubt. He'd never done anything to merit distrust, even if he was on the quiet side.

By the time the sun perched on the tops of the sassafras trees in her backyard, she had convinced herself of her folly in harboring suspicious thoughts about Miguel. Whomever she'd seen, if she'd seen anyone at all, couldn't have been her neighbor. Miguel was out of town. "Flying to Houston," hadn't he said?

After the night of tossing and turning she'd endured, Tina didn't bother to apply makeup before she left the house. No amount of concealer or foundation could hide the dark circles under her eyes anyway.

She tiptoed over the porch's rotting floorboards, taking care to watch where she placed her feet. The undeniable odor of alley cat burned Tina's throat, even though more than two years had passed since Spinster Gaynor's Alzheimer's necessitated her committal to a nursing home. Back then, Tina and Miguel spearheaded the campaign to farm out Spinster Gaynor's extensive feline collection. As reward for their services, they allowed themselves first pick of the kitties in Miss Gaynor's menagerie.

Tina worked through every key on her huge brass ring until she found the one that unlocked the Gaynor front door. Even so, after years of little use, the heavy oak entrance refused to budge. Tina put her full weight into her shoulder and gave three hard shoves before the door flew open. She grabbed hold of the doorknob to keep from sprawling face-first across the entryway tile.

Halfway through her klutzy pirouette, a car horn brayed. A late model, pearl white convertible, its top down, idled alongside the curb. A tanned and blond hunk of a guy waved to her from the driver's seat.

Tina wiggled her fingers in response, then raked them through her spiked hair to give it a quick comb. She glanced down at her tattered blue jeans and denim shirt. Her outfit looked like something she'd dug from the laundry basket and thrown on. Then again, that's just what she had done. When she hung up the phone after scheduling this walk-through with Mr. Princeton, she'd had less than ten minutes to dress.

The handsome stranger hurried up the walk. As he drew close, Tina couldn't help but notice that the color of his golf shirt brought out the azure of his eyes. Overdeveloped biceps stretched at the hem of his short sleeves.

If only the floor would open up now and swallow her whole. Judging by the structure's condition, her wish stood a strong chance of coming true.

"Miz Frank, I presume? I'm Hal Princeton." He flashed her a movie-star smile, and she accepted the firm handshake he offered.

He reached for his wallet, withdrew a business card, and handed it to Tina. While he spoke, she gleaned snatches of information from the card. . .Sales and Service. . .United Home Security. . .Home Office. . .904 Sahara Trail, Boardman, OH. . .44514.

"Thanks for agreeing to meet me here on such short notice. I really wanted to get the details of a lease agreement worked out so I can start moving in later today."

"No problem whatsoever." Tina brushed off the inconvenience like she would shoo away a fly. "I'm sorry I didn't get back to you sooner. I just returned from a conference in Kansas City last night, and I had some disturbing news awaiting me."

The man appeared to be studying the termite-ridden porch rafters, but he quickly jerked his attention back to Tina.

"I apologize if I've caught you at a bad time. We can postpone this walk-through if need be. I can manage out at the Canal View Inn awhile longer."

"No, of course not. After all, we're already here. But, Mr. Princeton, I do wish you'd let me show you the new duplexes I have for rent on the outskirts of town. I'm sure I can find you something better suited to your lifestyle than this old hovel." Tina glanced at the sports car parked out front. Where cars were concerned, she knew next to nothing, but she recognized expensive. "Such a dilapidated house needs more work than I can get out of it in rent. Besides, I'm currently without a maintenance man." She tried to sound nonchalant but couldn't keep from flinching at her offhanded mention of Lenny.

"No, this place is just right—an easy walk to all the local stores and services. And I'm handy when it comes to repairs. If you don't mind me doing the work myself, that is. I thought I might install a security system too—with your permission, of course. And at no charge to you. If you'd like, we could work out an arrangement to put one in your own home. I understand your little village has seen an increase in crime of late, and I believe our products and services can bring peace of mind to the residents here."

Tina hiked her eyebrows. "I know news travels fast in these parts, but I'm surprised a stranger like yourself would already be privy to news of our community's tragedy."

He shrugged off the comment she'd intended as a question. "Miz Frank, do you mind if we step inside and have a look around? My mind is made up, but I know you'd feel better once I've assured you I'm fully aware of what I'm getting into by renting this particular house." He grazed her elbow as he swept past her. Before Tina realized what was happening, Mr. Princeton guided her out of the open doorway and into the foyer. He kicked the door shut behind him with his heel.

She jumped at the resounding thud.

Leading up to today, she had shown dozens of prospective tenants through countless rental properties. Now, for the first time in all her years as a leasing agent, she feared for her safety. Tina conducted a frantic search for anything she might use as a weapon, but she came up void of ideas. She'd left her cell phone at home when she'd dashed across the street, so she couldn't even call to Sheriff Yocum or his deputies for help. If only Miguel were home, he would come to her rescue. Tina made a mental note to buy a small canister of mace and carry it with her wherever she went—if she made it out of here unscathed.

Chapter 4

"Yoh, Miss Tina."

Tina jumped in her office chair. Hal Princeton's lease agreement quavered in her grasp like autumn's last treebound leaf. After her self-inflicted scare at the Gaynor place earlier this morning, she found herself trembling at the slightest provocation or strange noise. But when she turned to see Vernon Peck hovering across her desk, her fear changed to repugnance.

"I understand you're needing a new handyman."

"How could you, Vern?" Tina set the paperwork down and stood, pretzeling her arms in front of her. She shot Vernon Peck the most disgusted look she could muster. "Poor Lennie's not even buried, and here you are after his job."

She doubted her angry stance made much impact on this bearded hillbilly who insisted on wearing his grimy Chief Wahoo baseball cap indoors as well as out. Even so, the faintest of smiles on her part would be all the encouragement Vernon would need to forget his waiting friends and camp out for the next hour or two in the seat across from her desk.

Willy Pritchard and Doug Fisher, Vernon's constant sidekicks and chums since school days, hovered outside her office window. The trio liked to refer to themselves as Canal Pass's Three Musketeers. "Three Stooges" better suited them.

Doug caught Tina studying him, and they exchanged nods before he dropped his gaze to study the sidewalk again. Not one of the members in this happy clan could look a person straight in the eye. Though that fact alone would rate the three the title "suspicious characters," Tina had never known any of them to cause real harm. Still, she squeezed her balled fists tighter in an effort to stop her shaky hands.

"I don't expect there'll be a funeral for Lenny here in Canal Pass. Do you?" Vern's question pulled Tina's focus back to real time, and she watched him trace around the geometric pattern of her office carpet with the toe of his shoe while he spoke. "Can't say as anyone besides you would attend if they did, considerin' the circumstances. Uncle Eli told me Lenny's kin in West Virginia asked for his body to be shipped to their place after the autopsy's done. I expect they'll hold a memorial service down there. His folks plan to bury his remains in the family plot on their farm. Do you suppose they'll send him UPS or through the post office?"

Tina fought to maintain her straight face. "I have no idea. No one's told me anything about the internment plans. Your uncle decided to give me the cold shoulder after I refused an interview for the article about Lenny's murder that's running in the *Courier*."

"I sure hope you won't hold the actions of my kin against me none. I really need this job." Vern lifted his head and glanced at her through hooded eyes. "Don't get me wrong. I think what happened to Lenny was a cryin' shame. But if you'd hired me over him in the first place, who knows but what none of this might have happened." He sank back into his customary slump-shouldered form, his flash of defiance spent.

Coming from any other man, his response might have been cause for alarm, but Tina knew that was just Vern.

"Boy howdy, Miss Tina, don't you know me good enough by now to know I wouldn't be here if I weren't desperate. My mama done put her foot down. 'Vernon,' she says, 'it's high time you found yourself gainful employment and became a productive member of society.' She give me 'til the end of the month to move out. Can you believe that? My own mama kickin' me out of my childhood home."

What Tina couldn't believe was that Vernon Peck graduated high school with her in the class of '93 and, save the *Courier* paper route his uncle let him throw, he had yet to hold down a steady job.

"You've got my sympathies," Tina said, but she prayed he didn't read more into her words than she meant. "Tell you what—if you haven't found another job by the time I'm ready to fill the vacant position, then I'll consider you. I give you my word. But I can't make any promises to hire you. Not today. Not this week. There's too much going on in my life right now to add a new employee to the mix, even if that employee is you."

Especially if that employee is you, she thought. Despite his standing several feet away from her, Vern's body odor filled her sinuses and made her eyes water.

"Good 'nough, then," he said with a nod. "I can prob'ly convince Mama to let me stay put another couple weeks if she hears I've been talkin' to you 'bout a job."

Tina had tried to be kind, yet vague and noncommittal, in her response to Vern. But she had a nagging fear that she had just pledged more than she could deliver to her fellow alumnus.

Gyrating squiggles of psychedelic color pulled her attention to her computer when the screen saver popped on. "You are going to have to excuse me now, Vern. I really need to get back to work. Besides, it looks like Willy and Doug could use a referee." Out on the sidewalk, Vern's compadres were exchanging shoves and arm punches.

"Oh, them nincompoops! Can't behave themselves more'n a minute if I'm not there to baby-sit." Chief Wahoo oscillated along with Vern's wagging head. "Well, all right, I suppose I best be going. . . ." His voice faded along with his obvious hope that Tina would change her mind and invite him to stay.

"I know where to find you. I'll give you a call if I decide to hire a man of your qualifications." Tina turned her back on Vern and returned to her desk, leaving him to see himself out. Only with Vern would she be so rude. Still, her lack of manners never seemed to stop him from coming around.

Before she settled into her chair, she pulled a can of industrial-strength air freshener from the desk's file drawer and saturated the room with its clove-and-cinnamon scent.

"Now, where was I?" Tina placed Mr. Princeton's lease agreement in the wooden box marked "Incoming" on the corner of her desk and rolled into position behind her computer monitor. When she wiggled the mouse, the screen saver disappeared and Tina clicked her way through cyberspace until the four-color graphics of her favorite Web-site search engine materialized.

This current research project had nothing to do with rental properties. Tina was on a quest.

With knowledge came a sense of control—a commodity she suffered a serious deficiency of today. So, for the purpose of research, both writing related and personal, she decided she ought to learn all she could about the workings of organized crime and its connection with the drugs known as methamphetamines. At present, her knowledge of both topics wouldn't fill a three-by-five card.

Lenny made a fool of her by capitalizing on her naïveté. Now she wondered who else among her acquaintances lived a secret life of crime. In all likelihood, she would share the streets of Canal Pass with at least one murderer when she walked home at five. Barring further interruptions from tenants or job-hunters, she planned to enlighten herself on these depressing subjects and know enough to be suspicious should she notice certain signs. No one would accuse her of being gullible after today.

She started her explorations by looking in her online dictionary for the proper spelling of the word *methamphetamine*, then she keyed the word into the appropriate blank. The search engine kicked out thousands of matches in response to her request for Web sites with information about the drug.

The more she learned, the more her skin crawled. She never imagined such vices lurked amid the sheltered environs of Canal Pass.

To think Lenny sold this awful drug right under her nose—or rather, right over her head. Tina tipped her head back and studied the ceiling tiles. She shuddered to think what other crimes had been committed up there. How many commandments had he broken while she sat, praying for his salvation, in this very chair?

According to the online information, the common household ingredients used to make methamphetamines could be easily and legally purchased without leaving their little town. For all she knew, Lenny could have even been operating his own "meth" lab upstairs. Then again, if he was dumb enough to tangle with an organized-crime family, he probably didn't have the smarts to manufacture his own drugs, no matter how simple the recipe. Tina was beginning to wonder if she had grossly underestimated the extent of Lenny's foolishness.

The further she read, the more she shook her head in disbelief. Her cram course on the drug trade proved eye opening, mind-boggling, and pathetic. She couldn't imagine anyone being so desperate to escape reality that they'd knowingly risk consuming such dangerous substances. Oftentimes produced in mom-and-pop labs under substandard conditions and with no quality control or smuggled across the border from Mexico, each dose of methamphetamines put a user's life in jeopardy. Yet the number of people willing to take the risk must be substantial. According to all reports, the trade of these illegal psychotropic drugs reaped huge earnings for those willing to chance arrest, jail time, and a permanent record as a drug trafficker. The methamphetamine business in Ohio must turn a tidy profit for the big names of organized crime to consider it a worthwhile gamble—which they apparently did.

If what she read were true, law enforcement and crime-fighting agencies that tried to stop all this drug trafficking thrived in her fair state as well. Tina followed one Web trail to the FBI home page and discovered their task force supported a division in Cleveland with resident agencies in nine surrounding cities. She scanned the list of addresses for the various offices in her area. When she came to the listing for the Youngstown agency, something about it gave her pause.

Sahara Trail. . .Boardman. . . The street and town rang a bell. She'd seen this address on something recently. Maybe she'd skimmed past the listing on another Web page in her speed-reading on drugs. She tried to dismiss the matter, but the question kept tapping at her thoughts. Where had she read this address?

While she searched her memory banks, her gaze rested on Hal Princeton's lease agreement, paper-clipped to the forms was his business card.

A tingle raced through her.

The card didn't list a suite number like the FBI Web page did. The phone numbers shared only the same prefix. But the street and city matched. Sahara Trail. . .Boardman. . .

Tina considered the possibility that the corresponding addresses posed a wild coincidence. Such things happened. Truth proved stranger than fiction every day. Mr. Princeton's company must occupy an office in the same building as the FBI. That was the only conclusion she could draw. Still, what were the odds that, in the course of an hour's time, she would connect a shared street and town address for two different entities in a place some seventy miles away?

A wild idea occurred to her. Tina acted on the impulse and picked up her phone. She dialed the number listed on Hal's business card.

"United Home Security. How may I direct your call?" The greeting, spoken by a cheery female voice, held a lilting, musical quality. The voice sounded young. Maybe twenty-five, tops.

Tina, intent on committing the voice to memory, failed to answer.

"Hello?" The operator came again.

"Oh, yes. Sorry. My name is Tina Frank with Frank Family Properties Management in Canal Pass, and I need to speak with someone in your office who can give me a reference for one of your employees—a Mr. Hal Princeton."

"Certainly. I can connect you with someone over in personnel."

Tina thought the operator was transferring her call, but she heard the same voice in her ear after a short pause.

"Actually, Miss Frank, our company is small. Mr. Princeton is one of only a handful of sales reps for our firm. I'd be glad to let you speak with the president, but I can personally vouch for Hal's reputation. You couldn't ask for a better tenant."

The voice took on a love-struck softness when she spoke of Hal. Tina crinkled her nose. She could picture the perky young receptionist batting big doe eyes at her heartthrob salesman whenever he came by the home office.

"You just told me what I wanted to hear. I won't bother to speak with anyone else at this time. Thank you." Tina hurried to disconnect the call, and as soon as she heard a dial tone, she punched in the number listed on the FBI Web page. As she waited for a response, she replayed a mental recording of the United Home Security receptionist's voice.

"Federal Bureau of Investigation, Youngstown."

Tina's pulse pounded like a bass drum in her ear. Though she couldn't be 100 percent sure, this voice sounded very similar to that of the woman she'd spoken with moments ago—especially in the little lilt at the end.

Her mouth felt so dry, Tina didn't know if she could speak,

but, figuring the FBI must have Caller ID, she fought off the impulse to hang up. "I'd like to speak with Hal Princeton, please."

A long moment of silence preceded the operator's response.

"I'm afraid we don't have anyone here by that name. Could someone else assist you perhaps?"

Of course! Tina winced. How silly of her. She should have stopped to think through the logistics before placing this call. Even if her suspicions proved true—even if Hal Princeton worked as an undercover agent for the FBI and used the job in sales for United Home Security as a front—he wouldn't have given out his real name. Hal Princeton would be an alias. To make matters worse, her prior conviction about the two receptionists being one-and-the-same person now waned. This voice held a much more serious tone.

Tina blubbered a lame apology about dialing a wrong number, then dropped the phone receiver onto its cradle as though it were burning her hand.

What if the so-called Mr. Princeton found out she'd been snooping around in matters of top security? She sure didn't want to anger an FBI agent by blowing his cover.

If only she could turn back the clock and stop her impulsive behavior.

Tina's zeal for her role as an amateur gumshoe deflated like a leaky helium balloon. She closed all the open Web site windows, then rolled her cursor toward the red squared X in order to disconnect from the Internet. However, before she could complete the task, her computer announced, "You've got mail!"

She clicked on the mailbox icon and followed the prompts to view the incoming message. When she saw the familiar

E-mail address, she stopped ruing her bungled attempts at playing telephone detective and broke into a smile.

> *From: FlyingAmigo920*
> *To:TinaSpeaksFrankly*
> *Subj:Change of plans*
>
> *Hey, Mi Pequeña! I'm sending this from my handheld PDA, so I'll be brief. I thought I'd better tell you, I've had a change of plans.*
> *I need to fly a client from Houston to Mexico City. Won't be home tomorrow after all. Can you fetch my mail and check on Sophia? I'd be much obliged! You know the routine.*
> *I promise to bring you a souvenir. Ha! Might be home Friday. Hope so. Sure miss seeing you.*
> *Your friend and neighbor, Miguel*

She longed to talk to him in person and let him dissolve her every remnant of mistrust, to look into his warm maple eyes and hear him say, "Everything will be all right." Still, his E-mail confirmed what she had all but convinced herself of earlier—she must have been hallucinating last night when she thought she'd seen Miguel.

Tina responded to his E-mail with a rambling message, detailing the horrific circumstances of Lenny's murder. She decided not to embarrass herself by telling Miguel the part about her false sighting of him, though. She would save that for a time when she could tell him face-to-face and they could share a laugh at her folly and paranoia. . .a moment somewhere out in the future when life returned to normal and the one who killed Lenny was behind bars. . .a day when she didn't view everyone with suspicion. . .when her faith in humanity was restored.

※

"Yeah, Boss. It's me. Checkin' in." He cupped his hand around the cell phone and kept his voice low even though he sat in the privacy of his car.

"Not a whole lot yet to report on this end, but I figured I'd keep you updated on what I do know. Seems your suspicions about Tina Frank are panning out. In the past twenty-four hours, she's made contact, in one form or another, with most of the creeps we've identified as associates of our late, great traitor Lenny. She must be sending them some kind of signal to lay low, because I haven't seen any money or merchandise change hands. No sign of our missing funds. We've gotta give her this much—she's sly. That sweet-and-innocent act of hers deserves an Oscar or an Emmy or whatever those big-shot actors get. I'm not picking up any useful information from the bugs yet, and my search of her place turned up dry. She's a pro at making all her business affairs seem legit. I do think ol' Lenny's demise must have shaken her up pretty good. She's as nervous as a turkey the day before Thanksgiving. I'll get back to you as soon as I've got something solid to go on. Don't worry. I'll get the answers we're looking for from Miss Frank—one way or another. Say, gotta go. I think I see her coming this way."

Chapter 5

At 7:42 A.M. on Friday, Tina scrambled out from under the warmth of her bed's down-filled duvet and wiggled into an Ohio State Buckeye sweatshirt and the rattiest jeans she owned. After shoving her feet in a pair of fuzzy-bunny house shoes, she raced downstairs and through the kitchen, headed for the side garage door. She wheeled her trashcan down the driveway and hoped upon hope that the trash truck hadn't yet come down their street.

When she saw still-full cans and bulging plastic garbage bags lining the curb, she heaved a sigh of relief. She'd almost done it again. Tina never understood how she could forget this simple task week after week.

"Good morning, Neighbor!" Hal Princeton strolled down his driveway carrying a stack of flattened packing boxes. He dropped them on top of his burgeoning trash mound, then waved to her. "Cute shoes."

A moan swelled in Tina's throat, but she swallowed it down and offered Hal her best smile. At this point, she didn't stand a chance of impressing this guy with her class and style. She might as well take the sweet and down-home-charm route instead—not that she wanted to pursue anything other than a friendship with Hal. She had to admit, though, she felt a certain degree of security knowing Hal lived across the street, especially with Miguel out of town.

"Thanks, and good morning to you too." Her first spoken words of the day sounded something akin to the honking geese that flew overhead. Tina wagged her left foot out in front of her. "Premier designer footwear for the finest of lazy bums."

Hal laughed, then checked for oncoming cars and started across the narrow street. Decked out in khakis with the collar of a plaid sport shirt peeking out from underneath a navy blue sweater, he could set the industry standards for casual Friday wear.

When he wasn't looking, Tina clawed at the back of her hair in a futile attempt to untangle the rat's nest that had built up in the night. "I'll have you know—I really do clean up pretty good. And I promise you, my wardrobe contains more than one pair of jeans."

"Oh, yeah?" He stood close enough for Tina to smell his woodsy aftershave above her trash's week-old potato peelings and moldy spaghetti sauce. "I'm skeptical. You'll have to prove it to me." He added with a wink, "What would you say if I were to ask you to back up your claim this Sunday? I'm looking for someone to go with me to church. I hate the idea of walking into a crowd of strangers all alone, and you appear to me to be the church-going kind. Am I wrong?"

"No, you're right. I'm just sorry I didn't think to ask you first." As she spoke, Tina chastised herself for thinking Hal didn't seem to be a church-going type of guy. She knew she had no right to judge what did and what didn't constitute such criteria. Even so, she couldn't shake off a prickle of doubt as to his motivation for wanting to go to Sunday services. Something about his twinkling blue eyes and teasing smile made her question whether his inquiry stemmed more from flirtation than matters of faith.

"Did you have a particular denomination or church in mind?"

"I don't have a preference," Hal replied. "I figured I'd just go where you go—if that's okay with you."

"Of course. I'd be delighted if you'd join me. That'll give me a chance to introduce you to Miguel Villarreal too—assuming he makes it home before then." Tina read the question in Hal's eyes, and she answered before he had a chance to ask. "Miguel is our neighbor who lives in that white frame two-story next to mine."

A pleasant warmth radiated through her when she nodded in the direction of Miguel's home. She wondered how Miguel would accept the idea of a new, good-looking stranger moving into their neighborhood. A spark of jealousy might be just what he needed to shift the progress of their relationship out of neutral and into overdrive.

"We usually walk together to church whenever he's in town—which isn't often lately. He's a pilot for an executive jet service, and it seems like they've had him hauling customers all around the globe this month. He was supposed to be home today, but he e-mailed me last night to say his return trip has been pushed back another day or two."

"Sounds like an interesting fella. I'll look forward to meeting him."

Tina didn't think Hal's tone of voice sounded all that sincere.

"If I don't see you before then, meet us right here at nine-forty-five on Sunday morning, and we'll start our little pilgrimage."

He nodded his understanding, but he looked past her toward Miguel's place, and his eyes held a far-off glaze. "Tell me, have you heard anything new about the search for your handyman's murderer?"

The sudden shift in subject matter threw Tina for a loop. "N–no," she stammered. "Have you?" She winced as soon as the question left her lips. No FBI agent worth his salt would divulge any information about a case, even if he knew.

"Only what I overhear being discussed down at Pearl's Café." Hal evaded her inquiry like a Buckeye quarterback doing an end run around a three-hundred-pound tackle, but he continued to send darting glances toward Miguel's home. "Listen, you be careful, you hear? If you ever need my help, call me. I can race over here in a flash. A murderer on the loose may make for booming business in my line of work, but I worry about you."

He pulled his focus back to Tina. His forehead crinkled as he held her gaze. Still, Tina questioned the reason behind his protectiveness. His lips curved ever so slightly into a sly smile that belied his serious words and tone. Again, she wondered if sincerity fueled his worry for her safety—or if he was merely flirting under the guise of concern.

She didn't think she liked the idea of Hal laying the groundwork for some future romantic developments in their germinating friendship. When she first figured out Hal Princeton must be an undercover agent for the FBI, she'd played with the idea of how she might respond if he ever asked her for a date. She didn't need to ponder very long, though, before she concluded she could never put herself in a position of falling in love with someone in such a dangerous line of work. Every time he said good-bye, she would worry she might never see him alive again. She fretted enough over a friend who faced the risks associated with flying planes. She could only imagine how she'd stew if someone close to her dealt with dangerous criminals every day. Besides, no matter how hard she tried, the only man she could ever really picture falling in love with was Miguel.

From the next block over, the rumble and squeal of heavy machinery sliced through the quiet morning air.

"Man, oh, man. Is that the trash truck?" Tina skittered backward toward the sidewalk as she spoke. "Listen, I hate to be rude and leave you standing here, but I have to run next door. I need to see if Miguel has any trash to set out. He'll never let me live it down if I forget again. I'm notorious. . ."

Hal's expression changed to one Tina couldn't read.

"Ah, no problem," he said with a nod. "Go on. I need to get to an appointment anyway. I'll see you right here Sunday morning at nine-forty-five if I don't see you before then."

"Sure thing." She threw him a good-bye wave, but he had already turned and started across the street.

Tina jogged around the corner of Miguel's garage and over to where he kept his trash cans, next to the side-entry door. While she owned only one trash container, Miguel had two. He never came right out and said as much, but she assumed he'd purchased the second receptacle as a concession to her frequent bouts of trash-day forgetfulness.

She lifted the hinged lid on the can nearest her and discovered it held only one half-full kitchen trash bag. The second garbage can appeared close to capacity, but Tina thought, with a little muscle, she could smush the contents of the other can into this one and save herself a second trip to the street. She reached for the drawstring of the lone bag and yanked. As she lifted out the plastic bag from the one can to make the transfer to the next, she glanced down to confirm it was empty.

A piece of black fabric lined the bottom of the can.

The dull patina of well-worn satin sparked a mental match.

Tina shook off the image of Lenny in his Vietnam Vet jacket. *My mind must be playing tricks on me again.* She piled the white plastic bag onto the brimming mound of trash.

"Go!" The trash collector's shout to his driver accompanied the clank and scrape of metal as the civil servants did their job. Judging by the racket's clarity and volume, Tina knew the truck was no more than three or four houses away. She gripped the handle of the full garbage can, then pushed it onto the walk and toward the driveway, ready to make a dash for the street before the truck passed by.

But only her mind raced. Her feet refused to move.

A host of wild what-ifs clogged her thoughts. What if that fabric piece really did turn out to be Lenny's jacket? What if Miguel's garbage held other belongings of Lenny's? What if she carted away the rest of the trash and, in so doing, risked destroying crime-scene evidence?

Even if she missed another trash collection, Tina knew what she had to do. She had to find out what that was at the bottom of Miguel's garbage can.

She tried to ignore the stench as she leaned into the refuse container. She squinted and shook the can in an attempt to get a better look at the suspicious article, but neither effort helped much. Tina didn't think she could stretch down far enough to reach the item. Besides, she didn't want to touch the dirty cloth with her bare hands.

In a quick survey of the side yard, Tina spied a fallen branch at the base of a wild cherry tree. The branch appeared to be the perfect length for her intended purpose. She used the skinny end of the long stick to stab the material, then she eased the item out of the trashcan and flipped it onto the grass. With the act, she verified she'd definitely found an item of clothing of some sort.

She poked at the garment, and red embroidery stitching came into view.

The blood rushed from Tina's head, and she felt faint.

She sucked air into her lungs and willed herself to stay alert. As best she could with her crude utensil, she smoothed the fabric out flat until the substantiation of her fears came into full view.

An intricately stitched eagle looked over an embroidered inscription that read:

Vietnam 1967–69
47 Confirmed Kills.

But why would Lenny's jacket be in Miguel's trash? Had Miguel put it there on purpose, thinking she would unwittingly dispose of the condemning goods?

Panic hit her with knockout force and shattered her thoughts like glass shards. Hard as she tried to think what she should do, she could not string together a coherent line of reasoning.

The trash truck squealed to a halt. Tina knew without

having to see it that the vehicle was next door, in front of her own house.

She couldn't risk anyone catching her with such incriminating evidence at her feet. She had to think. Decide what to do. Sort out her real and imagined suspicions. Allay this frenzy of fear.

From the depths of her soul sprang a desperate and sincere round-robin prayer—*Oh, dear Lord, please. . .give me wisdom. . . show me what to do. . . Oh, dear Lord, please. . .*

In that moment, Tina remembered. Miguel kept a spare key to the side garage door behind the shrubs and under a rock. She found it immediately, without having to dig or hunt. The garbage truck still seemed to be idling out front. Tina breathed a thank-you to Hal for his role in keeping the collectors busy as they carted off the heap of move-in debris he'd set out for removal. Then, in one fluid motion, she speared the jacket with the end of her stick and backed into Miguel's garage. The door clicked shut when Tina nudged it with the bunny on her slippered foot.

Her racing heartbeat thundered in her ears as she waited for her eyes to adjust to the darkness of the windowless garage. A paralysis of fear kept her from groping to find the light switch, but a slice of light seeped in from around the garage door, and Tina could make out the inky silhouette of Miguel's new motorcycle.

There had to be a reasonable explanation, she thought as she stared at the black-on-gray outline of Lenny's jacket dangling from the end of her stick. Maybe one of the days before Lenny's demise, he and Miguel had been working on the motorcycle and oil spilled on his coat. . .and maybe, just maybe, Miguel had convinced Lenny that any hopes of salvaging his war memento were nil. . .maybe Lenny, himself, had deposited it in the trash can on his way home. . . .

Then again, maybe Lenny had been wearing this very article of clothing when he took his last breath.

She dropped the jacket to the cement floor.

Miguel couldn't be a murderer. He just couldn't. Her heart crumpled at the thought. She couldn't bear to think Miguel might have been using her—leading her on in order to work all manner of evil while she opened her heart to him a little more with each passing day.

An unwelcome replay of every television interview she'd seen conducted with friends and family members of a convicted felon flashed through her mind: "He's quiet and keeps to himself. . . . I'm tellin' you, you've never met a nicer guy. He's not capable of such a horrible crime. . . ."

She always figured Miguel was too good to be true.

On the other hand, according to Drake Axelrod, the most obvious suspect never turns out to be the perpetrator in a mystery.

If only the rules of fiction applied to real life.

As desperately as she wanted to believe in her neighbor's innocence, the circumstantial evidence did not favor Miguel. From what she gathered from Agent Princeton's innuendos and inflections a few minutes earlier, she feared he ranked Miguel as Suspect Number One in Lenny's murder as well. Who wouldn't if all they saw were black-and-white facts?

In keeping with the information she had read on the Internet, Miguel did appear to fit the mold of someone who trafficked methamphetamines. The articles stated a good percentage of the drugs originated south of the border. By his own admission, Miguel made frequent trips to Mexico. And he certainly tried to keep a low profile whenever he was home.

If it were true that Lenny sold drugs as well, Tina could imagine a number of possibilities as to why Miguel might want Lenny dead.

She grimaced to think how easily she could be labeled an accessory to the crime. For the past several days, Tina had let herself in and out of Miguel's house to feed Sophie and carry in the mail. Now she wondered what other evidence or clues might have been right under her nose all along. Her gaze fell to the crumpled jacket. At the very least, she could be accused of tampering with evidence. She knew Sheriff Yocum well enough to know he'd throw her in jail first and get answers later. A wave of nausea washed over her at the thought of being a captive audience to that man.

Perhaps her best course of action would be to take Sophie over to her house, where she could keep an eye on her, and steer clear of Miguel and his home altogether until the authorities solved the crime. She would think about how to handle her discovery of Lenny's jacket while she collected the cat.

Tina inhaled a fortifying breath, then forced herself to move. She found the light switch and flipped it on. Sidestepping Lenny's jacket, she retrieved the cat carrier Miguel kept on a garage shelf, then tiptoed into the house.

Chapter 6

"Here, Sophie. Here, kitty, kitty." While she waited for the cat to emerge from her chosen hiding spot for the day, Tina set down the carrier and appraised the kitchen. Nothing appeared different or out of place. Miguel kept a clean house. Spotless, in fact. She always thought this trait of Miguel's a noble and rare quality compared to the other men she knew.

Tina used to love to imagine herself at home here. In that most secret inner spot where she saved her too-good-to-be-true dreams, she held an imaginary picture of her husband, Miguel, sharing life and conversation with her in these rooms. But today, that image dissolved in her suspicions that the money used to renovate Miguel's place came from ill-gotten gain.

Miguel supposedly used an inheritance when he hired Travis Simms, a local contractor, to remodel the inside of this hundred-year-old Victorian. The exterior boasted fresh vinyl siding in a pale yellow with white trim. Two white spindle rocking chairs and a porch swing adorned the wide verandah, which ran the length of the house's front. Miguel obviously possessed a tasteful sense of design as well as the money to support his style. To date, the most Tina had been able to accomplish toward the remodeling of her grandmother's old home amounted to new kitchen appliances and a cordless phone.

She rocked her head from side to side but couldn't shake off the overwhelming disenchantment and disbelief that filled her. The Miguel she thought she knew and liked so well might be nothing more than a fraud—not the real Miguel at all. But as hard as she tried, she couldn't picture Miguel as a drug dealer or murderer. Her heart refused to accept the indictment, regardless of the evidence.

In this muddle of confusion, one thing Tina knew for sure. She had to get out of here. Fast. And think things through.

"Sophie? Where are you, Girl?" Tina made a few puckering, kissy noises before she called out again. "Come here, pretty kitty. It's me, coming to take you for a visit with your ol' friend, Mr. Poe."

When all else failed, Tina knew she could get Sophie to come running by shaking the box of dry cat food. She crossed the kitchen and retrieved the box from the pantry. Then she gave it a good shake and listened for the *thud-thud-thud* of Sophie's paws.

A mew floated from the direction of the living room.

"Sophie?" Tina started toward the sound and gave the cat food box another shake. "Come on, Girl. Come see me."

A gasp sucked the air from Tina's lungs.

"Oh, Sophie! How could you? Especially now?"

Another meow filtered from behind the closed draperies.

"That's right," Tina called out as she set the cat food on the nearest end table, "you ought to hide in shame. Just look at this mess." A mountain of black soil coated the white carpet around the base of a potted weeping fig tree. "You've been a very, very bad kitty."

From time to time, Sophie had expressed her displeasure over Miguel's extended absences by pulling some act of feline mischief. On one such occasion, Tina followed a toilet paper trail back to an empty spool in the master bath. Then, for awhile, Sophie took to sneaking off with the coffee-table coasters and hiding them under the foyer's oriental rug. None of her pranks to date, however, had been this messy to clean up.

Tina knew it was silly of her to bother about such a little matter with all the major problems she had on her mind. But she couldn't very well just leave the mess for someone else to clean. If she should decide to call Sheriff Yocum about her discovery of Lenny's jacket in Miguel's trash, she could see the sloppy lawman tracking this dirt through the whole house as he searched for other evidence linking Miguel to Lenny's death. Who knew when—or if—Miguel would ever get around to the job. Even now, he might be on the lam or captured and under arrest for murder with no option of posting bond. She might as well vacuum up as much of the soil as she could. The deed wouldn't require more than a minute of her time.

She retrieved the vacuum cleaner from the kitchen pantry, wheeled it into the living room, and plugged it into the nearest outlet. Before Tina flipped the power switch, though, she wrestled with another panicky thought. Maybe Sophie meant to dump the potting soil, intending to reveal a hidden cache of Miguel's drugs.

Tina dropped to her knees and examined the loam from every angle. Flecks of silver shimmered among the rich earth, but the mess still looked like run-of-the-mill, store-bought dirt to her. She supposed, even if the soil did turn out to contain an illicit substance, the authorities could retrieve their evidence from the vacuum bag. She stood and dusted off her hands, then turned the vacuum on.

A dust cloud bellowed from the sweeper, accompanied by a high-pitched whirr. *That's just great,* Tina groused as she hurried to turn the power off. *The bag is full.*

She squeezed the fabric exterior of the zipper vacuum bag to confirm her diagnosis. But something didn't seem quite right. Instead of the squishy softness she expected to feel in a full dust bag, Tina felt the outline of something hard and rectangular. She crouched down and unzipped the bag's outer casing.

A brick of cash in a plastic freezer bag fell into her lap.

"Money!" She pinched the bag's zipper closure between her thumb and forefinger and slowly extended the contraband out at arm's length, then stood to her feet.

Tina stared at the stack of currency. This had to be the most cash she'd ever seen in one place. But why Miguel kept such an enormous sum hidden in his sweeper, Tina didn't have a clue. A cyclone of possible explanations swirled in her head—none of them good.

For a long while, Tina agonized over what she should do. Lost in her thoughts and pleading prayers, she began to rock back and forth, clutching the money to her chest with both hands.

The cat left her hiding place and came over to rub her thick, tiger-striped fur against Tina's ankles.

"I have no choice, Sophie. We have to call the authorities. I'm in way over my head." Her voice quavered on the last word. Welling tears spilled down Tina's cheeks. Sophie stopped her ankle massage, looked up at Tina, and answered with a short meow.

"A phone call won't be necessary."

Tina twirled in the direction of the deep voice. Through her tears, Tina made out the blurred form of Hal Princeton, brandishing a revolver.

"I'll take the evidence off your hands." Hal pointed his firearm to the bag of money Tina clenched to her chest.

Her relief at the federal agent's appearance outweighed her nervousness over the casual way he waved a lethal weapon about. He had saved her from having to make the most difficult decision of her life—the decision to betray her friendship with Miguel by turning him in.

"You guys are really on your toes. How did you know to come so quick?"

Hal offered only a smirk in response, but Tina's mouth dropped open at the dawn of a revelation. "You've been spying on me, haven't you?"

"I've had you and your favorite neighbor under surveillance for awhile now." Hal gave out a breathy snort. "The collars on those two mangy cats of yours provided an ideal site for planting bugs. I knew if I waited long enough, you'd lead me to the dough."

He shook his head and gave Tina a disgusted look. "So, you've discovered your buddy's been holding out on you, huh? I'm glad to see you've come to your senses about your partnership with a creep like Miguel Villarreal, but you may have realized the error of your ways too late. You're right. You're in way over your head."

Tina's insides wriggled under his severe scrutiny. The glint of condemnation in his eyes made her feel guilty, despite her innocence. She dipped her head and stared at the gaping vacuum bag from where the money had emerged.

"I figured all along that you were in on this," he hissed, all former pretense of friendliness gone from his voice. "No one is ever that nice in real life."

Hal's false accusations brought a fresh cascade of tears, but Tina's ballooning fear stopped her from arguing.

"With your overactive imagination, you really should be a writer. What a great cover-up!"

At last, indignation overcame fright. Tina squared her shoulders and lifted her chin as she prepared to defend her innocence. Hal leveled his gun at her head and muttered, "Uh-uh. Don't move."

She fought off a fresh attack of panic.

"B—but, surely you don't think. . . You've got to believe me. . . If you've been watching me, you must know already. . . I had nothing to do with any of this. . . ."

"You can explain all that later. First, we're going to take a little trip to Youngstown. There are a few unanswered questions we need your help with, and if you're smart, you'll cooperate." His growl conveyed the end of what little patience he had. "Now, I want you to pass me the money, then raise your hands. Slowly. I want no sudden moves. I'm warning you. Don't try anything funny. If I have to, I won't hesitate to shoot."

Tina slackened her chest-crushing squeeze on the package, but before she could complete the transfer, a commotion to her left made her tighten her hold again.

"Don't do it, Mi Pequeña! This thug isn't who he pretends to be."

An explosion of emotion shot through her when she recognized Miguel's Tex-Mex drawl. Old feelings die hard, even though she had him to blame for her current predicament—

and despite her growing assumption of his guilt. She wanted to ask him what he meant about Hal, make him explain himself, but the words froze in her throat.

She had no idea where he'd come from or what he was doing here now. She longed to believe he was her knight in shining armor come to rescue his damsel in distress, but her assessment based on the known facts indicated Miguel was making a last-ditch effort to take the money and run.

In light of Miguel's surprise arrival, Tina braced for Hal's gun to fire. She pinched her eyes closed. The muscles in her neck and shoulders tensed, and the sweat on her hands caused the bag to slip. She felt the money come to rest on top of her fuzzy-bunny slippers, but she dared not open her eyes or lower her head to look.

"You fool. Get that thing outta my face," Hal's voice snarled. "Do you think you'll get away with killing me?"

Tina relaxed one eye just enough to allow herself a sliver of sight. She saw Miguel with a gun aimed at Hal's head. He mirrored the pose Hal held as he pointed his weapon at her.

"We've got all the goods on you and Miss Frank here, and you'll never make it out of Ohio alive if you try to flee." Hal punctuated his threat by jabbing Tina's head with his gun barrel.

Tina squeezed both her eyes shut tight again.

"Not unless you have a death wish will you so much as wiggle that trigger finger of yours. I'll open fire the split-second I see you make a move." Miguel spoke in a slow and steady tone, as though he were discussing the matter over a cup of coffee down at Pearl's Café.

Silence sucked the oxygen from the room.

Her overpowering curiosity finally won out over her fear.

She opened her eyes full wide and studied Miguel. He kept his eyes trained on Hal alone, like a lion studying his prey.

"So. . ." Hal broke the tension-packed quiet and cleared his throat, but appeared to take great pains to keep his head and body statue-still. "It appears we've reached a standoff." His gaze darted back and forth between Tina and Miguel.

Now, there was an understatement if she ever heard one. Maybe they taught him to downplay these types of situations in crisis negotiation class at FBI school.

The loud ticking of the mantel clock above Miguel's fireplace marked another five seconds.

A bead of perspiration slid down the small of Tina's back. Afraid to draw a deep breath with a loaded gun resting against her head, she tried to inhale through her mouth. The effort made her parched throat burn.

"Miss Frank," Hal interjected again, "tell me. How did a classy lady like you get mixed up with a creep like this? Don't you realize, if he hasn't yet, he's sure to turn traitor against you, just like he did your friend, Lenny? I've had to deal with his kind all my career. He only wants you alive long enough to save his own skin and make off with the goods. Then you'll be next on his hit list."

"Don't listen to him, Mi Pequeña." Although Miguel addressed her, he kept his intense focus on Hal. "He's messing with your mind—stalling until the moment he can throw me off guard and make a move. You're my closest friend. I'll never forgive myself if anything were to happen to you." His shoulders lifted in a sigh. "I know it looks bad, but you've got to believe me. Just as sure as you know you're not guilty of anything other than being my friend and Lenny's boss, I promise—I'm innocent of the crimes this guy's trying to pin on me. I'll give you a full explanation once this situation is resolved. Hal is the bad guy here. Not me. Trust me. Please."

"Ha!" Hal's laugh didn't make it to his face. "Lady, if you believe this joker, you're a hopeless cause." He paused and sent Tina another darting glance. "If you're really innocent like he says, we'll get to the bottom of it once the situation is resolved. Don't try anything now you're gonna regret later."

With all her heart, Tina wanted to believe Miguel. To her knowledge, he'd never lied to her before. Even though his claims of innocence seemed absurd at first, the more she thought about the man she'd come to know these past two years, the more she found his declaration easier to swallow than the idea of him being a murderer.

She wished Miguel would glance at her, if only for a fleeting second. She longed to look in his eyes to judge his sincerity before she made up her mind. She studied the profile of Miguel's face for some signal, some clue. If she trusted him and he proved to be lying to her, she would be assured of doing prison time for aiding and abetting a felon at the very least— if she survived this current crisis. She had to decide if she was willing to risk such grave consequences to prove her devotion and loyalty as Miguel's friend.

A verse of Scripture raced through her thoughts. She and Miguel had worked together to memorize it just a month or so ago after church. *John 15:13. "Greater love has no one than this, that he lay down his life for his friends."* She'd been totally unworthy and undeserving of Jesus' friendship, but He proved His love for her by dying on the cross and taking on the consequences of her sin.

Whether Miguel was lying to her or not, she knew what her response must be. She chose to trust him despite evidence to suggest she should do otherwise. That's what true friends did.

"Miguel." She managed little more than a whisper. "If something happens to me. . ." She paused to gain control of her crumbling emotions before she continued. "I want you to know. I'll be waiting for you in heaven when your time comes. Everything's okay. I believe you."

If Tina hadn't been studying Miguel's face, she would have missed his almost imperceptible nod.

"Hey, you stupid cat. Get away from me!"

Tina felt the gun barrel jiggle against the side of her head. She shifted her gaze from Miguel to Hal.

Hal's mouth puckered into a grimace. His eyes bore a look of pain. He was obviously struggling to keep his body rigid and his neck stiff lest Miguel follow through on his threat to shoot if he moved.

She rolled her gaze downward to look at Hal's feet. Sophie was kneading the gunman's pant leg with her front paws. Whether by reflex or intent, Tina didn't know, but Hal kicked and sent Sophie hurling across the room.

Tina seized the moment to drop to the floor.

A double explosion of gunfire rang out.

An agonizing scream rent the air.

She braced herself to feel the hot pain of a bullet wound. Instead, the wind whooshed from Tina's lungs when a heavy weight fell across her back.

Two questions plagued her during the interminable time she waited for someone to speak or move: Was it Hal or Miguel who pinned her to the floor? Was he alive or dead?

Chapter 7

From her vantage point on Miguel's front porch, Tina watched a team of paramedics hoist Hal into an ambulance. His head and shackled feet poked out from either end of a white sheet. The way he moaned and carried on, one might think he'd been mortally wounded. She pitied the attendants who would have to listen to his wailing during the thirty-minute ride to Canton. However, Miguel had assured her that the injuries Hal sustained to his shoulder amounted to little more than a flesh wound. Aided by the bed rest he was sure to get in jail, he stood to make a full recovery.

The large yellow letters FBI emblazoned the backs of a trio of men in blue nylon jackets who huddled around Sheriff Yocum and Miguel. The clustered group had been absorbed in discussion for several minutes. Tina couldn't make out their words, but she watched as the agents, one-by-one, pulled out their credentials and passed them to the sheriff for examination. Yocum scratched at his bald spot, then shrugged his shoulders and shook his head. Finally, he offered a handshake to Miguel. Tina smiled. Without a doubt, the sheriff would be pondering the complexities of this case for years to come.

The ambulance sped off, engulfed in a conflagration of sirens and lights, and Miguel appeared to excuse himself from the clutch of men. He backed away. Then, waving to a crowd of curious neighbors nearby, he started toward the porch.

Tina wiggled her toes inside her bunny slippers as he approached. For the first time since her early morning trashcan encounter with Hal, she was aware of just how sloppy she looked. She plowed her fingers through her hair in two passes, but she abandoned the effort when she saw Miguel's wide grin.

He took the porch stairs two at a time and came to a stop by her side. "Forget the hair. You look great. Feel okay?"

"Um-hum. Glad to be alive." *Glad to be standing here next to you,* she thought as she looked up into his caramel eyes, but she didn't have the courage to speak the words.

"The guys can handle things from this point," he said, nodding to the team of agents. "I promised you an explanation, and I'd like to make good on that. Are you up for a walk down to Lock Five Park?"

"Sure, I'm pretty whipped, but I think I can manage to go a block. Would you mind if I ran into my place and changed shoes first?"

Miguel looked down at Tina's feet. He wore a grin when he looked up again. "I think I can spare a minute." They traveled together across the yard and next door to her place. Tina left Miguel sitting on her bottom porch step while she dashed inside to grab a pair of sneakers. On her way back out the door, she snatched a couple of bananas from the basket on her kitchen counter.

When the squealing screen door slammed shut behind her, Miguel jumped up from his perch.

"Here. I thought you might want one." She tossed Miguel a banana. "Stress always makes me hungry, and right now, I'm starved."

He accepted her offering with a "Thanks." As they headed down the walk, Tina peeled her fruit.

"I'm not really sure where to begin. . . ." Miguel let his words trail.

"Haow," Tina mumbled around a big bite of banana. She hurried to chew and swallow, then began again. "Hal Princeton." She used her finger to wipe the corners of her mouth. "I've already pretty much figured out that you are the under-cover agent—not Hal. But if he isn't with the FBI, then who is he and who does he work for?" Tina wagged her banana at Miguel. "You're not going to tell me he really worked for United Home Security, are you? Is he the one who murdered Lenny? If so, why? And how did Lenny's jacket get in your trash? Then there's all that cash. What on earth was it doing stuffed in your vacuum bag?"

"Whoa, whoa, whoa." The sound of Miguel's laughter sent joy splashing over Tina's soul. "Hush up and eat your banana while I answer this batch of questions. Then you can add to your list when I'm done if need be." Miguel paused in the mid-dle of the Williamses' drive and appeared to be collecting his thoughts, then he started to walk again. As he strolled, he cast frequent glimpses at Tina. "The man you refer to as Mr. Princeton uses a list of aliases longer than the Old Testament genealogies, but his mother named him Bernard. Bernard d'Angelo Kratz. Bernie for short."

"I can understand why he'd prefer an alias." Tina smirked and took another bite.

"I see your point," Miguel answered. "Well, ol' Bernie worked in, what I call for lack of a better term, 'middle management' for the Zamboni crime family over in Youngstown. The Zambonis have a corner on the drug market in this part of Ohio. Have had for years. They run a smooth operation—they'd even become so bold as to lease a suite in the same office complex as our Youngstown branch. They conducted the front for their legitimate business cover from there."

"United Home Security?" Tina knew the answer before she asked.

"Exactly." Miguel ticked his head in the affirmative. "My objective when I accepted this assignment was to not only collect enough evidence to convict the low man on the totem pole—who, in this instance, turned out to be Lenny—but to build a strong enough case to put away the boys at the top of the Zamboni family tree as well."

Tina polished off the last bite of her banana and stopped when they reached the walk leading down to the historic canal lock so she could toss the peel into a park receptacle. "Keep talking." She wiped her palms on her jeans. "I'm following you so far."

"Okay, but here." Miguel passed her the banana she'd given him earlier. "I'm not really hungry. Why don't you eat this one too?"

Tina took the proffered fruit. "Thanks, but I've had enough. I wonder if the squirrels would eat it?" She unzipped the peel and tossed it into the trash. "I guess there's only one way to find out." She broke off pieces of the bald fruit and left a trail as they walked.

Miguel led her toward a bench that looked out over the

canal. A large weeping willow tree stood between the canal and the footpath and afforded them a measure of privacy from the occasional jogger or dog walker who happened by. He sat close beside her, and she turned so she could watch him as he spoke.

"I had collected enough dirt on Lenny to put him away for life, but we were willing to negotiate a plea bargain and knock a few years off his sentence if he agreed to help us nail the coffin shut on the Zambonis. The day you left town for your conference, I confronted him, and in light of the evidence we had against him, he agreed to go along with our plan. We rigged Lenny's keyboard so I could monitor all his communications and track his activities."

An image of the pitiable Lenny flashed through Tina's mind. He never went anywhere without that portable keyboard, which served as his mouthpiece to the speaking world. She wondered if he'd been buried with it. A pang of regret accompanied the mental impression. If only she had been able to get through to him and convince him of his spiritual need. Tina dug her hands into the hand-warmer pocket on her sweatshirt. She crouched forward to stave off a chill, despite the heat from an Indian summer sun.

"Do you need me to stop, Mi Pequeña? Is this too upsetting to hear now?" Miguel laid his hand on her shoulder. His face telegraphed his concern.

"No, I'm fine. Please. Go on." She offered a weak smile and gave his knee a pat.

"Okay. If you're sure."

She urged him on with a nod.

"Well, that cache of money you found in my sweeper came

from Lenny. We'd 'borrowed' the funds from him, so to speak, and marked the bills in preparation for his final exchange with the Zambonis. We were within hours of making our big bust, and I hid the cash there, thinking I'd be handing it back to Lenny right before his scheduled meeting with his delivery-man. The job was scheduled to go down early in the morning on Saturday. Unfortunately, Zamboni sent one of his thugs the night before to settle a score with Lenny. I tried to intervene as soon as I read the feed from Lenny's keyboard that showed him pleading for his life. Hard as I tried, I flat-out couldn't get there in time."

"But why? What did he have against Lenny that warranted such a violent death?" Tina knew she shouldn't have sympathy for a drug dealer, but vengeance came harder when she could put a face with the deplorable title.

"Unfortunately, there was one factor I didn't know that proved fatal for Lenny. I hate to speak ill of the deceased, but you and I both know, Lenny wasn't exactly the brightest candle on the cake. For several months, he had been siphoning more than his share of the proceeds from his drug deals and shorting the Zambonis in his payments in order to help one of his brothers in West Virginia pay off a big gambling debt."

Miguel shifted to look Tina full in the face and took her hand in his. His grave expression sent a stab of worry into her chest.

"I have a confession to make and an apology to offer for not being honest with you. I wanted to tell you. Really, I did. But I would have jeopardized the mission if I had. I never went any farther than Canton this past week. I went below ground, working under cover of darkness until we could untangle the details of

Lenny's murder, gather evidence, and identify the perpetrator."

"There's nothing to forgive." Tina looked deep into Miguel's eyes, hoping he could sense her earnestness. "I understand. You were acting in the line of duty."

Some other time she would tell him she had seen him on the street. Not now. "So, was Princeton—I mean Kratz—the one who murdered Lenny?"

"No, from what I gathered from the transcription of Lenny's conversation right before he died, Kratz didn't actually commit the homicide. Another Zamboni henchman by the name of Santos did. Santos was only in town long enough to do the evil deed. Agents tracked him down and arrested him in Columbus yesterday."

Miguel kept Tina's hand covered with his, but he looked past her, across the canal. A light breeze sent strands of his black hair dancing in the sun. "Our friend Kratz was in charge of mopping up the operation, finding out what Lenny had done with all the money he'd stolen from 'The Family,' and making sure all his partners and associates were accounted for and dealt with appropriately before they assigned someone else—someone they could trust—to Lenny's territory. He started asking around town about who I was and what I did for a living. To do his research unhindered, Kratz even convinced Sheriff Yocum he was an undercover agent with the FBI, knowing that our local sheriff wouldn't go to the effort of checking out his story."

Even as Miguel spoke of Sheriff Yocum, a siren screamed from the direction of their homes. Tina figured the inept law officer had left Miguel's to travel the short distance back to his office.

"I'm certain Kratz had no idea I was with the bureau. When he learned Lenny used to hang out with me in my garage, he deduced Lenny and I were in business together, with me running drugs up from Mexico on the jet and Lenny working to set up our own clientele and cut the Zambonis out of our market share. He's the one who put Lenny's jacket in my trashcan. As extra insurance, he played several other little tricks like that to frame me for Lenny's murder and steer all suspicion away from himself. I believe the plan was to make my death, whenever he caught up with me, appear to be a suicide. I suppose, unfortunately for you, Kratz dubbed you guilty by association with the two of us. I never would have put you in such a position had I known what Kratz was thinking. I still can't comprehend how he was so misguided as to suspect you were involved."

"Unbelievable." Tina scratched her head. "This is all so confusing. I should have brought pen and paper along and kept notes."

"Who knows," Miguel said. "Maybe this will all end up as a plot in one of your mysteries someday."

"Nope. Not a chance. This is one of those times when truth is definitely stranger than fiction. Nobody would buy a word of such a farfetched tale.

"So what's next?" Tina dreaded his response, but knew she had to ask. "Will you stay here or move on with your next assignment?"

Miguel stood, and taking Tina's hands in his, he pulled her to her feet. He closed the gap between them so that she had to tilt her head back to look into his eyes.

She swallowed hard against a rising knot in her throat and

braced herself for another round of bad news.

"Soon after I moved to Canal Pass, I knew I had come home to stay. I told my chief a few months back that this assignment would be my last. I'm submitting my resignation to the bureau. I've used up a life supply of adrenaline in this job, and frankly, I've faced all the danger I can stand. I'm tired of having to live under a shroud of secrecy, and I think it's high time I settled down and found myself a wife." He shot Tina a quick glance, and his lips quirked into a smile. Heat radiated from her cheeks, and a wash of goose bumps covered her arms as the implication of his words sank in.

"I want a family. I want to live a quiet, peaceful life and spend the rest of my days right here in this sleepy little town." Miguel's breath brushed across Tina's cheek with his soft-spoken words. "There's one big problem, though, I have yet to solve."

She pulled back and looked into his maple eyes. "What's that?"

"I'll soon be unemployed with no real prospects for a job."

Tina released the pent-up breath she'd held in preparation for a serious dilemma. "I learned from good authority that you are mechanically inclined and skilled at making household repairs. You might have to take a cut in pay, but I know someone who's looking for a maintenance man. Would you be interested?"

His cheeks creased into deep dimples when he tipped his head back and laughed.

"Hum. I might be—depending on this company's policy on employees fraternizing with management."

"The current ownership just adopted lenient guidelines in that regard." She shot back the retort, and they shared another round of laughter.

He pulled her to his chest, and she nestled into his embrace.

When he released her, just far enough to look into her eyes, she watched an expression of tenderness transplant his merriment. Miguel gently traced the contour of her face with the back of his fingers and stroked her hair. His eyes revealed the depths of his feelings as he studied her.

He pulled her close to him again. So close, she could feel his heartbeat against her cheek. Miguel stooped and kissed her—tentative and timid at first, then growing in intensity.

In that moment, she solved the greatest mystery of her life. As she stood on tiptoe to receive his kiss, she knew she'd found the man of her dreams.

If Tina had any say in her life's plot, she hoped to keep all future villains locked within the pages of a mystery manuscript. And in writing the story's ending, she'd leave her heroine right here, along the banks of the peaceful canal, nestled safe and secure in the strong arms of a hero named Miguel.

SUSAN K. DOWNS

Susan lives near the fictional village of Canal Pass in the real-life town of Canton, Ohio. When she isn't writing, Susan works as a freelance fiction editor. She and her minister-husband raised five children and recently became the enthusiastic grandparents of one most-delightful grandson. Whenever the weather is fair and they can break away from their duties and responsibilities, Susan and her husband enjoy a Harley ride along the old Erie Canal routes and Amish buggy trails of eastern Ohio. Read more about Susan's writing/editing ministry, family, and latest motorcycle adventure at her Web site: www.susankdowns.com.

Suspect of
My Heart

by Pamela Griffin

The Makings of a Great Mystery
by Drake Axelrod

Chapter Two
Red Herrings and Other Fishy Leads

Rule: Thou shalt create a list of possible villains and keep the reader guessing as to which leads are false and which are real.

Exercise: Create a reason or reasons why someone might want to murder a person and a cast of characters to accompany the list.

Chapter 1

Cold-blooded murder wasn't Raine's style. She couldn't even stand to watch some unsuspecting soul gunned down or stabbed in the back in an old '30s mystery movie. Foreign espionage with a 007 flair was a possibility. But it would take more than the usual research, and there wasn't enough time. Maybe a jewel heist. . .yes, that had merit.

Studying the baggage claim area, Raine pressed the bottom of her ballpoint pen to her chin. She repeatedly clicked the silver button, thinking. In the constant flow of airport passengers toting luggage, surely she could find one among them for her most likely suspect. No, make that four, since she needed at least three red herrings to make her plot work, according to Drake Axelrod's lecture on how to write a mystery novel.

A bouncing brown spot under a connecting row of chairs opposite hers snagged her attention. She lifted her eyebrows in surprise, gazed at the spot harder, then smiled. Of all things. A small sparrow had found its way into the airport and was merrily hopping about on the blue carpeting.

"Mommy—ook!"

Raine turned her head to see a toddler drop her doll—almost

as big as the child herself—and run for the bird. "Petty bewd!" she exclaimed, falling onto her hands and knees in front of the chairs. With a panicky fluttering of wings, the sparrow flew a short distance to another set of chairs, eliciting a complaint from the dark-haired tot.

"Bandy get the bewd," she said decisively and trotted to pick up her doll. She ran, then threw the doll at the bird, just missing it. The sparrow rustled a few feet away in a flurry of feathers.

A husky security guard suddenly appeared and smiled at the child. "Do you like our little bird? He's become something of a mascot since he flew into our waiting room two days ago."

With wide eyes, the tot backed away from the gray-haired man.

He turned his attention to the bird and slowly approached it. Raine saw that he held a small carton from a nearby Chinese fast-food restaurant. "Come on, little fellow. I won't hurt you."

The bird gave several flutters of his wings but otherwise offered little resistance, as though knowing it would be safe, and allowed the large hands to scoop him gently into the box. Raine watched the guard walk to a nearby exit door.

The child started to cry. She ran to a nervous-looking woman with dark hair. "Bandy want the bewd!" she yelled.

"Shh, Brandy, everyone's looking! Hush now. Aunt Kara doesn't want to see you crying."

The child wouldn't be consoled and continued to sob against her mother's jean-clad legs. Embarrassed for the mother, Raine focused on her notepad and the doodles she'd made in place of the words that should be there. She sighed. Why was it so hard to think up good characters?

"You must be Brandy! Come here, Hon, and give your auntie Kara a hug."

At the sugarcoated words, Raine lifted her head. A woman with a pink-and-purple, tie-dyed and fringed jacket had joined the child and her mother. Huge gold loops dangled from the woman's ears, with shimmering earrings running up the entire lobe and over the top. Her dyed hair—resembling the color of days-old red carnations fading to black—looked as if someone had gone cut-happy with a pair of scissors and uniformity wasn't the name of the game. A tattoo of some sort could be seen below the collarbone, above her turquoise T-shirt. Yet her smile seemed genuine, and her violet-colored eyes sparkled with fun.

If Raine wanted an unusual character for her heroine's buddy, she need look no further. She had to fit this woman into her novel! She jotted down as many characteristics as she could in the short time it took the trio to walk to the exit. She gave up words for pictures and hurriedly penned an adequate drawing. As she stared at it, another idea came to mind, and she sketched a face that would have done Agatha Christie's Miss Marple proud, complete with a floppy flowered hat, and next to that, the face of an elderly gentleman with a white walrus mustache.

Her pen seemed to take off without her as she flipped the notebook's page and set to work on her fourth character suspect. This one had something of a pretty face, though she made sure the jaw was strong. She didn't like men with weak jaws. To her, a weak jaw denoted weak character. The nose was narrow, but a pair of frameless glasses sat nicely upon it—the type that used illusion wire to hold the bottom of the lenses in place so the eyes could be seen clearly. And the eyes. . .jade green. Oh, yes. Definitely jade green—like the fathomless waters of the South Seas. The face should be tanned so as to see the eyes even better. Too bad she didn't have colored pencils handy. She made a note to the side for eye color.

Now for the hair. . .hmmm. . .long, pulled back in a ponytail reaching just below the neck. Sandy blond—almost brown—wavy. She added a small gold loop dangling from his right ear, like a pirate would wear, and smiled at her composite. Perfect! Attractive, with a heady mix of boy-next-door and devil-may-care rogue. He would make a nice counterpart for her female character with the wild clothes. A peculiar sense of awareness hit. She stared at the drawing a little longer, gave a mental shrug, and forced herself to move from it and sketch her last character.

"Hello! Earth to Raine—or is it Raine to earth?" a joking voice said loudly.

Startled, she raised her head. "Chris!" She shot up to give her teenaged brother a hug. "It's good to see you! Have you been waiting long?"

"I pulled up front, spotted you through the glass wall, and honked—but you were in another world."

Heat rushed to her face. "I'm gathering information for my mystery novella."

He looked in amusement to the drawing in her hands. "Oh, is that what they call it—gathering information, huh? Well, let's get out of here. I'm double-parked. Got any luggage?"

"Just those two cases."

She slipped her carry-on over her shoulder and followed

her tall, football player of a brother out of the baggage claim area. He hurried through the automatic doors, his breathing not the least bit labored though he carried two heavy weights.

"There's something you should know before we get home," he said once they were in his beat-up Ford. "Mom phoned you about Great-uncle Harold dying last week, right?"

Raine sobered. "Yes. I'll miss him."

"Well, did she tell you in the letter she sent that it's rumored he left you something?"

"No. But I haven't gone through all my mail yet. I brought it with me. I'm a few weeks behind."

Chris looked at her strangely. "You don't open your mail every day?"

"Things have been crazy, what with getting canned, then going to that writer's conference—I paid in advance and didn't want to lose the money—and then moving out of the apartment. I haven't had time to sit and wade through all the junk mail and stuff. Kathy took care of the bills, though."

"I'll bet Mom will be interested to know her mail is junk."

Raine hit him on the arm. "Oh—you know what I mean! Now, tell me about Great-uncle Harold before there's one less brother in the world to worry about."

He grinned. "Threats, huh? Well, what else should I expect but flack from a soon-to-be millionaire. Of course you'll have to be at the reading of the will this weekend to collect."

Raine stared at him. "Pardon?"

"If you check that stack of 'junk mail,' you'll probably find an envelope from Mom containing something from the law offices of Uncle Harold's attorney."

Raine suddenly felt dizzy and was glad she was sitting down.

"It's probably nothing. Just a token gift he left me."

Chris snorted. "From a guy with his cash flow? I doubt it. Dad didn't get a summons, and he's Uncle Harold's nephew." He looked her way. "So, how's it feel to be filthy rich, Sis? Care to lend me a twenty to tide me over 'til payday?"

"Don't be a doofus." Raine couldn't think. Chris was assuming a lot. If Uncle Harold had left her anything, it was probably something of sentimental value. Yet why should her grandfather's brother single her out at all?

One week later, her mind a hodgepodge of jumbled thoughts resembling the painted shapes streaked across the canvas before her, Raine stood inside the cavernous Gladney Fine Arts Museum, with its almost cathedral-like silence, and waited to see a museum curator. She still couldn't believe it. Uncle Harold had left her something sentimental, all right—his entire art collection. An announcement that hadn't made his only child, Drew, at all happy.

Why? Why had he done it? True, Raine was as strong an art lover as her uncle had been. It had been the glue that bonded them together during her yearly visits with her parents to his seaside manor. Drew only cared about any money he could get his hands on to supplement his drug lifestyle, Raine was sure. Perhaps that's why Uncle Harold left the collection to her and not to his son.

Wondering what was taking so long, Raine moved to the next painting. To keep the collection was impossible. She couldn't afford insurance on such priceless art, though at least her uncle had left her enough funds to cover the inheritance tax, something he'd worked out with his lawyer ahead of time.

Raine fluctuated between thinking she should loan the entire collection to the museum and wondering if she should sell just one of the items and use the money to tide her over until she found a job. Uncle Harold stated in the letter he'd left her that the collection was hers to do with as she pleased, though he preferred it remain in the family. Raine wasn't mercenary; but she did need to eat and eventually find a place to live. Still, it would be difficult to let go of even one piece of the lovely art.

"Did you hear about the burglary in Melleville?" A woman's voice came from beyond a bronze sculpture of modern art, which sat on a pedestal on the marble floor. "They took off with the woman's wedding rings and their antique silver and collectibles."

"No?" another woman intoned. "How horrible!"

"Isn't it, though? My daughter lives in Melleville—in the same neighborhood as the people robbed—and is privy to information the reporters don't know. For instance, a brown van was sitting near the Thorntons' home two days before the burglary. Just sitting there. Whoever was inside never got out. And Nan's sure they were watching the Thorntons' place."

"Oh, my word. Did she tell the police?"

"She doesn't like to get involved. She's shy, you know."

"But I should think they'd want to know about that!"

As Raine listened to the women talk about the clues discovered at the robbery and the shy Nan, an idea came to mind for a scene in her mystery novella. Excited, wanting to jot down the concept while it was still fresh, she reached into her large hobo bag for the three-by-five notebook she always carried, but she couldn't find it.

Brow furrowing, she sorted through things, located a gel

pen, and snatched that up. Still digging through the many items she'd stuffed in her bag, which hadn't been cleaned out since her move back home, Raine trudged to a row of cushioned chairs along the stucco wall and took a seat. She darted a glance around the alcove. No one stood nearby. Quickly, she began to grab items from her purse, one handful at a time, and pile them on the chair beside her.

"Is everything all right?"

The warm, masculine voice coming so suddenly at her elbow startled Raine. She jerked her head up—to meet a pair of jade green eyes behind illusion-wire glasses. His thick, sandy blond hair was pulled back in a ponytail, hitting just below the neck, and a small gold loop dangled from his right ear.

Her purse, already in a precarious position, fell from her lap, scattering loose change, breath mints, and all the rest of the handbag's contents onto the polished floor and around his tan loafers. She hardly noticed.

"Ma'am?"

Shock held her speechless. Her pirate, boy-next-door, mystery-novella suspect had come to life!

Chapter 2

Concerned, Lance eyed the petite woman with the huge, tortoiseshell-colored eyes—a striking light brown flecked with gold. Her sleek dark hair was cut jaw length in a breezy do. The flipped-up ends brushed her cheeks as she shook her head as though denying something. Her stricken gaze scanned his face, then lowered, taking in his uniform coveralls, before she looked up again.

"No," she murmured, "it's not possible."

"Ma'am?" He leaned forward, putting his weight on the long handle of the steel dustpan he held. "Can I get you something? You don't look well."

She didn't answer, just continued to stare at him as if he'd walked out of one of the paintings on exhibition. Feeling helpless, Lance scanned the area for a female worker. Not spotting one, he set his broom and dustpan against the wall and moved through a nearby door, with a sign saying, "Authorized Personnel Only." At the water cooler, he snagged a cone-shaped cup from the dispenser, filled it, and rushed back to the stricken woman. He placed the paper cup in her unresponsive hand, which still rested on her lap. As though suddenly aware of the cup, she looked at it, lifted it to her mouth, and drank the liquid in one gulp.

"Are you here with anyone?" Lance scooped up the coins and mints and dumped them into her open purse.

The woman shook her head, her eyes wide as they scanned her lap.

Lance stood. "Is there anything else I can get you?"

"Raine?" a feminine voice called. "Raine, is that you?"

The woman jerked in surprise and looked over her shoulder. "Crystal?"

"Oh, man—it is you!" Laughing, a redhead in a skirt, sweater, and heels rushed forward and gave the seated woman a hug. "What are you doing in Gladney?"

The woman he now knew as Raine seemed to tense more, puzzling Lance. Her unusual behavior intrigued him, setting off all sorts of switches in his mind. Was it the question that upset her or the other woman's presence?

"Oh, this and that." Raine's gaze flicked his way, then down again.

Deciding he was the reason for her unease, Lance held out his hand for the cup. "I'd better get back to work."

"Thanks," she said in a hoarse voice, putting the paper container in his hand.

Lance nodded, disposed of the cup in a nearby receptacle, and grabbed his cleaning tools. As he moved away, Crystal loudly whispered, "Oh, sorry—was that a case of bad timing? He's hot!" A pause. "Is he a friend of yours?"

"I just met him."

"Then I guess asking you for an introduction would be out of order, huh?"

"I see you haven't changed," Raine said.

Lance continued down the corridor until he was out of hearing range. Before turning into a room featuring Native American art, he glanced back. Raine's wide gaze was fastened to him. Seeing she was caught, she hurriedly looked away. Thoughtful, Lance stared at her a moment, then moved into the next exhibit.

❦

"Hey," Crystal said, laying her hand on Raine's arm. "You're really uptight. What gives?"

Raine forced herself to relax, pushing what had just happened into a convenient slot in her mind to sort out later, and gave her old high school chum a smile. "Things have been crazy. I moved back home—but I guess my mom already told yours that I was fired from my job at the newspaper. Mom said they were on the same church committee."

"I hadn't heard! What happened?"

"Someone stole my story, then set me up to look like the bad guy." Raine began shoving articles back into her purse. "I really don't want to talk about it. I liked that job."

"Well, if you're looking for work, we need help at the gift shop. There're only three of us, and with the museum's fiftieth anniversary underway, the publicity has brought more business than usual."

For the first time Raine took in Crystal's professional appearance, different from the jeans and T-shirts she'd always favored. "You work here?"

"Three years now. I manage the gift shop." She eyed a gold wristwatch. "And I have ten more minutes of lunch. Walk me back? The shop is on the other side of the museum."

"I'd like to, but I'm waiting to talk to a curator."

"Oh?"

Raine hesitated, sensing Crystal's curiosity. "Remember my great-uncle Harold?"

"The rich guy who owns the chain of resort hotels?"

"That's the one. Well, he died."

"I'm sorry," Crystal murmured.

"Thanks." Raine fiddled with a folded piece of paper, still uncertain, then handed it to her friend. "It seems he left this to me."

Crystal took the paper and opened it. Her eyes widened the further she read. "Degas, Monet, Cassatt. . ." Her eyes seemed about to pop out, and she snapped her head up. "A Rembrandt etching and a drawing by da Vinci?"

Unease prickled through Raine at Crystal's response. "Amazing, huh?"

"I'll say!" Crystal leaned forward. "Do you have any idea what these are worth? We're talking in the multimillions— hundreds of millions even! Do you think any of them might be stolen? Did you run a check?"

Frowning, Raine snatched the paper back. "Uncle Harold wasn't a thief. I have bills of sale and papers of authenticity. I jotted all this info down from a catalog he kept. He was very wealthy."

"Don't be mad, Raine. But to have so many masterpieces in one private collection, he would have had to be a billionaire! That's a long list."

"It's not all paintings. I also jotted down the doll collection of my late aunt's and other things. Everything he left to me, anyway." Raine squirmed in her seat. "My great-uncle's grandfather started the collection, decades ago, during the postwar years. Uncle Harold once told me that, in those days, you never knew when a fantastic masterpiece might turn up on the market. His grandparents were both lovers of impressionist art and took advantage of the situation. Since then, both my uncle Harold and his father, who loved the Renaissance period, added a few paintings and a sculpture here and there." Raine realized she was rambling but couldn't stop. Crystal's gaping stare made her nervous.

"You have sculptures too? Give me names!"

Raine slipped the paper back into her purse, wondering if it had been a mistake to confide in her friend. Maybe even old high school chums stabbed you in the back, and not just trusted coworkers.

Crystal touched her sleeve. "Please, don't look at me like that. I have a reason for asking."

"The three I have are unknown, but papers classify them as coming from the Renaissance period. They're angels."

"Oh, my." Crystal rubbed her brow with her fingertips, as though she had a headache. "And my guess is that you were going to loan out the collection to this museum?"

"Where else? I can't afford the insurance on them."

Crystal sighed. "Listen, I'm telling you this as a friend, but if I were you, I'd hold back on talking to the curator. There've been some strange things happening lately, and your collection might not be safe."

"What do you mean?"

Crystal's gaze shot to the front desk, and she lowered her voice. "I can't talk about it now. Just trust me on this—have I ever misled you?"

Raine hesitated. "No. . ."

"Well, I'm not misleading you now." Crystal stood and smoothed her skirt. "So, you haven't found a job yet, right?"

"I've only been in town a week. I'm still getting settled."

"Then why not work for me? It's not the newspaper business, but I seem to remember you have experience in retail, and I could use someone savvy, art-wise. You could even put those investigative journalist genes to work and see if you can get a lead on things here." Crystal cracked a grin.

"Thanks, but I'm not going freelance, and I doubt I'll be applying at the *Gladney News* offices either. Actually—and don't laugh—I'm writing a mystery novella with three girls I met at a conference. We have yet to pitch our idea to an editor, but we've had fun working on it."

"Raine, that's fantastic! You always did have such a sharp mind and could put words together so well. I confess, I was jealous of how you aced all those unit tests with ease. That photographic memory of yours ought to come in handy in your research."

Raine attempted a smile. Unfortunately her photographic memory was selective. Locations, dates, faces—those things she remembered well. Where she'd put her mini notebook, on the other hand, was still a mystery.

Raine tugged hard at the stubborn zipper and closed her purse, inch by inch. Reaching a decision, she looked up. "When would you need me to start?"

Crystal glanced at her wristwatch and smiled. "How about now?"

After a week of working at the museum gift shop, Raine noticed suspicious goings-on too. Such as the behavior of Lance, the museum worker, and his avid interest in a temporary exhibit—a montage of paintings featuring the High Renaissance artwork of Raphael, Granacci, da Vinci, and others, many of which were on loan from private collections all over the world, as well as from other museums. It seemed every time Raine left the gift shop and glanced that way, Lance would be staring at the paintings rather than doing whatever it was museum janitors were supposed to do. Each time she saw him, she continued down the corridor, hoping he wouldn't see her.

During her fifteen-minute break, Raine glanced into the room where the exhibit was held. Not seeing Lance, she moved to the archway.

"I'll need to see your ticket," a young brunette said with a polite smile. Her gaze darted to Raine's badge. "Oh, never mind. Go on in. I didn't realize you worked here."

"You mean I can see the exhibit for free?" Raine asked, uncertain. "I'm employed at the gift shop."

"It's one of the perks of working here. The director likes all employees to acquaint themselves with what's being displayed. I believe it's so that any worker, no matter their position, can help a visitor who has a question." She held out her hand. "I'm Mona, a volunteer. Raine is such an interesting name. What does the initial 'E' stand for?"

"Elizabeth," Raine muttered, shaking the woman's hand. She never had liked her first name, Elizabeth, and started going by her middle name, Raine, once she entered high school. Later, she used the first letter of her given name as a middle initial to create Raine E. Wells, her excuse being that every writer needed a catchy moniker.

A couple with a stroller approached Mona. Raine stepped through the entryway, feeling as if she'd been transported back in time. The coffered ceiling and white columns, placed in peristyle fashion near the ivory walls where the masterpieces hung, contributed to the sense of living in another century. Only the hidden spotlights that focused on each painting hampered the sensation. Yet they were cleverly placed above so as not to detract from the overall atmosphere.

Raine walked along the peristyle, feeling as though she were living a dream to have the privilege of staring at such beautiful works of art. She especially liked the painting by Giovanni Bellini of the mother and Child; there was something so secretive yet sweet about the woman's eyes. Many might call the canvases "dark"; the oils used were a dark pigment. Yet Raine liked the paintings of this era due to the mystical quality they held. That most were biblical also appealed. When Raine stopped to consider that she now owned two such pieces of artwork, she felt awed. She had yet to see them; they were still at her uncle's manor. Yet her uncle's attorney, Mr. Rand, had advised their removal soon, due to her cousin's disagreeable behavior. But where? Where could she move such valuable works of art?

Wholly focused on the masterpieces in their gilded frames, Raine continued down the peristyle—and almost trod onto the heels of the person in front of her.

"Oh—sorry!" she exclaimed, turning her head. Her face grew hot.

"Well, hello." Lance's grin was wide. "You like the Renaissance period too?"

Raine nodded. Since their first encounter, she'd convinced

herself that the fact that his features matched the character sketch of her novella suspect was sheer coincidence, nothing more. Still, she felt nervous around him.

"It's interesting to see the many ways Italian painters of that day depicted the Lord Jesus as a child and His mother, Mary." Lance's gaze went to a detailed painting by Piero di Cosimo. "The works are so different, yet so alike."

Raine stared at him instead of at the canvas. By his words, he sounded as if he were a Christian. His actions in helping her the other day certainly pointed to that possibility.

Raine's gaze lifted to the richly hued painting and the Babe sitting on His mother's lap. "When I was younger, I studied the oils showing the Madonna and Child and wondered what type of relationship those painters must have had with the Lord. Some depict Jesus smiling, others give Him such a sad look, and a few almost make Him seem impish."

"I see what you mean." Lance continued to regard the painting. "I suppose, just as the eye is the window to the soul, a painting reveals the artist's true heart."

Touched, Raine smiled at him. "That's a beautiful analogy." Suddenly remembering that time had not conveniently stopped, she glanced at her watch. "Oh, my. I should go."

"But there are two more rooms of this exhibit."

"I work in the gift shop. I'm on my break."

"Ah. Well, maybe we'll see each other again soon and talk more about paintings."

"Um, yes, I'd like that." His words flustered her, and Raine quickly turned, almost mowing down the couple behind them. "Oh, sorry!" She hooked one arm around a nearby pillar to maintain balance so she wouldn't fall on top of their baby, who gurgled up at her from his reclined seat in the stroller. With a nod to the couple, she hurried away.

Lance stared after Raine, his smile dissolving. She was too jumpy, as if she were hiding something. Or maybe the problem was she knew something she shouldn't. . . .

"Excuse us," the man pushing the stroller said.

Lance moved closer to the velvet barricade rope to let the couple pass.

Maybe he should keep an eye on Raine. He doubted a quiet girl like her could do any harm, but it was best never to assume anything.

Outside the Renaissance exhibit, Kara stood in the lobby. She raised her brows in question, but Lance only gave a slight shake of his head and looked away. She frowned, walking past him. As she did, she whispered, "Meet me at Brentley's at three. We need to talk."

Irritated, Lance continued to stare at the wall mural, giving no outward sign that he'd heard her. He had cautioned Kara from the start that they shouldn't be seen together, but he supposed he should bend his rule this once. Her voice sounded urgent, and if a problem had arisen, he wanted to know about it.

Chapter 3

Raine scooped up her purse, preparing to leave.

"Off to lunch?" Crystal looked up from arranging a display of illustrated Renaissance books.

"Yes, but I'm just going to get something from the vending machine and come back."

"You must've found out about the museum café's steep prices. Even with our 10 percent discount, I don't go there often. I prefer Brentley's."

"Brentley's?"

"It's only been around a year, but they have the best food and cheapest prices. Remember where Sarge's Deli is?"

"Three streets north, turn to the right, take a left at the first light, go to Central, second building on the left."

Crystal shook her head. "How do you do that? You're amazing. Anyway, Brentley's is next door. You should try it. The lunch crowd should be gone by now."

The prospect appealed, though Raine was wearing borrowed heels until her first paycheck arrived and she could supplement her wardrobe with the required clothing for this job. Somehow she'd lost her one pair of good shoes in the move. Her mom's shoes were comfortable, but had a higher heel. Still, she figured she could walk the four blocks it would take without a problem.

Once outside, Raine took in a deep lungful of air. Though the Atlantic was miles away, the cool breeze seemed to carry with it the salty tang of ocean, ruffling her hair and invigorating her. She spotted gulls in the distance, cavorting in a blue sky. She smiled, almost able to hear their sharp caws over the traffic. Gladney wasn't a busy town except during tourist season. With its tree-lined sidewalks, historical storefronts bearing colorful awnings over the doors and windows, and lush gardens, the downtown area still held its old-town charm.

After a short walk, she spotted Brentley's. Raine glanced up and down the two-lane street and crossed after a yellow Volkswagen puttered by—something she never would've been able to attempt on Chicago's congested streets. She had to admit, it was nice being home again.

Inside the restaurant, which looked empty of customers, delicious aromas tempted her palate. She was pleased to see a buffet of salads, soups, meats, and vegetables, as well as a dessert bar. She paid a reasonable price, got a cola from the self-serve drink station, and slid her tray along the silver bars mounted at each side of the delectable buffet. She took a helping of crab salad.

"Just tell me, Kara. Do you want to stick to the original plan or not?"

Hearing a man's terse voice nearby, Raine halted in surprise. That sounded like Lance. The long hanging light fixture above the buffet prevented her from clearly seeing his booth, and she slowly slid her tray along as she walked, forgetting to fill her plate.

"I'm not sure what to do," a woman replied in a Southern drawl, out of place on the East Coast and sparking Raine's memory. "Tell me this, Lance, would it be dangerous to proceed with a new plan?"

"Any switch in plans would be dangerous at this point. But don't worry about that. Just tell me what you want me to do."

Raine reached the end of the bars but still couldn't see their booth. Hesitating, though she didn't know why—after all, she had as much right to be there as anyone—she picked up her tray and stepped to the other side. As she did, a dark-haired man came from the direction of the rest rooms and approached Lance's booth.

Raine's arms jerked in shock. Her drink toppled from the corner and went sailing to the floor with a loud crack and splash, as iced cola sprayed all over her mom's shoes.

From two booths away, Lance darted a surprised look her direction. His booth-mate turned her head of days-old carnation-colored shaggy hair, and her violet eyes met Raine's. The second man also stared.

Raine gasped softly. It was the woman from the airport! And the man—he looked like her fifth mystery suspect!

The three shared a few quiet words, then looked at her again.

Brain frozen in shock, Raine did a hasty, deep knee-bend to pick up the plastic glass. Keeping her focus on the floor, she mopped up the spill with a napkin on her tray.

Was it some crazy fluke that three of her mystery novella suspects knew each other and were having a weighty discussion? True, the woman character was created after Raine saw Kara in the flesh, but that didn't explain Lance or the other man. How did Lance know these people? Who were they?

"Here," a waitress said from above, a towel in her hand. "Let me get that for you. Go ahead and get another. Refills are free."

"Thanks," Raine mumbled. Her head was filled with a conglomeration of conflicting thoughts ricocheting off each other like a metal ball hitting the flippers of a pinball machine. Gathering courage, she rose to a standing position and lifted her gaze to Lance's booth.

All three of her suspects were gone.

After putting away his cleaning tools, Lance turned to the three men who worked maintenance with him. "What a day! Anyone up for a game of pool at the rec center?"

Rod, the tallest, huskiest, and quietest in the bunch, shared a look with the shortest guy, Frank, and shook his head. "Can't. Busy." He grunted his reply.

Frank gave Lance a narrow-eyed stare, then shook his buzzed head and slammed his locker shut. Phil patted his shirt pocket, as though checking for his cigarettes, then smoothed a hand over his slicked-back brown hair. "And I can't, 'cause I got me a date with the looker from the gift shop."

The words hit Lance like a slap in the face. Raine was going out with this guy? "Maybe next time then."

"You got a date?" Frank asked. "Tonight?"

Phil shrugged. "We're just going to grab a quick bite."

Lance counted the bills in his wallet. "I probably should go home, anyway. This job puts meat on the table, but the pay isn't all that great, is it? I sure could use a hefty boost to my income. At this point, I'd do almost anything—short of murder." He grinned, flapped the wallet closed, and stuck it in his back pocket. "Well, see you guys next week."

He exited the back room and went upstairs toward the museum offices. His loafers squeaked on the slick floor. The place always was eerily quiet after closing time.

Kara caught his attention where she waited near the west wing and nodded toward the registrar's office. Lance headed that way. Tia sat inside, typing on her computer keyboard.

Lance leaned against the doorjamb and smiled. "Hey, Tia. Mrs. Phillips wants to talk with you about one of the shipments. She asked me to tell you to meet her in storage."

Tia's brow wrinkled, and she stared at the phone. "Why didn't she just buzz me? I'm behind on getting the latest batch of Egyptian relics catalogued for the next exhibit."

Lance grinned. "You know Mrs. Phillips."

A sudden short laugh erupted from Tia, and she flicked back her waist-length, black hair. "Isn't that the truth? Okay, I need a break anyway."

Lance moved aside to let Tia by. She brushed past him through the doorway, giving him an interested half smile before heading for the east wing. Once she was out of sight, Lance moved into Kara's line of vision, gave her a thumbs-up signal, and watched as she hurried toward Tia's office. He moved to the lower level and the cavernous back room where the newly shipped paintings were stored, heard voices, and slipped into a storage closet to wait until he was sure all workers in that section of the museum were gone. Then he stealthily set to work.

❧

"Crystal, did you tell anyone about my inheritance?" Raine asked as they stayed after closing time to set up displays of new souvenirs.

Crystal fidgeted and looked away. "Define 'anyone.'"

"Crystal!"

"Last week, Mrs. Phillips, the curator, commented that her Tuesday, one o'clock appointment had vanished, and I mentioned it was because she got a job with me. But she's the only one I told. . .except Tia Monoham, the registrar, did overhear."

Prickles of unease jumped over Raine's skin. "So two people know?"

"Two of the most reliable people on the museum staff."

"I just wish you wouldn't have told anyone," Raine muttered. "You're the one who told me things have been fishy around here."

"Yes, but Mrs. Phillips has been working at the museum for seven years. I doubt she has anything to do with what's going on. And Tia is her right-hand girl, so I'm sure everything's okay on her end too." Crystal gave her a penitent yet encouraging smile. "Your paintings and sculptures will be safe in whatever vault you have them in."

"What makes you think they're in a vault?"

Crystal's eyes widened. "You mean they're just out in the open?"

Raine unbent from her kneeling position on the carpet and brushed lint from her navy skirt. "They're at my uncle's. Arrangements are being made to transport them." Raine paused, wondering if she'd said too much. She should have known better than to trust Crystal. Hadn't she learned that to trust anyone was to endanger oneself?

"Your uncle's lawyer will advise you of the safest measures to take in dealing with them, Raine, so everything will be fine. Okay?"

Raine eyed Crystal. "Just what sort of fishy things have you been noticing? You never did tell me."

Crystal stood. With her stockinged foot, she shoved aside a box of T-shirts emblazoned with the message: "I'm an art lover of the Gladney Fine Arts Museum, celebrating fifty years." "Go home, Raine. This display can wait 'til next week. It was a mistake to try to tackle it tonight."

"Why won't you tell me what you know?"

Her friend let out a noisy breath. "Oh, it's just things. Strange behavior of some of the newer workers, weird conversations overheard in the break room, things popping up where they shouldn't be and disappearing from where they should."

Raine tried to make sense of the addled words.

Crystal appeared to force herself to relax. "It's probably nothing. Go on home. I'm sorry I kept you so late."

"You should go home too. Didn't you tell me you have a four-year-old daughter?" Raine moved to the back room where they kept their personal items.

"Yes, and Frannie's all the world to me. We take care of each other since we're all we've got. But I still have invoices I need to look over and book work that won't keep."

Raine scanned the shelves and frowned. "Rats. I forgot my canvas bag with my loafers." After closing time, the high heels always came off, and grudgingly, she slipped back into them now.

"You're walking?"

"Chris can't pick me up tonight."

"I hope you brought your pepper spray," Crystal said, coming to the door.

Raine patted her shoulder bag, then realized the spray she

always carried while living in Chicago was in her hobo purse and not in the one she'd brought to match the shoes. "I'll be all right. This is a small town with a low crime rate. The house isn't far."

"I guess you didn't hear about the robbery in Melleville last week. That's a small town too."

Raine remembered the chitchat between the two ladies while she waited to talk to the museum curator. "You're not helping any."

"Good." Crystal grinned. "Did I scare you enough to change your mind and call a taxi?"

"No." Raine smiled. "It's nice to be back in a town where you can walk the sidewalks and not be afraid someone might mug you. I've missed my nighttime strolls." She didn't admit that until her first paycheck came, taxis were out of the question, and she didn't want to bother her parents, who were likely asleep. They usually went to bed early.

Crystal shook her head as though Raine were crazy. "You'll have to ask Joe to let you out. He's the night watchman in this sector. Look for a man with white hair and glasses. He's husky and walks sort of bowlegged."

"Or I could just look for a man in a blue security guard uniform," teased Raine as she headed for the arched entryway to the shop.

"Will you get out of here?" Crystal laughed.

Raine found Joe, a friendly man who, during their walk to the exit, gave her a rundown of his thirty-five years at the museum. Assuring the kindly guard she would be fine, she moved through the glass door, which he then locked behind her. She wondered about the security system in the old sandstone building but had been assured by Crystal that, though it might seem primitive to the naked eye, it was state of the art, or as state of the art as Gladney got. Once all workers left the premises and the art-maintenance technicians had finished dusting, alarms would be triggered. The place was rigged with a security camera system and wireless sensors—the touch of a hand on a painting setting off a siren so loud it would scare off any would-be thief. And night watchmen patrolled the area throughout the night.

Still, Raine hesitated about loaning her paintings out until she could investigate further. Crystal had made light of her suspicions in the store just now, but it hadn't escaped Raine that her friend seemed upset about something.

The street lamps gave off welcome pools of light, but were spaced far apart with stretches of darkness in between. All the friendly shops of earlier had closed, their windows reflecting like black eyes gleaming at her. The roads were mostly empty, with few cars driving past, their wheels making shushing sounds on the wet pavement. At the next street lamp, Raine checked her watch. Nine-forty-five. How had it gotten so late?

Her heels made hollow clacks on the cement walk, and she stuffed her hands in her jacket pockets. The sudden loud squawking of a bird from a branch directly overhead almost made her jump out of her skin. She deliberately calmed herself by taking a deep breath. Her earlier conversation with Crystal was making her nervous. Inhaling deeply of the crisp, cool air, Raine turned her gaze toward the ink-dark sky. Through the clouds, she could make out a half moon and sprinklings of stars. Suddenly she froze. Were those footsteps?

She strained to hear, but all was quiet. Swallowing hard, telling herself she was imagining things, she started walking again, crossed the empty street at the intersection, and continued down the sidewalk. Nearing the park, she heard the sound again and halted. A couple of footsteps crunched far behind her, then stopped.

Heart beating fast, Raine glanced over her shoulder and saw a dim form, about fifty feet away, standing in the patch of darkness between street lamps. She quickened her pace. Behind her, the footsteps came faster. She darted a look over her shoulder. The stranger was gaining on her.

Terrified, Raine clutched her handbag strap and ran as fast as she could toward the park. In the borrowed high heels, she was no match for whoever was pursuing her. In the next patch of darkness, she darted off the sidewalk and into a narrow opening between a long row of bushes. Huddling behind them, she pressed her face against the prickly leaves and tried to control her rapid breathing, while issuing silent pleas for God's protection. The footsteps slowed to a walk, grew louder, then faded as the stalker moved past her hiding place.

Her nose began to tickle. Alarmed, she pressed her finger underneath it, trying to stop the sneeze—but failed. The explosive sound shattered the stillness. Losing her balance, she made a wild grab for the bushes.

The footsteps abruptly halted, then came back, faster than before and growing louder until they stopped directly in front of the bush where she hid.

Chapter 4

Darkness obscured his vision. The street lamp stood far away, giving off faint light, but Lance was sure he saw the tall bushes move and heard them rustle.

"Raine? Are you okay?"

A pause, another rustle, then the upper portion of a face peeped over the top of the bush. "Lance?" She straightened until he could see all of her head and shoulders.

"What are you doing in there?" he asked.

She hesitated. "Why were you following me?"

"I saw you leave the museum. You shouldn't walk home by yourself this late. It's not safe for a woman to be out alone after dark."

"This is Gladney." Her words sounded uncertain. "Nothing happens in Gladney."

"You just moved here from Chicago, right?"

"Yes." She sounded uneasy.

"Times change, Raine. You need to be more careful."

At his well-meant warning, she backed up a step. "Thanks. I have to go."

"I'll give you a lift. My car's on the next block."

"No. . .I. . .thanks anyway." Turning, she fled deeper into the park.

Lance groaned. He obviously had scared her, which hadn't been his intention at all. "Raine?" He looked for the opening between bushes. "Wait up!" Finding the narrow space, he rustled between the prickly scrub until he was clear.

Since her awkward behavior at Brentley's earlier when she'd spotted him discussing plans with Kara and Bill, then later after hearing about Phil's date with her, Lance had decided to keep close tabs on Raine. Had she overheard their conversation? Did she suspect anything? Lance wondered why she wasn't with Phil now—relieved she wasn't, but curious, nonetheless.

He scanned the park, which was sporadically lit with black, wrought-iron electric lamps, though the closest one wasn't working. All around him, bushes and trees remained murky shapes against a background almost as black. In his line of work, he was accustomed to dark surroundings, but he didn't know the first place to look. How could she have disappeared so fast?

A sharp cry to his left was followed by a loud rustle, then a groan. He hurried in that direction. In the weak lighting of a lamppost several feet away, he found Raine sprawled in a shallow ditch some landscapers had left. Yellow tape was posted around the opening, half of it crushed by Raine's fall.

Lance moved to help her up. "Are you hurt?"

"I don't think so. But I broke my shoe." She walked a few steps, seesawing up and down as she did. "Now what do I do?" She groaned softly. "I can't walk home like this!"

"I'll drive you," Lance insisted. When she didn't answer, he continued, "Look, I didn't mean to scare you earlier, and I'm sorry. But I'm not about to let you walk home in this condition."

She hesitated, as though weighing her options. "I should call my parents and let them know."

Lance reached for his cell phone and turned it on. Once the screen lit up, he unlocked it, then handed it to her. "Just hit 'send' when you've dialed the number."

She took the phone but only stared at it.

"You still seem shaken up," Lance said more softly. "There's an all-night diner close by. How about we stop there, let you get cleaned up, then grab a bite to eat? It's on me. You don't want to worry your parents, and if they saw you coming home like that, they might be upset."

She looked down at her heel-less shoe, mud-splotched skirt and blouse, and torn hose. "Yes. All right."

"There's a bench over there. You make your call, and I'll get my car." He guided her over the uneven ground to the bench, helping her sit down. Beside them, a lamppost beamed white light over her strained features and stained clothing.

"Uh-oh. You've skinned your knee." Lance pulled a handkerchief from his pocket and knelt in front of her. Gently he pressed the cloth over her torn stocking and the scrape, blotting away the small amount of blood.

"I'm okay," she said faintly. "It only stings a little."

Leaning closer, he softly blew on it. She gasped, and he lifted his gaze. "Better?"

"Y–yes. . .thank you."

Lance felt entranced by the bewildered, wondering look in her huge brown eyes. Quickly, he stood and moved away. "Don't try to walk. I'll be right back with the car."

Twenty minutes later in the diner, Raine eyed the attractive man across the table while he talked about the town as though she were a stranger to it. Maybe she had misjudged him. Lance had been nothing but a gentleman, helping her in the park, tenderly dealing with her wound. When he'd blown on her scrape, her heart had given a mad flutter, and she'd melted like chocolate inside—all sweet and gooey.

Afterwards, he'd helped her to his car, which, to Raine's surprise, was an expensive newer model, and opened the door for her. When she hesitated, looking down at her muddy clothes, he assured her it was okay for her to sit on the blanket he'd placed on the seat. At the diner, seeing the patrons' shocked expressions, Raine limped straight to the washroom in her broken shoe—and gaped at the sight that met her in the mirror. With wet paper towels, she'd done her best to make herself presentable, all the while wondering about the man who waited in a booth outside the door.

Raine stared at him now, appreciating the way the incandescent lights brought out bronze-gold flecks in his hair and made his eyes a rich green like the fathomless sea, mysterious, deep. Dreamy ballads from the early '60s came from a radio behind the counter, adding to the old-fashioned feel of the place. Framed prints of '50s Thunderbirds at hamburger drive-ins covered peach-colored walls. Matching curtains hung at each booth window.

Raine clutched her elbows, which rested on the table, and leaned closer. "Tell me about you, Lance," she said. "I already know about the town."

"There's not much to tell."

Raine frowned. Was he evading the question? "How long have you worked at the museum?"

"Two months."

"And do you like it there?"

He grinned, a crooked, endearing, boyish grin that made her heart give that mad flutter again. "Are you interviewing me?"

"What do you mean?" Raine blinked.

"I heard you were a Chicago reporter before moving to Gladney."

Crystal must have blabbed again! Raine's gaze dropped to her half-drunk cup of coffee. "Did you also hear I was fired from my job?"

"Something to that effect." His tone was sympathetic.

All of a sudden Raine felt the need to spill. She'd kept the hurt and anger bottled in for weeks, but something about Lance and the gentle way he regarded her made her want to confide in him.

"It was a tough assignment that involved blowing the lid off a big corporation suspected of shady dealings. A lot of time, footwork, and research were required—something I loved and didn't mind one bit. I was the cub reporter to one of the best and oldest in the business. I trusted him. All through those months of investigating, he assured me that he'd help me in my career, that this would be 'the plum story every reporter dreamed of.' But later, when news leaked out that the newspaper was planning to let him go, he stole the story—took full credit for it—basically intimating that I did nothing and was an albatross around his neck. He saved his job, and I was released from mine." She shrugged, though the pain of the betrayal was still strong.

"I'm sorry," Lance said quietly. "It's hard to forgive people like that when they've hurt you so deeply, isn't it?"

Raine's gaze flew to his. She realized that she'd never forgiven Brady McMillan. Nor did she want to. The thought disturbed her.

The crooning song ended, and a jingle for the news came on, followed by a woman announcer's smooth voice. "Hello, I'm Roberta Harowitz, and you're listening to a WLAZ Newsflash. In local news tonight, thieves robbed a home off the coast hours ago, making off with thousands of dollars worth of priceless art. When asked to comment if this burglary was related to the one in Melleville last week, Police Sergeant Dale Clemmons responded with the following:"

"It's too soon to tell." A man's gruff voice came over the speakers. "There's been no real evidence leading to such a suspicion, but rest assured the Gladney police force will double their efforts to catch these criminals and keep our neighborhoods safe."

Raine was thankful her uncle's home wasn't local. Lance set his coffee cup down on the saucer with a harsh clink. "I need to take you home."

"But—the waitress hasn't brought our sandwiches yet."

"I'm sorry." He pulled a twenty out of his wallet and slapped it on the table. "I'll make it up to you another time. I have something I need to do."

Raine allowed him to steer her to his car, her mind active—both with the alarming newsflash and Lance's odd behavior. A stranger now sat in the driver's seat, one who barely talked or smiled, and he was exceeding the speed limit, as well. When she pointed out that he was driving too fast, he slowed, but the tense expression never left his face. Once he pulled up to her parents' house, she jumped out with a hasty good-bye.

The wheels of his car skidded as he roared away, and Raine stared after him, confused.

❦

Raine stayed home sick most of the next week. During that time, she talked over the phone with her uncle's attorney. He convinced her that she had no choice but to arrange for the transfer of the paintings. Her cousin was making threats, and Mr. Rand advised speedy removal of the artwork from the manor, telling her he would make all necessary arrangements.

Drew called long-distance from Florida the next day, offering Raine one million for the art collection, nothing close to what they were worth, but more money than Raine cared to think about. He told her she could keep the sculptures and doll collection, but he wanted to "cut a deal on the masterpieces." The temptation to accept his offer was strong, until she remembered the probable reason her uncle had left her and not Drew the paintings. Drew likely would sell them and use the money to buy drugs, maybe even move from being a user to a dealer. With what that collection was worth, he could easily become a drug lord and start his own crime chain. True, he could sell the manor and resorts to get the money, but Raine wouldn't be a contributing factor to his criminal dealings. She wouldn't sell him the paintings.

On Wednesday, Raine stood wrapped in her robe, sneezing into a tissue, and nervously watched two men arrive in a van and carry her inheritance into the only windowless room of her parents' home. Raine must have checked the security alarm box fifteen times that night to make sure everything was functioning properly. Their home security system seemed adequate, but Raine didn't know much about alarm systems.

Friday she returned to work. One of the maintenance men came into the gift shop and immediately started an argument with Crystal, who firmly told him to leave. After he stormed away, Crystal explained that she and Phil had had a date last week, but he'd stood her up, and she didn't need a man like that in her life.

That conversation made Raine think about her idea of the perfect date, which invariably led to thoughts of Lance at his most charming. On several occasions, Raine ran across him. Each time he seemed pleased to see her, though he never mentioned why he'd cut their time together short at the diner. Where Lance was concerned, her feelings were in a hopeless muddle. One minute she liked him, the next she wasn't sure how she felt.

After work Saturday, Raine hurried to the employee parking lot. Her father had insisted she drive her mother's compact once he heard about her scare in the park coupled with news of the recent burglary. Suddenly, Gladney didn't seem so safe anymore.

At home, she parked the car in the garage. She found a note on the kitchen table: *Your father took me out to dinner. Chris is on a date. Love, Mom.*

Raine tossed the car keys on the counter and hurried upstairs to the windowless room. Throwing open the door, she tugged on a metal cord, filling the cramped area with hazy light. Instantly, she spotted the canvas-wrapped rectangles propped against the wall and melted against the doorframe in relief.

Sinking to the carpet, she sat cross-legged, chin on her fists, and stared at the canvas parcels bound with twine. It was a horrible way to treat such priceless works of art, but Raine had insisted she didn't want the workers bringing it in anything that would attract unwanted attention, like huge wooden crates.

Long minutes passed while she stared. It was so quiet she could hear the clock ticking in the corridor. This had been the first real opportunity she'd had to see the paintings since they'd been delivered. Almost feeling as if she were trespassing, though it was legally her property, she reached out and worked the knotted rope loose from the first parcel. With shaky hands, she pulled the cloth. Grooves of a frame met her fingertips. Swallowing hard, Raine pulled the rough material the rest of the way down—and gasped at the beauty of the masterpiece before her.

Myriad flecks of color, appearing as light, mixed with darker colors, denoting shadow, in a peaceful garden display. In the far background, with the foliage of trees for a backdrop, a woman wearing a white gown smiled mysteriously at something off canvas.

"Claude Monet." Raine whispered the artist's name at the bottom, left-hand corner. To think that an actual Monet, and behind that a Degas, and other paintings by the masters were sitting propped against the wall in her parents' four-bedroom bungalow was almost impossible to fathom. Yet here Raine sat staring at one. She brushed a fingertip over a bed of flowers, then quickly withdrew her hand, feeling guilty to put prints on this lovely oil. These paintings didn't belong shut away in a musty, dark storage closet. They belonged in the open where many could have the pleasure of viewing them, as Raine had done with the Renaissance paintings at the museum.

Uneasy, she covered the artwork with the cloth, pulled the light's cord, and left the room, shutting the door behind her. She needed to get her mind off these past weeks. She needed to get to work on her novella. Her "Sleuth Sisters," the handle Drake Axelrod had given their group of four, depended on her to get her three chapters written soon so they could send off the proposal before the year was out.

Going downstairs and into the study at the back of the house, Raine flicked the power switch to the computer and settled on the office chair, using only a desk lamp for light. Getting into her Word program, she called up the file with her rough draft and worked on the fifth scene. After agonizing minutes, she made a frustrated sound, halfway between a growl and a groan. It wasn't coming together; one of her character suspects wasn't cooperating. It would have to be Lance's double, Phillipe, who was causing all the problems.

Raine stared at the words she'd just typed:

> *The icy breeze blew around Cynthia, as though whispering to her soul, forcing her to face the truth. Dead. Charmaine was dead. Phillipe's words came as softly as the north wind that blew at her back. "I tried to warn her, but she wouldn't listen."*
>
> *Angry, Cynthia faced him. Gentle green eyes appraised her. "How do I know you didn't kill her?" Suddenly frightened, wondering where Tom had disappeared to, Cynthia stepped back on the uneven ground and fell.*

Quickly Phillipe moved to help her, his tender touch bringing with it a spark that jump-started her heart.

"No, no, no! Cynthia isn't supposed to like Phillipe! Tom's the hero." Raine scanned the printout of her synopsis. Images of Lance's smiling face clouded her mind. Frustrated, Raine deleted areas and typed new words, forcing the nice-guy persona away.

The icy breeze blew around Cynthia, as though whispering to her soul, forcing her to face the truth. Dead. Charmaine was dead. Phillipe's words were as chilling as a north wind. "I tried to warn her, but she wouldn't listen."

Angry, Cynthia faced him. His green eyes raked her to splintereens. "How do I know you didn't kill her?"

With an evil laugh, he stepped forward and pushed her down.

This wasn't working.

Letting out a heavy breath, Raine minimized the screen and hit the shortcut to the instant-messaging Internet program she used. Maybe Cassie was on again tonight. Seeing her IM handle, Raine clicked on it, jotted a quick, "Hi, can you talk?" in the small white box that popped up, and sent the message.

Half a minute passed before a short musical-like computer bell dinged and Cassie's words showed on screen. "Sure, I'm just working on my novella. How are you coming along?"

"I'm not," Raine typed in. "Too much has been happening. I can't get my mind on the story."

"Want to talk about it?"

Raine paused, her hands hovering over the keyboard, then found herself madly tapping out the highlights of the past weeks, ever since the writing conference when she'd met Cassie face-to-face. Raine waited what seemed an interminable period until Cassie's message came back.

"Wow, I'll be praying for you and for your cousin to change his thinking. It sounds as if you've had it as rough as me."

Raine frowned. "Why? What's happening with you?"

"Oh, I've met this guy—Ethan. I told him about my idea with the murderer in the mystery leaving a dried bridal bouquet on his victims. Then there was a murder in my neighborhood. . . oh, I don't know. I'm too spooked to talk about it now. After I've had time to sort it all out, maybe I'll tell you then. In the daylight."

Raine puzzled over Cassie's jumbled words. The computer bell dinged and another message filled the lit screen. "So, who's Lance?"

Raine blinked at the purple words, then slowly punched the next three letters out. "Why?"

"Because you mentioned his name five times in the highlights of your week. Is he somebody special?"

Raine hesitated, unsure how to reply. For some reason— probably because she was afraid Cassie might laugh at her and think she was a nut—she had eliminated telling her the part about her character sketches coming to life in the faces of three very real people.

"He's a guy who works at the museum," Raine typed. She hesitated. "He seems nice. I don't know him all that well."

"Is he a Christian?"

Was he? Raine didn't know. He acted like a Christian,

though she knew that just because people said and did the right things didn't necessarily mean that Jesus was a solid part of their lives. She did know that he was kind, gentle, and thoughtful. . .and sometimes, when he drew near, her breathing went a little off and her heart did funny things—like when he blew on her scraped knee. That night she had to remind herself to just breathe.

"Raine?" The word flashed across the screen.

The sound of crunching leaves came from outside. A shadow crossed the drawn curtains, and Raine's eyes widened. Quickly she turned off the lamp and the computer monitor, plunging herself into darkness. A slight scraping skritched at the window. Something—a hand?—knocked against the curtains as though reaching to trip the lock from inside.

The security alarm remained silent while a scream huddled paralyzed in her throat.

Chapter 5

Heart pounding, Raine went through a mental list of everything she should do. Run across the room. Grab the phone. Call 911. Grab a weapon. Yet she sat, frozen, paralyzed. *Jesus, help me! What do I do?*

Ferocious barking sounded from the yard next door.

"You there!" Raine heard her parents' neighbor, Mr. Willoughby, shout. "Whaddya think you're doing to that window? Dagon—sic him!"

A vicious growl was followed by another series of barks, then a commotion of rustling bushes and running footsteps. Raine almost felt sorry for the intruder, whom she heard fleeing from Mr. Willoughby's trained Rottweiler.

Outside, near the front of the house, she heard a squeal of tires as a vehicle burned rubber down the road. A minute later, a knock sounded at the back door.

Realizing it must be their neighbor, Raine clicked on the lamp and headed that way. Hands still shaky, she unbolted the door and opened it a crack. Seeing Mr. Willoughby's lined face, she moved the door wider. Dagon stood beside him, on a leash. Raine nervously eyed the dog. He was calm now, but she knew that at one word from his owner, he could turn vicious.

"Guess you didn't know you had a thief trying to rob your house, did ya, Missy?" the elderly man asked. "Dagon, here, tried to grab a chunk o' him, but he jumped in a van before Dagon could get him a good, healthy bite." Mr. Willoughby looked down at his dog. "Dagon! Release!"

The Rottweiler spat something from between his sharp teeth onto the ground. Mr. Willoughby picked it up, offering it to Raine. "The police might want this. By the way, I called 'em already, so you don't have to. They should be here any minute."

"Thanks. I appreciate it. And thank you too, Dagon." Trying not to grimace, Raine accepted the proffered scrap of material slathered in dog drool, holding it gingerly with one finger and her thumb.

"Dagon and I will be going home now. If the police need me for anything, send 'em over."

Once Mr. Willoughby left and she securely bolted the door, Raine stared at the sodden piece of torn clothing, refusing to believe what her mind told her.

The scrap was the same color and material as the museum janitors' uniforms.

⚜

After church let out Sunday, Raine walked down the three shallow steps into the sunlit day. Instantly, she was swarmed by well-meaning citizens, most of them mothers and grandmothers, who inquired after her health and offered opinions, sympathy, and comments on what should be done to the burglars once they were caught. Thanks to the media, everyone knew that a glasscutter had been used on the window and the alarm's wires cut—as had been the case with the burglary in Melleville the previous week.

For the first time, Raine understood what it meant to be a victim. Being a reporter also, she knew that the media's job was to report the news. For that reason, she'd omitted telling either police or reporters that priceless paintings were being stored in her parents' upper room. Journalists were sharp, though. If they wanted to trail a story, they would, and Raine was sure it was only a matter of time until the truth came out. Unless she beat them to it. Raine fully intended to investigate and crack this case wide open. Instead of scaring her off, the burglars had only sharpened her interest.

"Hello," a familiar voice said, startling her. She whipped around and stared. She had never seen Lance in anything but uniform coveralls, but this afternoon he wore charcoal-colored slacks and a green print shirt that heightened the color of his eyes. His hair was pulled back in the usual ponytail, but the gold loop was missing from his ear.

"Hello." Nervously, she fiddled with the purse strap over her shoulder. "I didn't know you went to this church. I didn't see you earlier."

"I sat toward the back."

"Oh." Raine glanced at the parking lot, feeling awkward.

"I heard about what happened last night. You okay?"

"Whoever it was didn't hurt me."

"I doubt he even knew you were there."

At this, she grew alert. "What makes you say that?"

"Those men, if they're the same ones who struck Melleville, are burglars. Burglars steal when the house is unoccupied. Robberies are different. The robber steals directly from the victim."

Raine knew that from her days of reporting but wondered how he'd learned such information. "Where'd you hear that?"

Lance grinned. "Would you believe in the movies?"

"Not likely."

"No? Well, truth is, my grandfather was a cop."

"Really?" The news startled Raine.

"Yeah. I learned a number of useful terms and tricks of the trade while growing up listening to his career stories." His gaze turned to something above her head. He nodded, then looked at her. "I have to go. But I'd like to make up that lost sandwich to you. How about lunch Tuesday? Just tell me what time to come by the gift shop."

"Okay." She really did want to have lunch with Lance and get to know him better, for investigative purposes, of course. "My break is at three."

He smiled. "See you then."

She watched him walk away. A trigger of alarm clicked within her. "Lance?"

He turned.

"What happened to your right leg?"

He raised his palms in the air. "I rushed a workout and pulled a muscle. A dumb thing to do, I know."

"Oh," she said vaguely and watched as he continued his slight limp toward the parking lot. She wondered what pant leg Dagon had torn the scrap from, now in police custody. The left. . .or the right?

Suddenly Raine gasped. She took the few steps toward the church's brick wall, grabbed it for support, and stared hard, wondering if she were seeing things. She must be. . . .

Lance was opening his passenger door for an elderly woman

resembling a jolly Miss Marple with a floppy flowered hat. Next to her stood a man with a white walrus mustache. Raine shook her head in disbelief as she stared at her second and third mystery-novella suspects. The ones she had dreamed up at the airport. Only this was no dream.

"Chris!" she called, scanning the area behind her. She spotted him talking to a girl. "Chris!"

Her brother looked up, said something to the girl, and strolled Raine's way. "What's up? You look as if you've just seen Lazarus come back to life." He grinned. "Just in case you were wondering if I listened to the message."

"Never mind. Who are those people by that dark blue car?"

He looked at the parking lot. "You mean the pastor and his wife?"

Raine glanced that way. Lance's car was turning behind the church. She groaned. "I lost them. It was an older couple I drew—I mean that I've seen before, and I was wondering who they were and what they're doing here."

"What they're doing here?" Chris looked at her strangely. "My guess is that they went to church like everyone else here today."

"Maybe." She wasn't convinced.

"You know, Raine, since you inherited those paintings, you've become a basket case. Maybe you should take Drew up on his offer."

"If I did, I might be aiding him in his criminal activities. And anyone would be rattled after almost meeting up with a thief face-to-face."

"I'm not just talking about Drew or what happened last night. You don't trust anyone—it's been like that since you came home from Chicago. Maybe you're the one who didn't hear Pastor's message. It was on trust, by the way."

Miffed, Raine glanced at a line of cars. "Never mind. You're too young to understand."

Shaking his head, Chris rejoined the girl. Raine stared after him. Her brother had never been in Raine's position. He'd never trusted a person as a beloved mentor, one who turned into a self-seeking enemy ripping all one's dreams to shreds. So how could he understand? Truth was, Raine couldn't afford to trust anyone, except maybe God. And that was the only certainty on which she depended.

❦

"You're quiet this afternoon." Lance regarded Raine from across the booth's table at the museum café. A serious expression on her face, she pumped the straw in her drink and stared at the ice cubes tumbling around the glass. "Trouble at home? Or are you coming up against a dead end in your story?"

Raine's hand stilled, and she looked up. "How'd you know I was working on a story?"

"You told me. That night we went to the diner, when you fell in the park. A mystery novella, I think you said."

"Oh, that." Her brow clouded, and she set the cola down. "It's not going well. One of my suspects—Phillipe—won't cooperate. He's too nice, and when I try to make him meaner, he won't let me."

"Uh-huh." Lance gave her a hesitant smile. She spoke about her fictional characters as though they were real. "Well, I hope you get it all straightened out." He took a bite of his sandwich. "I hear you came into some paintings recently."

"Who told you that?"

Lance drew his brows together. "I don't remember; I heard it awhile back."

Raine frowned and took a long drink of her soda.

"What period are they from?"

"Why do you ask?"

"Why do you always answer my question with a question?" Lance forced himself to relax despite her suspicious stare. "I'm an art lover too, remember?"

Raine lowered her gaze. "They're just some paintings—not a lot."

Her evasive answer caused Lance to lean partway across the table and firmly grab her wrist. "With all the burglaries, lately—the attempted one at your home included—don't take chances with your safety, Raine. No painting is worth it."

A blur of vivid color caught his attention. Lance glanced out the booth's window, which faced the museum corridor. Frowning, Kara walked past with a nod of acknowledgment before she disappeared from his sight. Lance withheld a sigh. Inconspicuous, Kara was not. He had told her numerous times how important it was that she not give anything away by action or look. She just wasn't cut out for this type of work.

Raine gave a soft intake of breath, and Lance swung his focus her way. She averted her eyes, jerked her arm free of his grasp, and grabbed her purse. "I have to go. Thanks for the sandwich."

"But you've only eaten half of it."

"I'm not that hungry." Her smile lacked warmth. "It's been great chatting with you, but I really have to go."

Lance watched Raine hurry to the café exit, wondering what "chatting" they'd done. He'd hardly been able to get a word out of her. Worse, though he hoped to maintain only platonic relationships during his short span at the museum, he realized he was starting to care for Raine as much more than a casual acquaintance.

And that could prove dangerous for both of them.

✿

Raine hurried in the direction she'd seen Kara go. With her odd hair color and bright, canary yellow blouse, the woman from the airport shouldn't be hard to spot. Raine hadn't missed the silent interaction through the café window between Lance and Kara, either. Nor did she like the unexpected stab of jealousy that attacked. Ridiculous that she should have such feelings. For now she was sure of the reason she'd drawn her novella characters' faces before discovering they were flesh-and-blood people. God must be warning her.

He had given her the faces in her mind to warn her ahead of time to be on her guard—that these story suspects truly were suspects, up to no good. Maybe they were responsible for the burglaries in the area. Why else would Lance seem so interested in Raine's inheritance and go so far as to warn her— or had it been a threat? Moreover, if he knew about her inheritance, it stood to reason others did too. Some people killed to get what they wanted—such as a priceless art collection. And Lance had mentioned being concerned about her safety. . . .

Raine's footsteps came faster. She fisted her hands deep in the pockets of her cardigan. She didn't want to think badly of Lance. He seemed so nice. But she was a trained reporter. She must stick to the fundamentals of what she'd learned: Keep cool; don't get emotionally involved; stay professional and alert—and pursue, pursue, pursue.

She spotted a flash of yellow between some trees near a bench. Kara appeared to be in serious discussion with the man who'd approached her and Lance's booth at Brentley's.

Raine's fifth mystery suspect.

Confident she was on the right track, Raine moved toward a water fountain a few feet away from the couple and bent to take a drink.

"It can't be helped," the man said. "I have to do it."

"But this Saturday night?" Kara asked. "Does it have to be this Saturday night?"

"I can't change the plans." His words were curt. "You know that."

"Perfect," the woman quietly fumed. "Just perfect. I'm telling you, Bill, you shouldn't go—it's too dangerous. I have this feeling. . . ."

"You and your feelings. Everything will be fine. I promise." The man's sudden switch to lightness seemed forced. "Later, we'll celebrate." The sound of a kiss. "Maybe even take a few days off and go to Hawaii; you know how you love Hawaii."

"I can't leave. Not with all that's going on here. Lance might need me—and you too."

Bill sighed. "Yeah, right. Lance. I just wish this was all over and done with."

"It will be soon, Darling."

Raine was sure that if she drank any more water, she would become a fish. She straightened, pretending interest in her hobo bag. Shuffling things around, she noticed the couple walk away.

Raine followed, keeping a safe distance behind. Suddenly a large group of noisy middle school children cut in front of her. The teacher had them all stop where they were, scolding them to quiet down and not run. Frustrated, Raine raced around them, her heels clacking loudly on the tile, earning an admonishing look from the teacher. If Raine weren't following a lead, she might have offered an apologetic smile or even thought the incident amusing. But she was far from being amused.

Her suspects had disappeared.

Raine looked to the right and the entrance of an art exhibit, then to the left, where a pair of double doors led to authorized quarters. Glancing at her wristwatch, she saw that she didn't have much time. But she needed to write down what she'd heard to mull it over later. These past stressful weeks, her memory couldn't be trusted.

Her mini notebook was now in her purse where it belonged, but the pages had been filled days ago. Seeing a stand of free pamphlets ahead, she moved toward them. She grabbed each in turn, looking for white space on the back—letting those that didn't apply flutter to the floor, planning to scoop them all up in one pile before she left. It would take too much time to stuff each leaflet back into place; the slots were packed so tightly. Most flyers had printing on all sides, but she found one type that would work. She retrieved her pen, held the leaflet in her palm, and scribbled down the conversation as she remembered it. Out of space, she reached for another flyer.

"I noticed a whole carton of those in back if you want me to bring them out to you," an amused but puzzled voice said from behind her.

Raine's heart leaped, the pen jerked, and she made a hole in the slick paper. She turned to see Lance.

"Another idea for your story?" he asked.

"You could say that." In an attempt to remain professional, she offered a polite smile while trying to stuff the pamphlets into her hobo bag. She missed the opening and watched them flutter to the tiles.

Lance swooped down before she could and plucked the two leaflets from the floor. He glanced at the one she'd written on, frowned, but handed them up to her. Scooping up the pamphlets she'd earlier discarded, he folded them and stuck them in his pocket.

"I was going to pick them up," Raine explained, feeling less like a reporter every minute and more like an abashed schoolgirl. "I was trying to save time. I have to be back at work in a few minutes."

"I don't mind. It's my job." From his hunched position, with one knee propped on the floor, he gave her a heart-stopping smile and stood. "I'll walk you back."

Raine nodded, too flustered to speak. Once in the gift shop, she thanked him and hurried to put her purse away. She noticed that Lance didn't leave but instead appeared to be shopping for something. Raine stayed on the other side of the store, behind a stand of clay pots on glass shelves, straightening anything her hands came across. She watched Lance move toward the register, pull out his wallet to pay, have a brief conversation with Crystal, pick up a pen to write something down, then walk from the shop, empty-handed.

Curiosity about to eat her away, Raine approached the front. Crystal turned, an amused smile on her face. She handed Raine a thick, mini notebook with an adorable kitten hopelessly tangled up in a skein of red yarn on the cover. "He left this for you," Crystal explained and strolled away from the counter, chuckling. "There's a message inside. I'm going on my break."

Raine hesitated a full five seconds while Crystal moved toward the back, then flipped open the cover.

Raine,

> *Thought this would come in handy. The museum director might mind you using leaflets to take notes, and I wouldn't want you getting in trouble.*

Lance

P.S. The kitten reminded me of you.

Warmth rushed to Raine's face. The kitten reminded him of her—meaning cute and cuddly? Or always in some sort of dilemma? She flipped the book closed and stared at the black kitten with the wide "Uh-oh, I'm caught" eyes. A smile tipped her lips, and a laugh bubbled out.

She must be wrong about Lance being a burglar. She just had to be wrong. Because Raine wasn't sure she could bear it if she were right.

Chapter 6

Late Saturday afternoon, business died down, and Raine took her first relaxing breath. She froze when her fifth mystery suspect, Bill, strode into the gift shop and to the counter where she stood. He plucked a pack of gum from a carton and set it down. Raine didn't meet his gaze as he handed her the exact change after she'd rung it up, but she watched as he strode to the museum corridor where Kara waited, looking upset.

"Crystal," Raine said. "That couple outside near the display case—who are they?"

Crystal looked up from replacing a sale sign that had been knocked off a shelf of small curios. "You mean Bill and Kara Phillips?"

"Yes. Do they work at the museum?"

"You could say that." Crystal gave Raine an odd look. "Kara is the curator responsible for putting together the Renaissance exhibit. And her husband, Bill, is one of the conservators here."

Phillips. That had been the name of the curator Raine had been assigned to talk with that first day. This couldn't be coincidence. Her dreaming up the characters and drawing their faces, later meeting them, then finding out three of them had connections to this museum must be crucial.

She grabbed her purse. "I hate to do this, and I promise I'll make it up to you, but I have to go." She watched Bill kiss his wife's cheek and leave. Kara frowned and moved in the opposite direction.

"What's up?" Crystal asked. "You look like a light bulb just went on over your head."

"I can't talk now, but I may be on to something."

Crystal grinned. "Are those journalist genes at work again?"

"Maybe. If I do get a story and sell it, I'll owe it all to you, Crystal, and I'll be sure and mention your name in my article."

"You're just trying to butter me up so I'll let you go early." Crystal glanced at the wall clock behind Raine. "Oh, all right—go. But inventory is coming up next month, and I'll collect on that promise of you making it up to me."

A group of chattering children in the company of one harried-looking couple strode into the shop. The kids scattered to different areas of the store, all hands, despite their parents' warnings to "look, but don't touch."

Crystal groaned at the sharp crack of ceramic falling over onto a glass shelf. "You better believe you'll make it up to me, Raine E. Wells." Pasting on a smile, she moved toward the couple while Raine hid her own smile and scurried out the door.

Raine didn't see Bill in the museum, but once she made it to her mom's car, she spotted him slipping behind the wheel of a '30s Cadillac. Raine frowned and followed him out of town. If he were on his way to a burglary, he couldn't have selected a more conspicuous car—unless he thought he was Clyde Barrow looking for his Bonnie. At each stoplight, people eyed the glossy, antique, red-and-gray car with its red-spoked, whitewall tires, and children pointed and waved to the driver. Maybe Bill was meeting the other thieves and they planned to take another car?

Forty-five minutes later, Raine sighed. Where was he going? They were in the middle of the country, on a little-traveled road—Raine four car-lengths behind Bill's puttering car. Bored, she propped her elbow against the window and leaned her cheek against her hand.

Autumn speckled the surrounding trees and hills with dusky hues of crimson, brown, and gold, using a dove gray sky for a backdrop. The holidays would soon be here, and Raine wondered what to get her brother for Christmas. What did one get a teenager who thought he owned the world?

His words came back to haunt her: *You don't trust anyone. . . . You've become a basket case.* Raine snapped on the radio, glad for the distraction.

Suddenly Bill's car took a right onto a road seemingly leading to nowhere. Raine paused in the middle of the empty two-lane street, tapping her fingers on the wheel. She waited a full stanza of the song before pulling onto the tree-covered dirt road, keeping the speck of red and gray that was Bill's car far ahead.

The lane finally dead-ended into a circular drive, an ancient three-story home looming amid the trees. The grounds were a car-lover's paradise, shining chrome and glossy paint jobs gleaming from what must be more than fifty antique automobiles. She pulled her mother's beige compact next to a silver sedan whose elderly passenger was just emerging from the driver's side, and rolled down her window.

"Excuse me," she said, noticing his curious glance at her car, which looked like a baby wren next to all these proud old peacocks. "Can you tell me where I am?"

"This is a meeting of the Antique and Classic Car Owners' Club."

A car club? Well, this was certainly no burglary!

He smiled, displaying two gold teeth. "You're welcome to come in, rest a spell, and listen to the proceedings. Though they might bore you to tears."

"How long does the meeting last?"

"We break up around eight-thirty, but it being the final one this year, it'll likely be ten."

"That long?" Her mom needed the car at nine. "I can't, but thanks."

"Can't say as I blame you. Our keynote speaker had to cancel, and they got some young whippersnapper to take his place." He shook a gnarled finger at Raine. "William Phillips might drive a fine-looking automobile, but I'll wager I know more about 'em than he does. Just 'cause he restores paintings and the like at that museum his wife runs doesn't mean he knows a hill o' beans about antique cars."

Raine squelched a smile and drove away. She flicked on her headlights when dusk thickened. Trailing Bill Phillips would have to wait. This lead had proven to be another dead end.

Ten minutes from home, news of a recent burglary on the other side of Gladney came over the radio. There was no way Bill Phillips could have arrived ahead of her in his ancient automobile, even if he had left the meeting and taken another road into town. Which meant Bill was no longer a suspect on her list of five, and Raine was beginning to doubt that his wife, Kara, was burglarizing homes either. Her first day at the gift shop, Raine had discovered that most museum work went on after closing time, and Kara, being a curator, would likely stay. That left the elderly couple. And Lance.

Raine tightened her hands on the wheel and stared at the headlight's glow on the road before her.

"Lance, Honey, I could be wrong, but there appears to be a car following us." Mrs. Trundle put one age-spotted hand to her flowered hat and craned her neck toward the rear window like an excited schoolgirl. "That beige car has been behind us since we left church ten minutes ago."

"Ida," her husband said from the backseat. "You watch too many of those *Murder She Wrote* reruns. No one's following us."

Lance glanced in the rearview mirror and spotted the vehicle four car-lengths behind. Too far to tell who was driving it. Making a snap decision, he turned at the next street.

"No, I must be right, Harry," Ida insisted. "See! That car turned too."

Lance narrowed his gaze, made another turn, and looked in the mirror. The car followed. He didn't want to jeopardize the Trundles' safety, but he didn't want a tail either. He directed a smile Ida's way. "How about we take a little excursion before I drop you and your husband off?"

"Oh, that does sound like fun!" Her blue eyes were merry. "Will you put the pedal to the metal and outrun them?"

"Ida!" her husband admonished.

Lance chuckled. He loved this old woman. "Nothing so

drastic. But let's give whoever's following us some exercise."

The car coming from the opposite direction left only enough room for one vehicle to make a left turn. Lance took the opening, then made another quick turn at a residential street. At the following intersection, he made a right. Far behind, he heard squealing rubber as the unknown car turned onto the first street he'd left. Lance grinned and took another quick right, ending up on one of the roads he'd just come from, took a quick right to the main road, then calmly turned left.

He looked in the rearview mirror. No beige car was in sight.

🙣

Raine hit the brakes at the intersection, looked both ways, and slammed her hands against the wheel. Lance's blue car was gone.

He had known he was being followed—why else would he have taken off like he did and led her on such a chase? Which must mean he was hiding something. And Raine was determined to find out just what that something was.

Chapter 7

When Raine wasn't working at the museum or writing her novella, she searched out leads. Pursuing the elderly couple had proven to be another dead end—they lived at a retirement home, and neither could drive any longer. Through overhearing gossip in the break room, Raine discovered Kara was upset with Bill because he'd gone to the antique car club and given his speech on the night of their anniversary and also because she'd thought it dangerous for him to drive his old car such a distance. Yet Raine still didn't understand Kara's earlier reference to Lance "needing them."

So much pointed to Lance, he'd become Raine's prime suspect. Unfortunately that meant she must spend time in his company, trying to glean information. Unfortunately, because his answers to her questions were often vague, and the more time she spent with Lance—eating lunches or walking through the museum—the more she grew to like him.

Sitting on the floor in the gift shop, Raine lost count of some Rembrandt prints and bit back a groan, rubbing her temples. The museum had been closed for hours, but she and Crystal doggedly pursued the inventory list, not even halfway finished. One of the employees scheduled to work had called in sick with the flu that morning, one was on vacation, and another girl recently quit, so it was just Crystal and Raine.

Crystal's cell phone beeped. She plucked it out of her pocket and flipped it on. "Hello?"

In the few overhead lights they'd kept on, Raine watched her friend's features grow tense. Fearful concern darkened the blue eyes. "Is she hurt bad? Where are you?" A pause. "I'll be right there." Crystal stood, stepped into her heels, and hurried to the back.

"Crystal?" Raine called. "What's wrong?"

"It's Frannie." Shrugging into her coat, Crystal rushed back to where Raine sat. "She fell and cut her head open. I have to go to the emergency room."

"Of course," Raine agreed. "I'll stay and finish inventory."

Crystal pulled on her gloves. "You don't have to."

"The papers need to be turned in Tuesday, right? I've got the hang of how it's done. Besides, you let me take time off to follow my leads. It's the least I can do."

"Bless you, Raine. This is the first time my baby's ever been in the hospital." Tears sparkled in Crystal's eyes as she pulled her purse strap over her shoulder. "On my way out, I'll tell security you're here."

Watching her friend hurry away, Raine offered a prayer for both little Frannie's well-being and peace for Crystal, then again concentrated on the prints.

She was halfway through counting books when she heard a faraway noise in the museum corridor. Things had been quiet the past hour, the floor buffing machines whirring throughout the museum now silent. Raine had been so engrossed in inventory she'd barely noticed her surroundings. Now she looked through the glass wall facing the corridor to see that the main lights and exhibit spotlights were off, and only dim, concealed corridor lights remained lit. Raine glanced at her wristwatch. Ten-forty.

She set the inventory packet and pencil down and stretched her cramped limbs. A movement in the corridor caught her attention. Maybe the night watchman was making his rounds. Raine could use a break and hopefully a few minutes of idle chitchat. She wouldn't mind hearing more about Joe's grandchildren. The museum felt positively spooky.

Her stockinged feet made no noise as she stepped from the flat carpet onto the cold corridor floor. After moving a short distance, she slipped, gave an involuntary little yelp, and grabbed the windowed wall. Someone had done a great waxing job.

Before she could move, footsteps thudded behind her and a hand clamped over her mouth. A strong arm circled her waist, pulling her back against a male form. Her screams came out in muffled squeaks against the hand, which tightened over her mouth. He quickly moved with her backwards, struggling, until they came to the entrance of the gift shop.

"Stop it, Raine," Lance harshly whispered in her ear, startling her into becoming perfectly still. "I'm going to move my hand from your mouth, but you've got to promise me you won't scream."

She nodded, and he released his hold. Instantly she spun around.

"What are you doing here this late?" he whispered before she could speak. He didn't look happy to see her. "And why are you slinking around the museum in your stockinged feet?"

156

"I'm not slinking—I'm doing inventory," she fumed quietly. "But why'd you scare the daylights out of me just now? What was that all about?"

"Shh!" His eyes flicked down the darkened corridor. "Keep your voice down. I can't explain—just trust me."

"Trust you? When you pull a stunt like that?"

A crash followed by low cursing came from the Renaissance exhibit down the hall. Raine's eyes widened.

"Stay here," Lance ordered. Her mind suddenly registered that he was wearing street clothes and not his janitor uniform. "I mean it, Raine, no matter what you hear, stay in the shop."

"Not on your life," she muttered after he'd crept down the corridor. If anyone was "slinking," he was. Another thought hit: If he were up to shady dealings, would he have let her go so easily? Yet something was definitely afoot, and she sensed a story. She grabbed a notebook and pen off the counter and quietly sped after him, watching as he walked under the archway of the Renaissance room.

Running on the slippery floor was a challenge, but she managed to reach her destination without falling and pressed herself against the wall. Trying to control her breathing, she peered around the corner.

In the dim light, two uniformed men stood on the far side of the room, in the process of lifting a Raphael painting from the wall. Lance crouched behind a statue, watching them. All of a sudden, he put his hand inside his jacket, withdrew a gun, and stepped into the open.

Stunned, Raine lifted the notebook to her heart. The pen slid away and hit the floor, making a loud clatter. All three men looked her way.

One of the workers released the painting and withdrew a gun with a silencer from his belt. He aimed it at Lance and fired. Raine softly cried in alarm. The bullet made a loud ping as it hit one of the metal poles holding the cordon ropes. Lance dove behind a large statue. He waited, then moved his upper body into the open, firing off two quick shots. The gun with the silencer fired again. A loud smack hit the archway a foot away from Raine as the bullet tore up plaster.

She backed away from the entrance, her mouth and eyes wide. Dropping the notebook, she sped to the nearest alarm— a fire alarm—though with as loud as Lance's gun was, the night watchman must have heard. Lance's gun. . .Lance had a gun. . .someone—two men—were trying to kill him.

Shaking, Raine tripped the alarm and melted against the wall. Pressing her back to the plaster, she slid to the floor, clutching her elbows, and listened to the gunplay in the Renaissance room now mix with the alarm's shrill bell. There was little more she could do.

Dear God, take care of Lance. I don't know what's going on, but please take care of him. She drew her stockinged feet close and lowered her head to her upraised knees, feeling weak. Helpless. Frightened.

Remember the sparrow.

The soft words within her spirit brought the image of the airport sparrow to Raine's mind. The guard had rescued the tiny creature from the boisterous child, and the sparrow seemed to realize that it would be safe in the man's care.

Are not five sparrows sold for two pennies? Yet not one of them is forgotten by God. Indeed, the very hairs of your head are all numbered. Don't be afraid; you are worth more than many sparrows.

The comforting verses from Luke whispered through Raine's heart. Suddenly the sound of running footsteps came from all directions. With relief, she watched men and women in police and security uniforms converge and race toward the exhibit room, guns drawn. A young policeman, obviously a rookie, moved her way, his expression a mix of uncertainty and suspicion. His hand remained on the butt of the gun in his holster.

"I work at the gift shop," Raine blurted out. "I sounded the alarm."

"Are you hurt?" he asked, eyeing her huddled form.

Raine shook her head. "I'd like to get up, but I don't think my legs will obey me." She gave a half-cry, half-laugh and wiped the back of her hand against her cheek, surprised to find it wet.

"You can't stay here." He helped her to stand. "You'll have to come outside with me. I need to ask you some questions."

She looked at her stockinged feet. "My shoes are in the gift shop."

He hesitated, then nodded. "I'll come with you."

He allowed her to get her purse and coat too, first examining them and obviously deciding she wasn't a dangerous criminal. The shooting ceased, and Raine was astonished to see by the clock that only five minutes had elapsed since the moment Lance had stopped her from walking into certain danger. Lance. . .

"Please." She turned to the policeman. "Could you find out if Lance is okay?"

"Lance?"

"He works here." She paused, trying to think. "He's. . .a

friend. They. . .they shot at him."

"I'll see what I can find out." He led her outside to a waiting patrol car, one hand on her arm to steady her. Blue and red lights flashed from the tops of emergency vehicles and police cars all around. Icy drizzle fell from a dark sky; Raine didn't even know such weather had been forecast. The policeman instructed her to get in the back of a police car, then joined another man in uniform. Raine sat sideways on the cushioned seat with the door open and stared at the mammoth stone museum building. The chilling drops hit her legs, but nothing felt real.

Someone pushed a cup of coffee into her hands. Gratefully she sipped it, allowing the warmth to soak her insides and the steam to heat her face. The shock began to wear away, and she was able to think more clearly. She was taken to the police station, where she answered their many questions. But her panicked questions about Lance, they could not, or did not, answer.

Her parents arrived at the station to collect her, and gratefully she fell into their comforting embrace.

Raine sat cross-legged on her bed and stared at her drawing of Lance. So much had happened this past week, since the last time she'd seen him.

The day after the would-be museum heist, she slipped into her journalist mode and typed out the story. Other reporters had only the basics: that three men from maintenance—two of them wounded in the shooting—one man from the works-of-art crew, one security guard, and Tia, the registrar, were involved. To Raine's complete shock, Mr. Rand, her uncle's attorney, had been implicated by one of the thieves as the chief instigator. It stood to reason that he was working for Drew, though nothing of that nature had been divulged. The night watchman, Joe, had been found tied up in back, not seriously hurt, much to Raine's relief.

When living in Chicago, Raine had gleaned what information she could after crimes took place. This time Raine had inside information; she had been there. Remembering everything her mentor taught her, she typed up the events of that night, printed the story out, then drove to the *Gladney News* building on Monday morning. Once she finally made it into the editor's office, sidestepping the secretary sent to waylay her, she slapped the story on his desk and promised him an exclusive if he would give her a chance and hire her on. He squashed his cigarette in the overflowing ashtray, raised his shaggy dark brows at her boldness, but picked up her story and skimmed it.

Without a flicker of expression on his haggard face, he told her, "If all your stories are as good as this one, you've got yourself a deal."

Immediately Raine located a pay phone and contacted Crystal. After her friend assured Raine that Frannie was back to her cheerful self, though she constantly tried to rip away the bandage hiding the four stitches, Raine relayed her news. Crystal was ecstatic. She told Raine that she belonged in a newspaper office, not working retail, and was glad Raine had made the decision to forget the past.

That made Raine think of her mentor. If it hadn't been for Brady McMillan, she never would have learned to write the story that secured her this job. Of course, if it hadn't been for Brady, she never would have been fired in the first place. But

Raine was tired of nursing grudges and made a decision to forgive—and to trust again. Those who deserved it. Besides, if she hadn't come home, she never would have met Lance.

Raine frowned as she stared at the pen drawing of his face. She had called police headquarters, the hospital, and the museum, once it opened again, seeking information. But no one seemed to know where Lance was—much less who he was—and it didn't help that Raine didn't know his last name. How had that happened? The two times she'd asked him, they'd been interrupted. Why had she never pursued the question? It was as though the man never existed. When she was tempted to worry, Raine remembered the sparrow and clung to the Lord, trusting Lance to His care.

"Elizabeth," her mother called from the bottom of the stairs. "Aren't you leaving soon?"

Raine glanced at the clock, not really wanting to attend her reunion, but supposing she should make an appearance since Mother's committee had helped with refreshments. Whoever heard of a grade school reunion—and one three days before Christmas, at that? Her mom had explained to Raine that it was planned that way to honor the principal, who'd been hired on December 22, forty years ago. Raine watched the icy moisture pelt the window, doubting there would be much of a turnout on a miserable evening like this.

She slipped into a black calf-length sheath and zipped it up. For the occasion, she attached a pair of rhinestone drops to her ears and added a matching bracelet. A quick brush of her hair, a dab of ruby lipstick, a coat of mascara, and she was ready. Deciding her black hobo purse would go much better with the dress than her mother's tan clutch, she slipped it over her coat and rushed downstairs. After a quick kiss to her mother's cheek, she hurried outside.

While she drove to the hall where the reunion was being held, she wondered if anyone would question her decision to attend alone. If she'd had a choice, she would have asked Lance to accompany her. . . .

Raine frowned and tightened her hands on the wheel. She wouldn't travel that road again.

Inside the hall, lavishly decorated with twinkling white lights, groups of people congregated. Raine experienced her first attack of nervousness. After all, she hadn't seen her classmates in fifteen years, and some of these people she didn't know at all, since the reunion covered all the years the school had been in existence.

"Elizabeth? Is that you?" a blond squealed from nearby. "I'm Hillary. We were in the eighth grade together."

Raine smiled. "It's good to see you again."

"Oh, you too!" Hillary hugged her, then grabbed her arm and began leading Raine through the throng. "Jeanne and Amy are here, and Robert—you remember how I had such a crush on him and you helped me write that anonymous love note? Oh, here's someone else you might remember—Karaleen?" Hillary tapped the shoulder of a woman wearing a shiny crimson dress. Her hair was the color of days-old carnations. "Karaleen, you remember Elizabeth Wells from Mrs. Rottmeir's class?"

Raine's mouth dropped open as Kara faced her.

"You're Karaleen?" Raine whispered. "Karaleen Foster?"

Kara laughed. "I changed my last name when I married this hunk." She grabbed Bill's arm, and he gave a polite smile to the women, looking decidedly uncomfortable. "Bill didn't go to Gladney, though he did help pull this thing off. I'm Kara Phillips now. But it's no wonder you didn't recognize me. I had brown hair and hazel eyes as a kid." She tapped her finger under one eye. "Violet contacts and three attempts to get the right color in hair dye did this." Her brow furrowed. "But you're not Elizabeth Wells, are you? I feel as if I've seen you somewhere recently. . . ."

"I, yes. . ." Suddenly Raine stopped talking—stopped breathing—as another man moved into view. Stunned, she whispered his name.

Kara gave an odd smile, then looked his way. "Lance? Do you know Elizabeth? She appears to know you."

Lance's jade eyes showed as much surprise as Raine felt. He looked striking in a dark suit and tie, his gleaming hair pulled back in its usual ponytail, the tiny loop shining in his ear. She noticed his glasses were missing.

"Elizabeth?" He shook his head in obvious confusion. "I thought your name was Raine."

"It is—now." Raine wasn't sure where she found her voice. "My given name is Elizabeth Raine Wells."

"No way. . ." Lance's soft words came out as though he'd made a startling discovery. "I'm Lance Rowoski. I sat behind you in the eighth grade."

Raine shook her head, still not believing that after her long, desperate search, here Lance was, standing before her at her school reunion.

"I was the fat blond who couldn't run very fast and never got picked in sports," he said with a grin. "My family moved here toward the end of the semester, so I'd be surprised if you did remember me."

Raine vaguely recalled a boy fitting that description. He hadn't talked much, and she'd been a social butterfly, so there'd been little interaction between them. Now that she dwelt on it, she did remember a plump blond boy with glasses tapping her on the shoulder and shyly asking to borrow paper or a pencil a few times. No wonder she hadn't drawn a comparison between them. This trim, well-built man in front of her was nothing like the chunky boy of the eighth grade. . .except they both shared the same gentle green eyes.

"Would you like something to drink?" Lance asked. "We have a lot to talk about."

Feeling off balance, Raine nodded. He took her elbow, leading her through the tightly packed room. A poster on a pedestal near the buffet table caught her eye, and she abruptly halted. Her mouth fell open.

All five of her mystery suspects stood in a row, smiling from a blow-up of a picture. She blinked, and the missing links in her memory clicked into place.

"Is something wrong?" Lance asked as she rapidly began sorting through her purse's contents. She unzipped an inside zipper and pulled a folded leaflet out, one she'd briefly skimmed before the move and had stashed in her purse. It was a flyer from the school, announcing the reunion. Inside was a smaller version of the picture that sat on the pedestal. A picture of those volunteers who'd worked to pull the reunion together, standing next to two teachers—her elderly couple. God hadn't been warning her. Her photographic mind had sorted the picture into a cubbyhole in her brain, and she'd sketched her suspects from memory! Suddenly she laughed.

Lance looked at her strangely. "Raine, are you okay?"

"I'm fine." She let out another gasping giggle.

"Let's get some punch and sit down," Lance suggested, sounding uncertain.

Once he retrieved their drinks, they found a quiet alcove with a love seat outside the main room.

"Before I tell you what had me laughing, I want to know what happened last Saturday." Raine set her punch glass on a low table in front of them. "And where did you disappear to?"

Lance hesitated. "Off the record?" At her surprise, he explained, "I heard you got a job working for *Gladney News.*"

Raine nodded. "Off the record."

Lance took a sip of his punch, stared at it a moment, then looked her way. "I'm not a museum janitor, Raine. I'm a private detective. Kara hired me to work undercover when she noticed problems in the museum—accession numbers not matching items shipped, that sort of thing. She got wind that something was going down concerning the Renaissance exhibit and was worried."

"A detective," Raine softly repeated. "I thought you were a burglar."

"I know." Lance's eyes twinkled. "At the beginning, I thought the same about you."

Raine gasped. "You knew I suspected you?"

"I had a feeling. But only after I saw you in your car Tuesday—the same car you tailed me in after church when I was taking the Trundles home."

"You sure led me on a merry chase," Raine groaned. "So you suspected me too?"

"Only at first. Later, I knew there was no way a sweet girl like you could be a thief."

His words embarrassed her. "Back to the museum heist, can you tell me anything I can put into print?"

"For obvious reasons, I don't want my name mentioned." She nodded.

"The thieves used the museum storage area to hide items stolen from other burglaries. I buddied up with three of them and eventually learned they were planning to take what they could from the Renaissance exhibit and blow out of town that night. That's why I was there—to stop them. Just today, the FBI took over jurisdiction, and the police are no longer on the case. It turns out that those same crooks are wanted for transporting stolen art across the state line."

Raine wrote the information in her notebook as fast as she could and groaned when her gel pen stopped working. She jabbed it into the paper a few times, making mad scribbles and trying to get the ink to flow. Lance's hand on hers stopped her, at the same time sending electricity through her arm. She looked up into laughing green eyes.

"Tell you what, Raine, I'll give you an exclusive interview later, but I'd like to change the subject now."

"You would?" Her throat felt suddenly dry.

"I still can't believe I didn't know you were Elizabeth Wells." Lance's voice was soft. "I had a crush on you in eighth grade. You were the prettiest girl in class and the only one who didn't make fun of me. When we went to different high schools, I thought I might die." He grinned.

Heat inflamed Raine's face. She wasn't sure what to say.

"These past months, getting to know you has been the highlight of my job," Lance continued. "At first I trailed you because I thought you might be involved with the burglaries—you were so jumpy all the time. But soon I just wanted to spend time in your company. I still do."

Raine felt a lump form in her throat. "I was worried when I tried to find out what had happened to you. No one would tell me anything."

"You were worried about me?" Awe laced his voice.

"Yes. Until I made myself turn it over to God. I had to trust Him with your safety, or I would have gone insane."

"Raine." His word sounded as a mere breath, and his hand on hers tightened. "I think I'd like to kiss you."

"I wouldn't mind," she whispered back.

Lance's expression softened as his fingers lightly swept her hair away from her cheek, and he leaned toward her. When his lips touched hers, Raine closed her eyes, feeling as if she'd been given a little piece of heaven to share with this dearest suspect of her heart.

Six months later, Raine stood beside Lance and stared at the museum's newest exhibit—her uncle's art collection. A brass plaque was mounted on the wall next to each item with the words, "From the private collection of Harold Wells III and Raine E. Wells," with the year inscribed beneath.

Inside her hobo bag, now cleared of its clutter, were the mini-recorder and extra tapes Lance had given her—along with his teasing remark about how it might be easier for her to take notes speaking into a machine. She reached for the recorder, an idea for a story coming to mind. Despite her plum job at *Gladney News*, as one of its fast-rising, up-and-coming reporters, she managed to find time to work on her fictional mysteries, which she loved just as much as searching out the real ones.

Nearby, a child with pale lips and a straw hat on her burred head, obviously a recent hospital patient, smiled up at her mother and hugged her. "Oh, Mommy. It's just like looking into God's garden, isn't it? I love that picture!"

Tears clouded Raine's eyes, and Lance raised her hand clasped in his to his lips. Yes, this was where her collection belonged. She'd made the right decision to indefinitely loan out the paintings to the museum so that everyone could enjoy them.

Seeing that her recorder was empty, Raine plucked up the plastic case with four blank mini-tapes from her purse. She fumbled to get the container open with one hand. Suddenly it sprung apart, sending tapes flying to the tiles.

Lance knelt to the floor on one knee and gathered the tapes, handing them up to her. His eyes sparkled with mirth. She grinned and took the tapes, slipping them in her purse, but shook her head. "Don't you dare laugh at me, Lance Rowoski."

"I won't. But as long as I'm down here. . ." He pulled something from his pants pocket. "I'd planned to do this over a romantic dinner for two, but somehow, in this place where we first met—this seems right."

His expression turned serious, and Raine struggled to breathe. Other people nearby must have realized what was coming too, for they stopped gazing at the paintings and stared at Raine and Lance.

"Elizabeth Raine Wells, I can't think of a time in my life when I didn't love you. When you were a girl in junior high, yes, but even more as the wonderful woman you are now."

He opened his hand to reveal a velvet box and flipped it open. The miniature diamond that sparkled up at Raine and what it signified were more beautiful to her than any museum masterpiece she'd ever seen.

"Will you marry me?" Lance asked quietly. "Together, we can work at unraveling life's mysteries—and make the best stories."

Raine brought her fingers to her mouth, laughing and crying at the same time. Her throat constricted, and she could only manage a half-sob, half-laugh.

"Is that a yes?" Lance asked, standing up. Suddenly he looked like an uncertain schoolboy, and Raine's heart melted.

She threw her arms around his neck and kissed him hard on the mouth, almost knocking his glasses off. Around her, people clapped, and one elderly man chuckled, "I'd say that looks like a yes to me!" The little girl giggled.

Raine pulled away, heat singeing her cheeks. But she kept her arms wrapped tightly about his neck and smiled. "I love you, Lance Rowoski, and my answer is most definitely a yes!"

After giving her an endearing grin, her suspect-turned-hero kissed her again.

PAMELA GRIFFIN

Pamela Griffin lives in North Central Texas and divides her time among family, church activities, and writing. Her main goal in writing Christian romance is to encourage others and plant seeds of faith through entertaining stories that minister to the wounded spirit. She has contracted twenty novels and novellas and would love for you to visit her Web site at: http://members.cowtown.net/PamelaGriffin.

Love's Greatest Peril

by Susan May Warren

Dedication

To Darlene Guinn. Not only did she befriend a sassy Yank,
but also she loved her well and taught her to love
her brothers and sisters in Christ who spoke with a twang.
You are a gift from God in my life.
To my dear friends at the *Elizabethton Star*
and First Baptist Church of Elizabethton.
Because of y'all, I left a piece of my heart in Tennessee.
To Melissa Anderson and Tracey Bateman—soul mates
who remind me of God's abundant provision.
To the Lord Jesus Christ, who taught me that wherever
I go—from East Tennessee to Eastern Russia, He is there.

Be strong and courageous.
Do not be afraid or terrified because of them,
for the Lord your God goes with you;
he will never leave you nor forsake you.
DEUTERONOMY 31:6

The Makings of a Great Mystery
by Drake Axelrod

Chapter Three
Tighten the Suspense Screws

Rule: Thou shalt plunge your protagonist into increasingly menacing situations until death is imminent.

Exercise: Create a list of increasingly perilous "accidents" that could befall your protagonist and write a final "escape from death" scene.

Chapter 1

"Thou shalt plunge your protagonist into increasingly menacing situations until death is imminent." Drake Axelrod's words seemed eerily prophetic as Justine Proof clung to the steering wheel and pumped her useless brakes. Fighting panic, she wrenched back the emergency brake. It caught, and the whine of her back brakes sliced through her thundering heartbeat. Justine fought the shimmy of the wheel, her hands turning slick and white as the Volvo began to slow. On each side of the ditchless highway, the Blue Ridge Mountains threw shadows across the road, as if in silent ratification of her doom.

Someone was trying to kill her.

She smelled the acrid heat pouring from her rear brakes and a desperate prayer flew heavenward as she wrestled the car across a bridge. The sheer seventy-foot drops flanked the highway, taunting her fatigued arms. If only she'd listened to the voice of reason shouting in the back of her brain.

What was she doing eight hundred miles from home, alone in the middle of back hills Tennessee?

The car negotiated the bridge, lurched another thirty feet,

then shuddered to a halt. Justine gulped in the first real breath she'd taken in what seemed like a year. Her arm muscles quivered as if connected to high voltage, but her hands refused to abandon their death clutch on the wheel.

Propping her forehead against the steering wheel, Justine felt perspiration drip down her temples and tried not to let suspicion take possession of her thoughts. Panic already had a heart-crunching hold.

"Ma'am!"

The voice made her jerk, and the car inched forward. She forced the Volvo into Park and shut off the car. Now, at least she wouldn't be screaming down a mountain like the General Lee on a *Dukes of Hazzard* rerun.

"Ma'am, are you okay?"

She glanced in the rearview mirror and tried not to yelp.

Although she'd always been offended by the unfair stereotypes of the South—bootleggin', big-hair, chaw-chewing, kissing cousins—everything she'd dismissed as prejudice rose like a specter to stalk her as she watched a bona fide redneck stride toward the car. The man looked blood-chilling in a pair of ripped-at-the-knees fatigues, a matching shirt with threads dangling where the sleeves had been, and hiking boots. To complete the renegade aura, he sported a dark blond smattering of whiskers and a fop of sun-burnt hair that surely hadn't seen a comb for weeks.

Cranking the window shut, she fumbled for her cell phone in the black hole of her leather bag. Lipstick, a tape recorder, notes from her seminar and—there! The Nokia. She dug it out and held it like a stun gun as he rapped on her window.

"Ma'am, you all right in there?"

"Yes! Fine." She glanced at the phone and wanted to cry at the "no signal" display.

"Ma'am, come on out. Let me see if I can give you a hand."

Oh sure, right into the river roaring below. She shook her head. Out of her peripheral vision, she saw him shrug, then saunter over to her front wheels. He crouched, palmed the hood as if feeling for a heartbeat, then looked up and—smiled? Not even a hint of brown between those pearly whites.

Her heart jumped. So he had a genuine, friendly grin. That didn't mean he wasn't an axe murderer planning to drag her into the hills.

Rising, he shoved his hands into his back pockets, cocked his head, and smirked.

Did he think this was funny? A flash of anger made her crack open her window. "Go away."

"Nope."

She had the idiotic urge to hit him. "I have a cell phone. I've already called for help."

He quirked an eyebrow. Mountain shadows hid the texture of his eyes, but she had a feeling they were tinged with humor. "You can't get a signal up here, Ma'am."

She threw her phone on the seat in disgust and blinked back the burning in her eyes. Now what? A little voice in the back of her head, sounding much like her father, screamed at her to stay put. *Don't. Get. Out.*

But short of smoke signals, she had no way to call for help. Besides, didn't she want to prove that she could stand on her own size-seven feet? She may have slaughtered some pride letting Daddy land her the noon anchor job at KMPR, but the millisecond she signed her first mystery book contract was the second she snuck out of his hovering shadow. She wasn't going to let her rattletrap Volvo send her running back across the Mason-Dixon line into Daddy's arms.

Even if common sense told her to wait for the cavalry.

As if reading her despair, Mr. Dangerous moved to the window and spoke through the crack. "I promise—I'm all bark and no bite."

She attempted a halfhearted smile and slowly unlocked the door. He opened it as she pried herself out of her seat.

The breeze ran over the magnolias, ferns, and oaks that blanketed the hills. The rush of a nearby river made her long for a Minnesota lake.

"Looks like you're in a fix," he said, by way of introduction.

What a discovery. She smiled, fighting a withering look. With her wheels bellowing out smoke like Mount Saint Helens along the side of the highway, it took a real genius to figure out that she wasn't going anywhere in the near future.

"Yep. I guess I've overheated."

She meant the brakes, but it easily described her personal misery. Tennessee was supposed to be. . .well, moderate, right? In politics, in southern culture, and in temperature. Hadn't she read that in the "Welcome to Stoney Creek" packet the Chamber of Commerce had sent her? But the September afternoon felt over one hundred degrees, which meant that after wrestling her car down Roan Mountain at life-flashing speeds, she felt as deep fried as the catfish she'd choked down last weekend at the party thrown for her by her new boss. She must look ridiculous in her long-sleeved, pinstriped suit, plastered by the heat to her body.

"Let me have a look-see at the engine." He moved toward the driver's seat, stepping so close that she blinked twice at his blue eyes and the mischief hinted in their depths. Like a country western tune, the phrase "good ole boy" sang through her mind, especially when he asked in a lazy drawl, "You aren't from around here, are you?"

She opened her mouth, somehow found her voice. "Uh, no." *Oh, witty, Justine.* So the man had eyes with stun power. He also looked like an underpaid mercenary.

"A Yank, huh?" He popped the hood. She jumped at the sound, and he glanced at her with a frown.

So she wasn't completely at ease standing next to a man who looked like he might live under a log. Truth be told, her heart had leaped from her chest and fled for the hills. She feigned a smile. "Yes, I guess so. I'm from Minnesota."

"You're far from home. What's a pretty lady like you doing driving like you're on the Bristol Speedway?"

She rubbed her temples. They felt oily. "I wasn't speeding. The brakes, they just. . ."

He frowned at her. Perhaps this wasn't the right time to mention that her failing brakes counted as the third suspicious circumstance in two weeks. Starting with the theft of her car radio on her first night in town and the attack dog behavior of her ancient collie around midnight last weekend, she could hardly be blamed for cultivating a healthy paranoia. Especially when all the unfair Southern stereotypes suddenly appeared in terrifying six-foot, three-inch, flesh-and-bone 3-D.

"I'm on my way home from Charlotte. I was probably going too fast. Tired after a big conference." She didn't add that the weekend included midnight plotting sessions with her fellow writers or that only the screech of rubber ripped her brain away from sinister scenarios.

He narrowed his eyes as if scrutinizing her story. "Are you okay?"

"Just a bit rattled. I'll be fine."

Using the edge of his shirt—to keep his hands clean?—he tucked his fingers under the hood and unlatched it. "What kind of conference?"

The car smelled like it would combust on the spot. Spewing oil fumes made her feel grimy to her marrow. Obviously, it didn't faze him for, again using his shirt, he screwed open the radiator cap.

"Oh, just a bunch of friends and me getting together." The last thing she needed was to lay open her dreams for this fraying redneck to laugh at.

The car radiator hissed, and GI Joe jumped back as if he'd been bit. "You're going to need a tow."

She bit back a sarcastic word. She didn't have a long list of friends in this town, and her cynical tongue would have to behave itself. "How far is it into town?"

He eyed her, high-heeled boots and up. The lazy smirk reappeared. "Too far for those shoes."

"You're a huge help." She reached into the car, grabbed the cell phone, and held it up, hoping, oh please, for a signal.

"I live just up the road. Come on. I'll call Jerry and fix you a glass of sweet tea while you wait." He smiled innocently, as if she'd love to run into the hills and vanish forever.

"No, thanks," she said, trying not to anger him. He might look like something the cat had played with, but underneath all that grime, sweat, and tatters, she saw muscular arms and a lean build. He probably wrestled bears in them thar hills.

To her utter shock, he replied, "No problem, Ma'am," and

ducked his head in leave, Rhett Butler style. "I'll get Jerry's to send you a tow quick as a wink." He paused, looked at the sky. " 'Til then, I'd get myself to some shade. At least until that thunderstorm passes."

What?

Justine shaded her eyes and stared at the sky. Sure enough, thunderheads gathered just over the mountain peaks.

Rhett Butler smiled boldly, a grin that could turn a woman weak. "By the way, welcome to the South."

"Glad to be here," she mumbled as he turned and strode down the road.

Chapter 2

I am a complete fool," Justine said to Maizey, the collie sprawled at her feet. The dog didn't comment on the humiliating realities of yesterday's near-death disaster. Justine sat on a worn leather sofa and tried not the think about the way she'd nearly dissolved into a puddle of tears right in front of the local wildlife. Thankfully, the renegade had disappeared before she'd unraveled in a soggy mess, just minutes before the thunderstorm rolled in and completed her drenching.

It should have been the perfect opening to her mystery novel. Who is trying to kill the schizophrenic writer sobbing by the roadside? She wanted to climb into bed, turn on a rerun of *Murder, She Wrote,* and forget that she had an assignment due. "Create a list of increasingly perilous 'accidents' that could befall your protagonist and write a final 'escape from death' scene." Accidents wouldn't be hard to dream up after her two ugly weeks in Stoney Creek. Justine crinkled a candy bar wrapper—thankful that the local Winn Dixie carried white chocolate—joined it to the wad of scribbled paper, and tossed the ball in a perfect arc into the wastebasket. At least she hadn't lost her basketball arm along with her senses.

Why had she ever thought she could make it alone, in the South, no less? More importantly, why had she believed her mother when she told Justine she could do anything she put her mind to? Justine had been seriously putting her mind to conjuring up a list of suspicious scenarios all night, and so far, nil.

"C'mon, Maizey," she said and rose from the sofa. The little cinder-block house seemed cool when she stepped out onto the porch and into the September heat. The low sun embossed the clouds hanging over the hills, and gray shadows striped the nearby schoolyard. The cicadas had already begun their harsh evening buzz, and someone in the neighborhood had fired up a barbecue grill.

With her Volvo jacked up at Jerry's Auto Repair, she had to wonder if her paranoia had merit. Or had she simply inherited a few too many suspicion genes from her investigative-journalist father? She hadn't been in town long enough to make enemies, especially the type who might want to do her in.

Maybe her overactive imagination would tame after some coffee. While driving home from work last week, she'd noticed an enticing coffee shop located on Main Street, squished between a jewelry store and a stitchery emporium. Housed in an ancient brick courthouse that looked like it had been used to condemn Yankee spies during the Civil War, the coffee shop had a beguiling wooden sign dangling over the door: The Right Cup. She envisioned creativity abounding under the nursing of a white chocolate latte with a shot of raspberry sauce, her favorite mix from her coffee hangout up north.

Going back inside her house, she shoved a tape recorder into her backpack and grabbed her bike helmet. "Stay," she said to Maizey, who looked like she might cry.

As she pedaled, Justine felt the tepid wind lift her short hair. She relished the beads of sweat that slicked between her shoulder blades. There was nothing better than fresh air and exercise to jump-start her brain. It would have to rev into gear soon if she expected to write a best-selling mystery.

Coasting down Broad Street, she turned past Fellowship Church and pedaled down to Main. Although the sun hovered just above the western hills, the street lamps shone, adding romance to the darkened shops. The marquee of a relic, one-screen theater listed some PG-rated show she'd never seen. At the end of the street, the War Monument turned gold against the sunset, and a slight summer wind reaped the heady redolence of the Doe River winding through the park.

Something about a lamp-lit main street, ducks quacking, and the whimsy of the streetside flowerpots spoke to a quiet place inside her. Braking at The Right Cup, she locked her bike and opened the door.

The bell jangled, and a few locals looked up from their clumps of conversation. Justine stood, entranced for a moment by the blue-and-white nautical theme, the miniature sailboats hanging from the walls, the hurricane lanterns lit on the pine tables, and the smell of rich ground roast embedding the brick walls. A reading nook complete with white wicker beckoned her, but Justine went to the counter. The tall cashier hummed softly, a tune that tugged at Justine's memory. She tried to place it as the woman smiled at her. "Can I help you?"

"Uh, do you happen to make white chocolate lattes with a shot of raspberry?" She knew by the cashier's grimace that she'd have to improvise. "Okay, how about a mocha latte?"

"For here or to go?"

"Here, definitely."

"You're not from around here, are you?" the cashier asked as she frothed the milk.

"It's my accent, isn't it?" Justine made a face. "As soon as I open my mouth, I stick out like a cactus."

"My name's Lisa, and we love cacti of all sorts in here." Her green eyes twinkled as she handed Justine a mug. "Enjoy."

Justine found a spot in the reading nook, set her coffee on a knotty-pine end table, and dug her recorder out of her backpack. Tucking the pack under her chair, she turned on the recorder, then dropped it into her shirt pocket. Now, how did one escape from death?

⚜

Patrick closed his chat program, sat back, and stretched in his leather desk chair. Fourteen hours staring at his computer had fused his joints. He needed a hike and a stiff mountain breeze, rich with the smells of autumn. Unfortunately, he'd have to wait until Sunday afternoon, his only day away from the store. He never thought he'd tire of the scent of ground coffee, but today it saturated his brain, pressing his thoughts into compact knots. Between the buzz of the grinder, the smell of the roaster, the online coffee order forms, and the memory of one very upset and forlorn city slicker, he felt as if he'd gone on a twenty-mile run with a full pack.

He couldn't erase the Yankee from his mind. Bless the woman's heart, she looked whiter than his laundry yesterday, and he wondered if it was due to her brake-burning careen down Roan Mountain or his sudden emergence from the trail he'd been hiking. She'd jumped as if he were Bigfoot, or worse, the Texas Chainsaw murderer. He gave a huff of disbelief and humor. Ten years ago, all her assumptions might have been true. But the navy and then the SEALs had turned him into a real Southern gentleman, something he wished he'd been all along.

The sounds of the shop had quieted to only the voices of a few evening regulars. He checked his watch. An hour left until closing. Before he could surrender to the urge to reopen his chat box and resume dialogue with his sister, he shut off his computer. These evening chats with Carma briefly filled the hollow place inside him. No one understood him like his big sister. And, in this town, no one ever would.

"Patrick, we just got an order for a white chocolate latte." Lisa ducked into his office. "Know how to make it?"

"No. Who asked for it?" He picked up his briefcase, crammed full of roaster brochures.

"A new face." She arched a sleek eyebrow. "A Yankee, I think."

A Yankee. Patrick kept his voice low. "Short blond hair, freckles? Kinda fancy?" The lady may have looked wrung out yesterday, but her blond hair frizzed out in a Big Apple sort of do, her sleek pinstriped suit, and her spike-heeled calf boots screamed high-society.

What was Miss Spiffy doing in East Tennessee?

"Not fancy, but yes on the rest. She's sitting in the book nook talking to herself."

Patrick peeked out of his office and spotted the woman sitting on a wicker chair. With her arms crossed over her navy sweatshirt, eyes closed, and head tilted back, she looked enmeshed in repose. Except her lips moved in private conversation. He couldn't hide a smile if he wanted to. This woman was intriguing, if not schizophrenic.

"How long has she been here?"

Lisa shrugged but wore a smirk. "Half hour or so. Been chatting up a storm with someone invisible." She leaned toward him. "Know her?"

He wanted to. The lady hadn't left his mind for the better part of twenty-four hours, and if he had half the sense of a hound dog, he'd find out her name before she exited his shop. "Sorta."

"Hmm. Then I'd track down a recipe for a white chocolate latte," Lisa said slyly as she sauntered back to the bar.

He hesitated, not sure if he should intrude. What if the woman was psychotic? She did seem to wear her emotions on her sleeve. After he'd called Jerry, he'd snuck back to make sure no other "heroes" stopped by to harass her and had seen her sob into her hands. He didn't blame her for crumbling, not after her near-death flight down the mountain. Still, something about her—perhaps the way she fought her tears or the look of desperation on her face—wheedled under his skin.

He went around the bar, poured himself a cup of Costa Rican decaf, and nodded at Virgil McGaff and Joel McKinney deep in conversation at a window table. They gave him a wave and nodded to their empty chair. He smiled and glanced at the woman in the corner. Virgil rolled his eyes, a gesture that twisted Patrick's gut. Ten years, and he still couldn't escape his reputation. Wild Irish Patrick. Never mind that he had been a decorated soldier. Never mind he took over his sister's shop when she moved overseas, and he'd done a bang-up job. Never mind that he made a public declaration of his faith and been baptized in the bone-numbing Doe River a summer ago. He'd always be Wild, the kid who set loose a greased pig in the homecoming court his senior year.

Okay, that had been one of his tamer pranks. Thankfully, only a handful of sworn-to-silence renegades knew his full and blushing history.

God's grace felt exceedingly abundant when he endured eye-rolling smirks from his childhood schoolmates.

He took a deep breath, then crept up behind his northern visitor, not sure if he should scuff his feet so as to alert her or tiptoe to afford her privacy until she was ready to open her eyes. Perhaps he could peruse the books while she—

"Maybe poison. I wonder how long that would take, and would there be an antidote handy?"

Patrick stopped, frowned.

"Or hanging. That's quick, and probably painless if there are a lot of drugs in the system." She had her fingers steepled under her chin, an expression of serenity on her pretty face.

"If I go with something bloody, I'd have to deal with the mess, and the scars—"

Maybe she was schizophrenic. Or homicidal? He stumbled, spilled his coffee, and cried out in dismay.

She sat upright and turned. "Are you okay?"

No, definitely not. Especially when she looked at him with those coffee-colored eyes, rich as French roast. His heart took a diving leap for his knees, but the word "bloody" lodged into his brain like a knife. What had she been talking about? "Yes, thank you." He forced a smile over a sick feeling welling in his chest. "Remember me?"

Her confusion gave way to recognition, surprise, then a chagrin that made him want to slink away.

"You," she said.

"Me." He stared at his cup of coffee, excruciatingly aware that the last time he'd seen her, she had tears dripping off her chin.

Two points for her, she made an excellent recovery. "You clean up well."

He suddenly remembered he'd also been groomed like a bobcat. So much for annihilating his bad-boy rep. He managed a wan smile. "You know us hillbillies. A bath and a shave once a year, whether we need it or not. You caught my last fling before the suds."

She quirked an eyebrow. "Honestly, I'm not sure which I like better, the pressed khakis or the cut-offs. Don't tell me you tossed them."

He had to fight a stupid grin. "Oh no. They have years of good wear left. They're in the wash, waiting for next Sunday. Where are your pinstripes?"

She considered him while a real smile edged up her face. "Touché." She motioned to a chair. "Would you like to join me?"

He tried not to look giddy as he nodded. But as his pulse raced, her murderous words flashed through his brain, along with a voice that warned, "Danger!" Aside from the fact that her smile made his heart jump to life, the sum of his knowledge about her centered on the facts that (a) she feared he might be some sort of backwoods murderer and (b) she enjoyed full-fledged conversations with invisible friends.

Perhaps, she needed a real friend. As in flesh and blood with two-way conversation. And if he unraveled a few of her mysteries, perhaps he could uncover whatever murderous thoughts lingered in her heart.

Hadn't he asked God for just this opportunity to make a difference? To redeem his past and show the world he could be a gentleman?

He sat down and crossed his legs at the ankles. "So, now, Miss Mario Andretti, tell me why you were racing down my mountain."

"No." Justine clicked off the tape recorder in her jacket pocket. She wasn't about to open her heart and show him her dreams. What if he laughed? Didn't every other person want to write a book? "I don't tell my secrets to strangers."

His blue eyes, lit by a nearby lantern, seemed to sparkle with mischief. "Patrick Bells, local good ole boy and coffee-shop manager."

His warm, solid, and slightly roughened hand hinted at outside pursuits.

"Justine Proof. Yankee invader."

"Who likes white chocolate, I hear. Lisa told me you ordered a foreign specialty. I'll have to track it down for you."

Justine made a face. "No, that's okay. I knew life here would take some adjusting. I'll just have to make do with my mocha latte." She lifted her mug. "And it's pretty tasty, so I'm not suffering."

"We aim to please. Part of our Southern charm."

Oh, he had that, in a dangerous mix, Justine thought. Starting with a drawl that sent a curl of delight to her toes. He took a sip of his coffee, and she watched him, wondering what happened to her rough-hewn rescuer from yesterday. This man sitting in the glow of twilight looked like he might have stepped out of a Land's End catalogue in a blue oxford and khakis. However, in place of the innocent model smile, he had scallywag written all over him—in the unruly, beckoning curl of his blond hair, a hint of whiskers, and a cocky grin. Good thing she was sitting because that smile still had the power to knock her clear off her feet.

"So, Yankee, tell me everything. You know, we have ways of making you talk, so don't get sassy."

She giggled like a love-struck teen, then wanted to cringe. "I'm working at KMPR, doing some reporting. It's sort of a favor for my dad."

That wasn't the complete truth, but how did she tell him that she was on the lam? Escaping from her father's shadow while trying to eke out a writing life. She knew if she didn't run now, she'd never break free of Monty Proof's reputation. Yes, she appreciated her father's leg-up in the journalistic world, but late at night, when she plotted in her head, she knew fiction, not fact, ran in her blood.

Something she dearly hoped she'd inherited from her mother.

"A favor?" Patrick invited her exposition by his raised eyebrows.

For the first time in two weeks, the ache to confide, to see understanding in the eyes of anyone but her faithful canine roared through her. And Patrick, now free of the 'dishonorably discharged' attire, did look relatively. . .safe.

"I think he'd call it his favor for me," she said, staring into her coffee. "He thinks I want to have a career traipsing in his footsteps. Joe Bob Trippett, the station manager at KMPR, is an old journalist buddy. Covered the Persian Gulf war, among other things, when they both worked for the Associated Press.

Joe Bob had a job opening and called Dad. He, of course, offered his firstborn daughter."

"I'm sensing the sacrificial lamb wants to crawl off the altar?"

She shrugged. "I'm thankful for the job—who wouldn't be?"

"You sound so thrilled. Especially the way your voice sinks into the low tones of despair. I can barely contain my glee for you."

She gave him a mock glare. "I am thrilled. Really. It's just. . ." She sighed, more deeply than she intended. "I have other dreams."

He stared at her with a silence that allowed embellishment. She couldn't surrender. Even for those searching blue eyes. "So, are you a hometown boy?"

He narrowed his eyes, then mercifully smiled. "Yep. Born and raised right here in Stoney Creek. Actually, I went to school in Hampton, up the road yonder."

"And your parents grew coffee beans?"

He chuckled, and a surge of warmth rippled through her.

"No. Pa was a sheriff in Johnson County. I think it was a parenting move. Once my brothers hit the school system, he figured the very real threat of lock-up would keep them on this side of the law. My ma was a teacher, another strategic move."

"Did it work?"

Patrick's smile dimmed, and he stared into his coffee cup as if it held the answer. "Eventually."

O—kay, so she'd hit a nerve. Way to go, Yankee. Come down from the North and stir up old feuds. "So. . .is this your store?"

His glance held the faintest etching of relief. "My sister's. She's a missionary in the Philippines."

"You're kidding. Wow. Is she single?"

"Yep. Went over a year ago. Asked me to run the shop while she's gone."

"That took some guts." Moving to the South had taken every last scrap of Justine's chutzpah.

"Faith, mostly. Carma really trusts God, and because of that, she knows she's never alone."

She offered him a smile, not quite believing his words. She'd trusted God her entire life and still felt that if she fell into a dark hole, not even heaven would notice.

"Do you agree with her?"

He nodded, his gaze tight. "I believe it to the depth of my soul. Since I met God, I know I'm not alone."

She felt darkness, as thick as tar, smatter her soul. What would it feel like to know she wasn't alone?

The bell over the door jangled. Patrick waved farewell to the exiting patrons.

"I suppose I should head home before it starts getting too dark," Justine said. "My car is still in the shop."

He leaned forward, balancing his elbows on his knees. "Did you walk?"

"Rode my bike. I live just up the hill on Happy Valley Street."

He turned his empty cup in his hands. "My car's parked out back. I can throw your bike in and drive you home if you want."

Sirens blared in her head. Just because Patrick looked civilized didn't mean he didn't have "stalker" in his blood. Besides, growing up in the big city had taught her to look twice over her shoulder and keep virtual strangers—even gorgeous ones—at a ten-foot-pole distance.

"No, thanks. I need the exercise after this chocolate." She held up her cup, trying to keep her voice light. "Don't want to encourage any extra layers."

He considered her a moment, all tease gone from his face. "Justine, I think you're just right."

Oh, Rhett Butler had returned, and for a second, she was Scarlett, running down the staircase, reconsidering her rebuttal. Then sanity grabbed hold of her brain and propelled her to her feet.

"Thank you. Right. Okay. Um, great coffee." She held up her cup, then set it down on the side table, turned, and beelined for the door. She wondered if the blush on her face turned her purple.

"It was nice to meet you, Justine." Patrick's voice held the slightest tinge of surprise, and she turned midstride.

"Yes, you too. Thank you."

He looked devastatingly sweet standing there, holding his coffee cup, his brow furrowed. She turned before she could give in to the temptation to grab onto his friendship with both desperate hands. It would behoove her to remember that she knew nothing about him other than he had excellent taste in coffee and knew how to drive all thoughts witty from her brain. He could be exactly the dangerous hillbilly she suspected.

She waved, turned on her heel, and fled the shop.

Unlocking her bike, she hopped on, rounded the corner, and cut through the back parking lot. It was deserted, save for a dirty white van backed up to the entrance of a neighboring shop, and a green, older-model sports car parked directly behind The Right Cup. Why had she thought he'd drive a pickup, complete with gun rack and deer antlers on the hood?

She peddled through the lot, watching as a man emerged from an alley, carrying a white bundle over his shoulder like Santa. Tall and thin, with a shock of snow white hair, he threw the bundle in the van, then turned to watch her. She waved. He smiled, waved back.

Yes, her overactive imagination had her conjuring up villains at every turn, and if she didn't crank it down to low, she'd never make a single friend south of Chicago.

Chapter 3

Patrick's bad-boy history picked the worst of possible times to roar to life. He stared at the blue backpack sitting on his desk chair and longed to open it. In the pit of his stomach, he knew it belonged to the Yankee girl from Minnesota—the Golden Gopher mini mascot hanging from one of the zippers gave it away—and only the gentleman inside kept him from plowing through her things. It smelled like her perfume, tangy, sweet, mysterious. Great. Just when he thought he'd exorcized the woman from his mind after a particularly restless night, her scent had to fill his office and tangle his brain.

He set the backpack on the floor, not sure whether to deliver it to her at KMPR television or keep it with the hope, oh please, that she'd be back today to claim it.

If he had the slightest inkling how to read her skittish response to his offer to drive her home last night, he might tuck a secret admirer letter into the pack, one that told her how her sheepish smiles had tugged at his heart, and her cryptic answers to his questions only baited the inquisitive male lurking inside him.

Then again, if he moved too fast, invaded her life like he wanted to, he might just scare her back North to the frozen wasteland.

For the sake of a substantial friendship, he'd let her retrieve her backpack. Meanwhile, he'd track down an online recipe for a white chocolate latte with a splash of raspberry flavoring.

The morning ticked by, and his cup of pecan decaf had turned cold before Patrick found the recipe and ordered a case of raspberry flavoring. Moseying out to the front, he noticed the lunch crowd had emptied. John Bowers, his daytime cashier and Lisa's husband, busily washed mugs. The early afternoon sun pushed through the large, plate-glass windows. A nutty popcorn smell, the residue of the beans freshly roasted in the morning, saturated the brick walls. Patrick noticed Grace Richardson sitting in the reading nook with her back to the counter, one hand on her lap.

"John, does Grace have Bluebell on her lap?" Patrick kept his voice low.

"I do believe she does. I found the animal sitting outside our back door about an hour ago. I think she left it here yesterday."

"I appreciate your tolerance, John, and I can understand Grace's love for the animal, especially since Charlie passed on, but I'm the one who has to face Fancy down at the health department."

John picked up a mug and began to towel it dry. "Then you'll have to be the terminator. I can't abide hurting the woman. Besides, she probably doesn't remember the rules. That's the third time she's forgotten the animal here in the last month."

Patrick nodded, starting toward the elderly woman. "Miss Grace?" He kept his voice light and touched her shoulder.

"How about if I put Bluebell in my office, just until you're finished?"

The fat Persian looked at him with the warmth of a pit bull. "Are you sure he'll be safe?" Grace Richardson had the face of a pumpkin, round and lined.

"Yes, I'm sure." He reached down, but the cat hissed. "How about if you do the honors?"

Grace flipped the cat over her shoulder like a newborn and waddled back to the office. Patrick spared her a scolding. Besides being his former Sunday school teacher, the woman deserved a bit of mercy in the face of her recent widowhood. Grace deposited Bluebell in the office, and Patrick closed the door. "I promise to take good care of her."

Grace gave him a look the biblical David might have given to the Philistines and returned to the reading nook.

Patrick picked up the television remote, hoping to catch the local news as he grabbed an egg salad sandwich from the refrigerator case behind the bar. "How was the lunch crowd today?"

"Busy. We're out of wild rice soup, and you'll need to order more bagels—they went faster than Miss Hildey's fried chicken at the annual church picnic."

"I'll call The Loafer today and put in a larger order for the morning." He poured himself a cup of Columbian decaf.

"Johnny Fair called. Said he was going to run up to the Goodwill in Mountain City this week. Said he'll leave the clothing for the children's shelter in his back room for you." John angled him a grin. "Still trying to redeem yourself?"

Patrick chuckled. "Naw. There's no hope. I'll never be anything but Wild Pat. But it doesn't hurt to make up for lost years. Besides, I like volunteering my time." Behind his eyes he saw the grimy faces of Chase and Kailee Wilkes. Bundled in tattered cotton blankets, neighbors had dumped the children off at the doorstep of the Stoney Creek child shelter after digging them out from their garbage-filled, lopsided trailer home back in the hills. Patrick had no doubt they had seen and heard things that would make a sailor flinch. The secret fact that The Right Cup funded much of the shelter's daily expenses gave Patrick purpose beyond roasting beans to perfection.

John clamped him on the shoulder. "The redeemed rebel. You're a testimony to God's grace, Friend. Don't listen to the devil's whispers. You're not the man you were, and no one has the right to tell you otherwise."

Except me. He managed a rueful smile. "Thanks, John. Give me thirty years or so. Maybe then some of my teachers will have lost their memories."

"Yeah, right. There's a reason you'll be giving out free coffee to the local police force for the rest of your life. You've heard the saying, legends never die?" John gave a slow nod and grinned at Patrick. "You're immortal, Pal."

Patrick scowled, then turned up the volume as he found KMPR. The cable station didn't broadcast more than three or four programs—community announcements, a "what's new in Stoney Creek" sponsored by the Chamber of Commerce, and a craft program hosted by his business neighbor, sewing expert Ida Schaeffer—but Patrick caught the daily noon news when he could. Thankfully, they rebroadcast it at three o'clock every afternoon for people like Patrick whose to-do list dictated his free time.

"In other news," said a flat, Midwestern voice, "the Fair

Jewelry Store suffered another break-in last night, the third this month."

Patrick stared at the reporter, and a bubble of teenage euphoria built in his chest.

"According to officials, nothing of value was taken, and the thieves escaped without detection. Fair said that he attributes their empty-handed failure to his newly installed security system."

Justine Proof smiled into the camera, her golden hair in trendy perfection, those rich, coffee-brown eyes just as piercing as they had been last night when she'd considered him and his questions. She looked snappy today in a trendy lavender suit. He knew a stupid smile had overcome him when John sidled beside him and gave him a hard look. "You know her?"

He gulped back his emotions and kept his voice light. "Yep. Met her a few days ago. She nearly drove off the road near the Watauga River Bridge."

"Huh. Now isn't that an interesting morsel of news." He untied his apron. "Lisa is meeting me for a late lunch, so I'm taking my break now. Can you handle the store?"

Patrick's gaze stayed on the television as she finished her news segment and signed off. "Sure."

John crumpled his apron, tossed it under the cash register, and headed to the door.

"John, wait. What did you mean by that?"

John turned, frowned. "Lunch? Something normal folks, with the exclusion of you and me, eat every day."

Patrick gave him a mock glare. "No. What did you mean about 'interesting news'?"

"Pat, it would do you well to push yourself away from your

computer occasionally and check in with the world. Didn't you hear about Harley Miller? KMPR's previous announcer?"

"No. . . ," Patrick said slowly, somehow dreading the answer.

"He died. Car wreck. Went over the Boone Bridge."

❧

"And. . .you're out." Bobby Boyd pointed at Justine from his perch behind the ring of cameras. "Good job."

"Thank you." Justine gathered her script, relief rushing over her. She'd nearly survived week three without any major catastrophes. KMPR might be only an affiliate cable station, and she might only be announcing the lunchtime news, but she didn't need to give the local population reason to start hunting her down at night.

They seemed to be doing just fine in pure daylight.

Her mishaps had started to spook her. Yesterday, she'd lost her backpack. . .or maybe it had been stolen. The last clear memory she'd had was wearing it home from the coffee shop. Like an idiot, she'd probably left it on the porch, handy for a thief to saunter by and scoop it up.

Thankfully, it only contained the very unimaginative death scene ideas logged into her recorder. It made her more than queasy to think, however, that someone had been lurking close to her front door.

She spied the station owner striding toward her, a grin as big as Grandfather Mountain on his thin face.

"I just knew you were the gal for the job. You've got Monty's knack for telling it like it is." He gave her a hug around her shoulders as if she'd just exposed the Pentagon Papers instead of taping a sixty-second update on last night's burglary of Fair Jewelers. "Thanks, Mr. Trippett."

"I told you, call me Joe Bob." He released her. "I think you're going to blend in just fine."

She didn't comment as he strode away, not believing for a second that her fly-away, cropped hair and high-heeled boots would fit into the society of the South. And they'd have to tar and feather her before she said, "Y'all."

"Justine, can you read over this copy?" Missy Scalf trotted up and handed her an update on the robbery at Fair Jewelers. "I just love your outfit today."

Justine blinked at her. "Thank you." And here she thought the lavender leather suit would have them running for the hills. She wished she could afford a new wardrobe, but on her salary, buying writing how-to books and eating came before blending in.

Missy hovered around her, blue eyes twinkling as Justine read the copy. "This is a good piece, Missy. Where did you graduate?"

Missy blushed. "Oh, no, I didn't go to college. I started here in high school and just, well, worked my way up." She shrugged. "Toad helped me a lot."

"Toad?"

"Oh, I mean Jeffrey. I forget that he doesn't like to be called that at work." She wrinkled her nose, along with a generous smattering of freckles. "Jeffery Brubaker, the station cameraman?"

Oh sure, tall and thin, with an Adam's apple that looked like a golf ball in his neck and stabbing brown eyes that didn't seem to miss a thing. Justine remembered him from the company party, along with the way his sweaty grip held her hand just a little too tight. The flash comparison of Patrick's grip in hers, wide and gentle, kept her from shuddering. "Why do they call him Toad?"

"It's a nickname his brothers gave him. I don't rightly know why." Missy took the page from Justine. "He says that someday I might be an announcer." Her grin made her shine, and Justine had to agree with Toad's prediction. For a stinging moment, she wondered why Missy hadn't filled the position of noon anchorwoman. With her size-six figure, her teased and highlighted hair, those stunning blue eyes, and an accent that sounded like well-played bluegrass, Missy would be perfect for the position.

"I'm sure he's correct," Justine said. She followed Missy back to the newsroom, found her desk, and logged onto Fox for some real news. She noticed the AP had picked up an article her father had written on a leaking chemical plant in Minnesota. A twinge of homesickness burned her eyes. Silly. Twenty-eight years old, and she still missed home.

Downloading her mail, she noticed two messages from her online mystery group. At least Raine and Tina had chapters written. She felt like a literary loser. She'd composed all of three sentences last night after returning home. A regular Agatha Christie.

Of course, it didn't help that thoughts of Patrick moved her into molasses motion. More than once she found herself tangled in the memory of his blue eyes and the smile that hinted at trouble. For the smallest, sweetest of moments, she'd actually felt like she might have found a friend.

Justine clicked over to the in-house mail system and read her list of developing stories. Rosie, society editor, had sent her a rough copy of an article about a city proposal to add a dilapidated homestead to the historical register.

At least someone could write.

ElHannon IV, son of Bisty and ElHannon Murphy III, has returned home. Nearly a decade to the day he left town, the last living relative of the first ElHannon Murphy, Civil War hero and local legend, has returned from his defection in the North to take up residence in the Murphy mansion. The oldest standing building in Carter County, the mansion and its land border the newly built Golden Golf Acres. Mr. Murphy refused to sell the land, a long sought-after property, which he claims was used as a way station along the Underground Railroad and later housed Yankee soldiers.

Justine vaguely remembered reading something in the Carter County literature about this section of upper East Tennessee supporting the Union.

Murphy has spent the last twenty years learning the profession of environmental design and assisted in the restoration of such notable locations as the Chicago Art Gardens, the Gardens at Whitley Park, the estate of Chicago Governor Mitchell, and the Henly Center Rooftop Gardens.

"I hope to light the home fires," ElHannon said of his return. "I'll be restoring the home to its original grandeur and put the Murphy mansion back on the map."

Rosie had put the last quotes in a box, noting that they had a clip from this interview. After scanning the rest of the article, Justine meandered back to the video room. At her knock, Frank Ketchum swiveled in his chair.

"Can I see the ElHannon interview?" Justine asked.

Frank dug through the stack of videos on his desk while Justine scrutinized the face paused on his screen. "Hey, I've seen that guy before."

Frank looked up, "Oh, that's Johnny Fair."

"As in Fair Jewelers? The store that got robbed last night?" The picture of a lean man, a bag flung over his shoulder, flashed through her memory.

Frank nodded, then with an "Aha!" he popped a tape into the player. A moment later, ElHannon's face filled the screen. Sounding elegant, with just a hint of a Southern drawl in his deep voice, the man appeared fresh off the cover of some upscale business magazine holding a rose in one hand like a jewel. The faintest tinge of a smile added to his mystique, and Justine couldn't decide if his blond ponytail complimented his Southern charm or made him seem an avant-garde Yankee. Under his urbane appearance, however, she saw a definite good-ole-boy glint, the same one etched in Patrick's eyes. Underneath Mr. Murphy's suave demeanor just might be hidden the makings of a story.

Needing a shot of caffeine to clear the late-afternoon fog from her head, she stopped in the employee lounge and popped some quarters into the coffee machine. A cup fell into the slot and a semi-liquid, reminiscent of Mississippi River mud, spat out of the machine, over the cup, and onto her leather skirt. Justine jumped back with a cry of frustration.

"There's only one place to find a decent cup of coffee in

this town," said a low voice. Justine turned. Toad Brubaker sat at one of the long tables. "The Right Cup."

Justine grabbed a handful of napkins from the counter. "I was there last night. Met the owner." She dabbed her skirt, frowning at the stain.

"Wild Pat?" Toad laughed, a huff that didn't sound like humor. "Yeah, I suppose he would have met you."

Justine stared at him.

"He's the local ladies' man. Had a pretty good reputation a few years back, before he joined the military." Toad folded the newspaper he was reading, then stood up. "Came back a couple years ago and took over his sister's shop. She went to Africa or something."

"Wild Pat? That's what you call him?" She noticed a shrill of panic in her voice.

"Well, down at city hall, I think they called him, 'Here again'? It's a good thing his dad was a cop." Toad smiled, but it didn't touch his eyes. "He's pretty harmless if you don't pay any mind to the trail of broken hearts he's left around town."

Justine's voice completely deserted her as Toad sauntered past her.

"By the way, if you're looking for a good story, you might want to ask ElHannon Murphy about Wild Pat. There's a reason old Han left town twenty years ago."

Chapter 4

Why was she standing outside ElHannon Murphy's estate, the wind hissing in her ears, the afternoon sun just below the hills? Justine wondered if she could call it "the people's right to know."

Or she could tell the truth. Justine Proof, ace reporter, hunted secrets. Specifically those involving Patrick Bells.

She wouldn't ask herself why it mattered. Why she'd called up Jerry and begged to get her car back, paying extra bucks for speedy service. Why the thought of Patrick being anything but sweet and slightly mischievous made her ill.

The Murphy mansion rose grand and glorious in a field of unkempt weeds. An outbuilding, probably a barn, hinted at a wealthy history. She imagined gleaming buggies pulling up to the massive porch, unloading debutantes into the care of white-gloved butlers. She easily saw the ivy winding up the white columns, lamps glowing from the round window in the third floor. Restored, the place would be a treasure. Beyond the house, tucked halfway up Murphy Mountain, the grounds tapered off to an overgrown trail that jagged into a clasp of sweet gum, mountain maples, dogwoods, and yellow birch. Already, fall had painted the leaves, hinting at a brilliant palette of October color. Smoke laced the air from some unseen coal chimney, despite the warm evening, and over the mountain, the lonely echo of a dog's bark gave her the spooks.

A woman using all her brain cells would wait until daylight before snooping around a man's home, especially one who might have a sinister history. The place had plenty of nooks and crannies in which to hide a nosy—and dead—reporter. She had no doubt that she would starve long before someone discovered the Yank in town had vanished.

The breeze whipped through her hair, and she shivered. One hand on her cell phone, she approached the dark house. The porch squeaked in expected menace as she climbed the stairs. Gulping her courage in a deep breath, she rapped on the door.

The night caught the sound. She opened the dilapidated screen door, jumping at the screech of the hinges, and tried the knob. It turned.

With a sweaty hand, she pushed the door open. "Hello? Mr. Murphy, are you here?"

No one responded as she stared into the dark foyer. Textured shadows and the bulk of a staircase ascending into the chasm of darkness made her wonder if ElHannon simply worked here in the relative sanity of daytime. She couldn't imagine anyone sleeping here. Not with the dust gathered in the corners and the smell of age curling her nose. She patted the wall, hoping for a light, and her hand slid across a cobweb. Her outcry echoed through the house like a gunshot.

"ElHannon?" she shouted again just to confirm her suspicions, then stood and listened to her own thundering heartbeat.

So, if the man wasn't home, would it be a crime to wander through his house?

She didn't let her conscience answer the question and instead moved into the foyer, leaving the door open both for quick exit and light. Shuffling forward, she aimed toward a dent in the darkness. As her eyes adjusted to the grayness, she made out a kitchen, including a pot-bellied stove, a countertop that looked like it might have been updated in the seventies, and. . .a microwave? She flicked the light on, bathing the kitchen in a dirty yellow glow.

Justine's heart stopped right in the middle of her throat.

Inside the microwave lay a convenience store hamburger in its yellow wrapper.

And, as if in response to her muted outcry, a figure appeared in the doorway to her left. Justine easily recognized the outline, much larger than the videotape hinted, of ElHannon Murphy.

"Can I help you?"

Patrick slammed down the telephone. "I missed her."

Lisa perched on his office desk, wearing a goofy smile.

"Just friendly worry," Patrick said. "Don't jump to any conclusions."

"Not jumping. I'm already there." She waggled her eyebrows and his bad-boy side wanted to toss her out of his office on her ear. "Well?"

"Jerry said she picked up the car an hour ago."

"And?"

"He said her front brake line looked weather checked and had a good crack in it. She probably leaked brake fluid all the way down the mountain."

"Any sign of sabotage?"

Patrick lifted his hands in frustration. "Hard to say."

Lisa began to hum, an annoying habit she utilized when trying to make a point. Her current tune seemed to be a rendition of "What a Friend We Have in Jesus." He stared out the window, noticing the departing sun had draped long shadows over the back parking lot. A merciless mountain wind had littered the lot with shredded oak leaves.

"So, did you ever figure out what she was mumbling about last night?" Lisa asked.

Patrick endured a stab of guilt over discussing Justine's secret musings with Lisa. The poor lady didn't need the town thinking she was a few bricks shy of a full load. Besides, he didn't want Lisa to read more into his concern than pure. . . friendship.

Who was he kidding? Between the secreted tears on Roan Mountain, the cryptic monologue, and the way Justine had giggled at his jokes, it didn't take a psychology degree to figure out the woman did dangerous things to his heart. "No. She wasn't telling her secrets. But there are some things I haven't forgotten how to do."

Lisa angled him a dark look. He gave a puff of embarrassment. "No, I don't mean anything corrupt. Years in the service taught me to dig in and wait for the right opportunity."

She folded her arms across her chest and nodded slowly.

"Really. I promise, my intentions are honorable. You should know that by now." How he hated it when his past rose like a specter.

"I know. But does she?" Lisa looked pointedly at the sagging blue backpack propped against his desk. "Seems to me she might need a hometown hero."

Patrick grimaced, wondering if he'd spent the last two-plus hours in useless worry. Harley Miller's death had been an accident, the fatal combination of a late-night curve and a half-bottle of whisky. Still, Jerry's hesitant answer to Patrick's question about Justine's car had him buzzing with concern. And a real hero would make sure she got home safely.

Justine gave ElHannon credit for patience and Southern hospitality. She sat in his restored office, drinking hot tea, still trying to wrestle her body back into her skin.

"Are you sure you're okay?" he asked as he sat across from her in his leather office chair. A scattering of blueprints, topographical maps, and computer printouts with accounting columns were spread over his desk, lit by a pool of lamplight. Justine managed to drag her gaze off the mess and meet his dark eyes. They held the texture of kindness despite his hard-edged jaw and renegade ponytail. With his broad shoulders and open-collared jean shirt, he reminded her of some sort of Revolutionary War patriot, plotting the advance of Washington's troops.

She somehow coaxed her voice from hiding. "Yes, thank you for the tea. Again, I'm so sorry to just barge in. . . ."

He lifted his hand. "Not a problem. I didn't hear you knock. You're from KMPR?"

"Yes." Justine felt purpose, albeit feeble, surge into her veins. "I wanted to ask you about. . ." Patrick Bells? Not unless she wanted to take out her heart and pin it to her sleeve right next to her fear. "Your absence. I'm not from around here, and

213

I was curious as to why you left town." She tried a smile, wondering if those dark eyes could see right through her.

He arched his eyebrows. "Personal advancement. I went looking for. . .other opportunities. I moved to Chicago and hooked up with a professional landscaper. Finally earned a degree in environmental design."

"And you've done well. Why did you leave it?"

He leaned back, grinned. "Guess I just missed Stoney Creek."

Homesickness panged in her heart. "I read your interview. But I have to know. Did you return for more. . .personal reasons?"

His smile grew. "You're not from the South, are you? A true Southerner would dance around that question for a good two hours while drinking sweet tea or even let it ferment for a day or a week until they worked up the. . ." His smile dimmed. "The relationship to ask such a forward question."

She winced. "Okay. How about I return in the daylight and you show me around the place and tell me why Murphy mansion is worth giving up your career in Chicago? And in the meantime, I'll promise not to snoop around town. You give me your story, and I won't write anything else."

He blinked at her. "So what you're saying is that if I don't unlock my secrets, you'll dig up twenty-year-old gossip and print it?"

She stared into her tea. No, that wasn't exactly what she meant. She wasn't out to destroy the man's life. In fact this had so little to do with ElHannon Murphy, she found herself shaking her head in disbelief.

"That sounds pretty ugly, doesn't it?"

"I think you should leave. Now." He stood, his face fierce and hard.

Justine's chest tightened. "The truth is, I met Patrick Bells, and well—"

ElHannon gave a throaty burst of disbelief. "This is about Patrick? And me?"

Justine made a face, completely disgusted with herself. How had she disintegrated into a suspicious, dirt-digging, fatal attraction? "I'll go."

"No, sit, please." His smile spoke of forgiveness. "You met Patrick. That's great. Well, you're not going to dig our past out of me, but let me tell you, if Patrick is half as interested in you as you are in him, you're in a heap of trouble."

Those words and ElHannon's warm handshake and invitation to join him on a tour of the grounds eased Justine's tension as she wound her way back down Murphy Mountain toward Stoney Creek. One sentence in particular, however, had her squirming. "When Patrick knows what he wants, he goes after it like a hound dog."

Justine gripped the wheel until it pinched her hands. She'd been right to turn down Patrick's offer of a ride home. Just think where'd she be if she let herself enjoy his pearly smile or opened her heart to his Southern charm. She shot off a prayer of gratitude, wondering if God had used her investigative snoopiness to wave her off.

It suddenly felt like a small eternity since she'd been on her knees, talking with the Almighty, seeking His friendship, asking for His help. Then again, with her father doing a bang-up job, she supposed she hadn't needed God.

But now that she did, what if it was too late?

As she motored into the city limits, her steering wheel shuddered, then, with a shot that sounded straight from a double-barrel, the car lurched sideways. Justine cringed at the rhythmic slap of rubber against the pavement as she muscled the car onto the shoulder. Now what?

Climbing out, she didn't know whether to kick the flat tire or sink into a ball and sob. Had she pumped up the spare? The dark feeling in her chest told her no. Digging her cell phone out of her bag, she was staring at it, her mind blank, when a car pulled up opposite her. Its headlights illuminated the highway behind her and, as the rescuer got out of the car, Justine squinted at the figure, not sure if she should slam the door or stand up and do a jig.

The answer became clear as she watched with widening eyes. Patrick Bells looked both ways, then swaggered across the deserted highway, wearing a cocky grin.

He dangled her backpack from one strong finger.

Justine jumped into her Volvo and slammed the door.

Chapter 5

It took Patrick's last reserve of patience and Southern coaxing to pry Justine out of the car. Even so, she regarded him with thinly veiled suspicion as he changed her tire, filling her spare with a can of aerosol flat-fixer. Her attitude annoyed him more than he wanted to admit.

He wasn't the local thug, despite what she might have heard. And he had no doubt she'd heard plenty by the way she hiked her fists on her hips and hawked his every move.

He tightened the last lug nut on the wheel. "Tomorrow, take your car into Jerry's. He's got retreaded tires. And get yourself a can of flat-fixer." He didn't look at her as he opened her trunk, tossed in the tire iron, and reached for the damaged tire. Turning it, he had no problem discovering the reason for her blowout. "Where did you say you were?"

"I didn't."

Okay. So she didn't want him poking around her life. "Well, I'd advise you to stay off the back roads. The mountain rocks can get pretty sharp, and this one made an ugly slash. Good thing you'd made it to the highway where someone could find you."

He left off who that someone was. He closed the trunk and forced himself to look at her.

Oh, this was silly. She stood, proud chin up, staring away from him like he'd just insulted her instead of having searched the city for two hours for her rusted-out Volvo. Not that she had to know that.

"Have I offended you in some way? Like by showing up and trying to get your car on the road—again?"

"Thank you," she said with the warmth of a bobcat.

"You're welcome." He shook his head, starting to stalk past her. He'd get into his car and sit there, just until she started home, and then he'd follow at a safe—

"You're just too. . .nice." Her voice held an edge of desperation. It caught him like a right hook.

"Nice? Well, Lady, I have to admit, of all my crimes, I didn't think I'd ever be accused of that one."

She turned, and her eyes held a tinge of fear. "And just what are those crimes?"

He opened his mouth. Nothing emerged. He hadn't meant to dredge up the past. . .now or ever.

She must have read his shock because she shook her head. "I'm sorry. I've just had a long day. I want to go home, walk my dog, and climb into bed."

She looked so forlorn beneath all that Northern spit and polish that his anger softened. "Listen, Yankee. I know we might talk a little funny down here, but believe me when I say I'm just trying to be your friend. Forgive me if I've scared you."

Were those tears edging her eyes? He felt like something that lived under a log. He took a deep breath, fighting the impulse to curl her into an embrace. "How about if I follow you home to make sure you're okay, and then, I promise, I won't bother you again."

"You're not bothering me." She closed her eyes, pressing beautifully manicured fingers over them. "I've just had a rough day."

"I'll call you tomorrow and maybe I can buy you a cup of coffee," he said, pitifully aware that she had the ability to tie his feelings into knots.

The invitation earned him a feeble smile. She opened her eyes. "Or I could buy you one tonight. You did save me a hike into town."

Uh oh, was that his heart jumping up and down like a kindergartner in his chest? "What?"

"Do you know how to make a brevé? Espresso and—

"Half and half. I know it." Just because he'd never made one in his life didn't mean he couldn't learn between now and The Right Cup. He did have a cell phone and a very cooperative employee.

"Okay then. I'll go home, grab a bite of supper, walk the dog, and then come down to the shop—"

"No." The look of surprise on her face sparked the old Pat, the wild one who enjoyed charming a lady. "I have a better idea. I'll pick you up in, say, an hour?"

Now that was a real smile, the one that he'd been hoping for.

An hour later he had raided the store of two ham-and-cheese croissant sandwiches, a tub of potato salad, and two iced coffees. Throwing the picnic into a brown bag, he dug a flashlight from the backroom and tossed it, along with a blanket, into the back of his car. Porch lights, barking dogs, and the crisp smell of fall nourished his hope as he drove to Justine's little cinder-block home on Happy Valley Street.

She was sitting on her whitewashed steps when he drove up. She'd changed out of the lavender leather and instead wore a pair of faded, flare-leg jeans and a light blue cotton sweater that made her seem like the girl next door. She waved almost shyly, and he tried not to spring out of the car like a giddy teen.

Her collie greeted him with more exuberance.

"Her name is Maizey," Justine said. "She's old, but faithful."

Patrick slowly rubbed behind Maizey's ear. The collie groaned and moved into the pressure. "I think she likes me."

"Well, she's old. Can't smell trouble anymore."

"I'd say she's an excellent judge of character."

Justine laughed, and it felt like an embrace.

"Ready to go?" He crooked out his arm and, to his delight, she took it. He helped her into the car.

Justine ran a hand over the wooden dashboard. "What kind of car is this?"

He climbed into the front seat. "A 1967 Carmen Ghia. It's a Volkswagen. I bought it a couple years ago and restored it."

"It's beautiful." She touched the ancient radio like she might be touching fine china. "I'll bet the ladies love it."

"You're the first one who's ridden in it, but I'm hoping it works that way."

She said nothing as they drove toward Main Street, but a smile tweaked her lips.

He motored down Main, over the Watauga River Bridge, and parked just beyond the monument. "Have you ever seen a covered bridge?" he asked as he pulled out the picnic fixings.

"No." She freed Maizey, who bounded out into the park like a puppy.

"Great. Let me be the first, then, to show you the Carter County Covered Bridge." He wished his hands weren't full—he might just offer her his. Then again, it was enough to have her strolling beside him, the river adding a harmony to the breeze playing the dogwood while lamplights pooled gold along the paved walkway.

In the distance, the covered bridge gleamed white under the thumbnail moon. He felt like he'd stepped right into the past, no, further—into someone else's past, the history of a Southern gentleman wooing his belle. This is how it should have been, what he should have waited for.

Justine's voice broke through to the present. "Do they still use it?"

It took him a moment to find his voice and unravel her question. "Oh, the bridge. Yes. It still works. Although only one car fits through it at a time."

"It looks ancient." She reached over and took the blanket from him, as if they were a longtime couple. He felt a rush of pure delight.

"They built it in 1882." He angled off the path and stopped underneath a towering oak. "How's this?"

He took the blanket, spread it out, and began to unload the supper. She stood quietly, her hands folded tightly in front of her, as if suddenly tense. Then, in a tight voice, she said, "Thank you, Patrick. For changing my tire, for this starlight picnic, and for putting up with my. . .thinking you were a redneck."

He stopped unwrapping the croissant and looked at her. She faked a smile, but underneath the attempt at humor lurked vulnerability.

"Come here." He reached out his hand, and she knelt next

to him. "You probably know that I don't have a stellar reputation in this town."

She paled, her eyes wide, and suddenly he wished he didn't have a past that intruded into all his golden moments. His throat felt like sandpaper. "I'm not that person anymore."

She nodded, but her expression spoke doubt.

He hooked his arms over his drawn-up knees and stared out over the river. "About a year ago, I asked Christ to forgive me, and I gave Him control of my life. To some people that doesn't sound like a big deal, but it changed my life."

He saw in his peripheral vision that she, too, studied the scenery. "I visited ElHannon Murphy tonight, Patrick."

He tried not to wince. "I knew he was back."

She picked up a twig and began to dig into the grass. "What is between you two?"

A friendship he'd thought would last forever. A betrayal so deep he still felt sick. "What did he tell you?"

"Nothing."

"Maybe it should stay that way." He closed his eyes when he said it, knowing that wasn't the answer she'd hoped for. For the first time, he truly understood the depth of ElHannon's fury and grief. Emotions that combined to drive him out of town.

"Please?"

Patrick forked a hand through his hair. If he didn't tell her, someone else would. And it could be ugly.

Then again, it couldn't be any uglier than the truth.

"I, um, stole ElHannon's girl."

She stayed silent. Too silent. He glanced at her, terribly aware that his heart was in his glance.

Eyebrows up, she wore a half grin, as if somehow the situation held a fragment of humor.

"I realize that where you come from, that may not be a big deal," he said. "But let me enlighten you on a bit of Dixie truth. We Southern lads love our women. Blood feuds have ignited over love. Believe me, ElHannon had his reasons to hate me."

"I don't think he hates you, Patrick. He seemed pretty forgiving when I talked to him."

"No. He's not going to forgive me." Patrick closed his eyes, wanting to run. "ElHannon was my best friend. I grew up deer hunting and hiking his mountain. We were like two bugs on a log." He opened his eyes and picked a tuft of grass. "Our senior year, we loved the same girl. Well, not loved. . .you know what I mean. Sequa Bowers. Cheerleader, blond. A smile that could kill a man." He pushed past the thickening of his voice. "She chose ElHannon. And for ElHannon's part, he truly loved her."

"And your friendship?" Justine asked softly.

"It took some hits. But we were tight. I didn't think a girl could ever come between us." How did this romantic setting turn into a night of soul flogging? "I was wrong."

Justine touched his arm. The kindness in her gesture buoyed his courage.

"He planned on taking her to the prom, but a week before the big event, he was injured. He was the high-jump champ, but he went over the bar wrong and broke his leg. Three months of traction at the Carter County Hospital."

"Ouch."

"He asked me to fill in for him on prom night."

"Oh."

He hung his head, sick to his soul. "Yeah, well. . .we were

all drinking, and one thing led to another. . . ." He closed his burning eyes. "My parents found us in a fairly compromising position, and the rumor mill churned. I think she was looking for a reason to dump ElHannon, but he took it hard."

"He severed your friendship?"

"I left for basic training before we made peace. When I returned, he'd left town."

"You haven't talked to him since?"

Patrick gave a self-deprecating grin. "I couldn't face him."

"Patrick, you can't let fear stand in the way of friendship. You have to smooth things out with him. A true friend is a treasure."

He touched her hand, aware of how soft it felt, knowing he didn't deserve to sit here in the embrace of moonlight with a lady who gave out second chances. "I'd like to be your friend, Yankee." He looked at her, saw her swallow. She started to tug her hand away, but he held it. "Don't be afraid. I promise I'm not that man anymore. You won't find yourself in any compromising positions with me."

She smiled, slow and sweet. "I believe you."

For a breath, he feared he might cry. "Thata girl." Then he took a deep breath and released her hand before he did something incredibly foolish—like kiss her.

Chapter 6

Justine propped her chin on her hand and stared at her computer screen. Only the buzz of the fluorescent light kept her company in the dark office. Even her online mystery group had abandoned her. Her stomach growled like a springtime grizzly, and she felt grimy and wrung out.

The day had started painfully and worsened, fast. At 9:00 A.M., horribly late and with a headache to rival any Excedrin ad, she'd just pulled on her hosiery when the doorbell chimed. Three times.

She still had to think hard to dredge up the woman's name. Grace. Richardson? Her elderly neighbor stood on the porch, eyes red rimmed, a wretched picture of despair. "Yes?" Justine asked as she tied her bathrobe, glancing at the merciless clock.

"I've lost. . .Bluebell." The woman's voice shook.

Justine invited her in.

"It's my cat. I can't seem to find him. It's so not like him to run off. . . ."

Justine didn't miss the wary look at the collie sleeping in a ray of morning sun. "What kind of cat?" She kept her voice light.

"A Persian. He's old, but he's all I have." The woman's eyes filled.

Justine felt a stab of pity. "No, Ma'am, I haven't seen him, and I assure you, Maizey hasn't either. But I will keep an eye out for him."

For the sake of community relations, perhaps she should hunt through her overgrown row of rhododendrons when she returned home. They did look like they could snare an animal whole.

She'd arrived at KMPR thirty minutes later, her hair in rebellion, looking like she'd put on her rumpled coral suit in the car.

The only thing that made the day bearable was the letter she found on her desk after taping the news. She had a moment's pause as she opened it and stared at the small square sheet of paper:

Justine,
Thank you for letting me show you the covered bridge.
Trust me.

Your friend, Patrick

ElHannon's words crept into her mind: *When Patrick knows what he wants, he goes after it like a hound dog.*

Except, Patrick certainly looked better than the local canine population, even if he seemed tenacious. Under the moon's kiss, his hair had turned pure gold, and she felt nearly jealous of the wind as it teased it and sent his coffee-brewed masculine scent her direction. He'd unraveled his history for her scrutiny, and the vulnerability hidden in the good-ole-boy guise spiraled right to a soft place in her heart.

It had taken all her Norwegian breeding to choke down her sandwich. She yearned to figure out a way to snuggle closer, but she couldn't even work up a decent chill to offer as an excuse. He'd done a bang-up job of making her feel warm clear to her toes.

She'd made a friend. It felt like a gift.

She propped his note next to her computer and spent half the day glancing at it and smiling. At least until Jerry's telephone call in the midafternoon.

"Missy, I'm sorry to tell you this, but this tire has been slashed."

Justine rubbed her temple, where her headache camped. "I was in the back hills and must have driven over a rock."

"One with a serrated edge that cuts in a six-inch straight line?" Jerry's voice held enough sarcasm to get the point across.

"Are you saying someone deliberately cut my tire?"

"That's what I'm saying, Lady. The car will be ready tonight after seven." He hung up.

Someone is trying to kill me.

She stared at Patrick's letter, wondering just how tenacious a hound dog could be to nab his prey. As they stood out on the road, he had paled when she'd asked him what crime spree he'd been responsible for. His horrified expression made her feel like a slug at the time. Now it turned her cold.

She shoved the letter into her drawer and spent the rest of the afternoon reading about ElHannon's landscaping company. He had an impressive Web site, including pictures of his work. Why had he tossed it aside to move back to the South? He'd purposely dodged her questions—not that she'd handled the interview well. But something, perhaps the way he folded his hands on his desk. . .

The maps. Of course. It came to her as she ate a mealy apple from the lunchroom vending machines. He'd had a wide map of Golf Course Acres spread underneath the topographical specs of Murphy Mountain. She'd glanced at it twice, surreptitiously, as she sipped her tea.

Did ElHannon plan on selling Murphy mansion after all? It was no secret Golf Course Acres hoped to expand, and Murphy Mountain would go for a pretty penny. But such a sale would not happen if the mansion were to be listed on the historic register. The city could bar the sale on grounds of national interest if someone discovered his plan. Someone like a nosy reporter who ran her mouth like a faucet.

Justine groaned and had imprinted her keyboard onto her forehead before she noticed the beeping that came from her confused computer. Just how long had she been skulking through ElHannon's house? Long enough for him to slash her tire in hopes she might careen off his mountain?

Swallowing hard, she opened her word-processing program and began jotting down scenarios. At least she'd be able to finish her assignment from Drake Axelrod's book in preparation for the novella collection she and her friends were going to propose.

She wrote "suspicious events" at the top of the page, then listed them in sequence:

Stolen car radio
Damaged brakes
Missing backpack
Flat tire

Below that column, she scribbled "Suspects." Justine ran her brain over the possible villains, finding it disconcerting that she so easily conjured up Patrick. Honestly, the man hadn't done anything but appear, albeit opportunely, to save her. It wasn't like he was stalking her or lurking in her backyard.

How about ElHannon Murphy? He certainly had reason to stop her from discovering secrets. And. . .her brain tracked back to the night she'd seen the man unloading his bundles into the white van outside the back entrance to Fair Jewelers. She'd looked straight into his beady eyes and waved like an idiot. Didn't Frank identify the fella as Mr. Fair himself? Could he be robbing his own store? She scribbled his name on the list. Maybe he didn't want her to delve deep enough to find out.

And what about her neighbor? Granny Richardson, or whatever her name was, didn't seem the type to prowl around in the darkness and steal her radio or slash her tires, but the lady surely had opportunity, what with their streetlight out. And after this morning, motive.

Justine printed her name.

That left. . .Patrick. With great dismay, Justine added him.

Her stomach roared. Closing the program, she found her car keys and headed out the door for Jerry's. Her car sat parked in front of the shop, a bill tucked on the front windshield wiper. Justine wrote a check, slipped it into the envelope, and shoved it under the front door before unlocking her car and driving down Main toward home.

She turned at Sycamore and drove behind The Right Cup, too tired to wrestle with her confusing emotions about its owner.

Of course, she couldn't stop herself from searching for his

sports car. No sign of him. And somehow, that added fact stabbed the soft tissue of her heart.

✿

He drove by her house. Again. He agreed that his actions bordered on obsession, but after Jerry's telephone call today, Patrick knew he wouldn't sleep tonight until he knew Justine had returned safely, even if he had to circle her block until morning. After leaving several messages on her answering machine, he resorted to drive-by surveillance.

He couldn't dodge the feeling someone hunted her. Even more unsettling was the idea that she knew it. He'd replayed her disturbing monologue from the first night a thousand times in his brain and couldn't decide if she had been speculating on her demise or plotting revenge.

Friend. That word took on new meaning since a lady flew down his mountain and crashed through the barriers of his heart.

He drove the length of another block, turned past Grace Church, and headed down G Street, the road parallel to her house, wishing he could see through the dry cleaners to her porch lights.

He could hardly believe he'd bared his soul, and she hadn't cringed. Not one flinch. A friend? After last night, with the wind playing with her hair, the moon in her sweet brown eyes, and the way she'd smiled, as if she trusted him, as if his past didn't matter, he'd passed right by the friend category and was moving up on. . .

Emotions swept his breath away.

This panicked, giddy, chest-filling feeling couldn't possibly be—love? He wasn't, couldn't be falling for her. He punched his brakes, turned onto Williams Avenue, and pulled over, sweat beading at his temples.

Okay, so he had feelings for her. But love? His pa would accuse him of dipping into the local 'shine.

Still, when Justine stepped into his world, the sun shone brighter, the air smelled sweeter. Life seemed. . .rife with second chances.

He took a few quick breaths, needing to focus before this feeling knocked him completely off his feet.

Turning onto her road, he felt nearly delirious with relief to see Justine's Volvo parked out front. Slowing, he debated whether to stop in and invite her out for a cup of coffee, realizing that was the last thing he should do if he wanted to wrench free of the grip she had on him. He crawled by, noticing that the streetlight above her car had gone out. While he pondered that and Jerry's latest information, he saw movement, a shadow in the jungle next to her house.

Patrick crunched his brakes and sat there, eyes squinting, peering into the bushes. Yes, definitely, someone creeping along the rhododendrons. . .

He slammed the gear into park and jumped out of the car before he knew what his legs were doing. Fury pushed him low and quiet as he crouched at the edge of the house.

He heard breathing.

With a roar, he pounced.

Justine saw the figure springing before she could scream. In a painful blink, she'd been flattened onto the cold earth, her head spinning and her heart in her mouth.

"Please, don't hurt me," she choked. The bulk had one arm

against her throat, the other pinning back her arm. "Please."

"Oh, no."

The voice sounded horrified. The man jumped up like he'd been shot, his face white, his blue eyes as wide as hers felt. "Oh man, Justine. I'm sorry."

She blinked. Sat up, blinked again. "Patrick?"

He was on his feet, backing away, running his hand through his hair. "I'm sorry, I'm so sorry."

She gave an incredulous huff that sounded horribly like a laugh. "What are you doing here?" In the dim, remaining light of the day, she saw his pain.

"Did I hurt you?" he asked, his voice tight with anxiety.

She shook her head. "I've been tackled before. Powder-puff football. But I have to say, it was the first time I've been pinned."

He advanced and held out his hand. "Forgive me. I was driving by and I saw—what are you doing, hiding in the bushes?"

"The neighbor thinks my dog ate her cat, and I'm trying to dispel that myth."

He was brushing debris from her arms and checking to make sure nothing was broken. His expression of agony went straight to her heart. "Really, I'm fine, Patrick. I promise."

"Wow, what a jerk I am. Pouncing on you in your own yard."

She reached out and pulled a twig from his hair. "Or incredibly sweet. I mean, you thought someone was lurking in my bushes. I'd say you went out of your way to protect me."

He opened his mouth, but nothing came out. Then he smiled.

Whoa. If she still harbored ideas that he might be trying

to do her in, they scattered with that grin. She felt herself blush. "You know, you seem to be making a habit out of saving my skin."

"It's a new hobby I've picked up. Save the Yankee girl from herself."

"I like it. Is there a club?"

"Nope," he stuck his hands into his khaki pockets. "It's a lonely job."

The fall breeze snared a bit of his masculine essence—a heady mix of coffee and cotton—and if she didn't do something fast, she just might forget his scribbled name on her list of villains. What was she thinking, villain? The man had "chagrined hero" written all over him. And now, with his linebacker tackle, he upped his status to something more. . .significant. "We can't have that. How about if I help you 'save the Yankee girl' and buy us both a cup of coffee? Do you happen to know a good coffee shop around here? One that serves decaf espresso?"

"I just might," he said in a devastating drawl.

Justine sat, legs tucked up on the wicker sofa, the lamplight from a hurricane lamp turning her hair gold. She held a cup of decaf espresso in her hands, blowing on it softly.

He felt like a rattlesnake. She still sported grass stains on her elbows from his stellar, soldier-class takedown.

Forget love, he'd be thrilled if she still considered him a friend. He leaned forward in his chair, rested both hands on his knees, and tried to pry words out of his knotted chest.

"Really, Patrick. You can stop sighing. I'm fine. I'm not made of ceramic, you know." She smiled, and he wanted to climb under the weathered floorboards.

"It's just that. . .well, Jerry called me today."

"I know. He thinks someone cut my tire."

He peered at her. No death pallor, no shaking. Definitely no tears. She even wrinkled her nose in his direction. He felt a sharp pang of pleasure right behind his sternum. "You don't believe him?"

She shrugged. "I should probably stop looking for villains in every face I meet. My father read the riot act to me before I moved here, and I suppose it made me a little. . .jumpy." She took a sip of her coffee, then stared into the cup. "But I think I've been overreacting." Her gaze met his, held it. "You see, I'm a. . .writer."

He saw her flinch, as if he might give a puff of disbelief or even laugh and realized that she also harbored deep secrets. He nodded, his heart leaping with the sheer joy at her trust.

She took a deep breath. "I want to be a mystery writer someday, and when I met you, I was on my way home from a writer's conference. Three other writers and I are planning to propose a novella collection to a publisher, and I'd been writing a list of perilous disasters that might befall a victim and then plotting her narrow escape from death." She laughed, a self-deprecating chortle. "In creating suspects, I think I might have drawn too freely from a few Southern stereotypes. I'm sorry, Patrick."

His mouth opened as his brain engaged. A writer? He tried not to laugh at his stupidity. She'd been fleshing out a mystery, not plotting first-degree murder.

Still, she hadn't slashed her own tires. Nor had she tried to drive off the mountain for the sake of research. "Justine, you have to level with me. Do you think someone is after you? I mean, first your brakes, now the tire."

"And don't forget my stolen backpack—"

"Stolen backpack? But—"

"Exactly my point." She set down her mug, then to his surprise, touched his hand. "I was breeding bad guys like fruit flies. You didn't steal my backpack any more than you slashed my tires or stole my car radio."

"Your radio was stolen?"

"Long before I ever met you." Her thumb moved over his hand, shooting fire right up his arm. "I don't have anything to fear from you, do I?" For a second, vulnerability flickered in the back of her eyes, that same raw fear he'd seen as she'd sat in her sweltering car, refusing to open the door.

"No." His voice sounded like it came running from Milwaukee.

She smiled, slow as sweet honey.

He couldn't help it. Dropping to his knees, he took her hand in his. "Frankly, I think I have more to fear from you." Her eyes were wide, and he could feel her pulse slamming against his thumb. "Can I. . ."

In a moment that swept the breath clean out of his chest, she kissed him. He closed his eyes and felt only the explosion of joy, tasted only her soft lips, smelled only the fragrance of coffee and sweet cream. He heard a murmur of pleasure and didn't know who had uttered it. But, as he cupped her neck and tangled his hand into her silky hair, it didn't matter. If this was friendship, then he was the luckiest pal alive. When he finally drew away, his heart was trying to escape his chest and leap out into her arms.

She smiled with one corner of her mouth, blushing.

He ran his fingers lightly over her cheekbone. "You sure know how to invade a man's world, Yankee."

"I thought you were supposed to be the stalker."

He kissed her lightly, right in the softness under her beautiful cheekbone. "Listen, Justine, do me favor. Call Sheriff Childress. Tell him what's been happening."

"Why?"

He held her hand and sat on his chair. Already she felt a billion miles away, and his arms ached to hold her. "Because I'm. . .nervous. Jerry told me that he thinks someone might have tampered with your car." He shook his head, panic filling his chest. "And I don't want anything happening to you."

She squinted at him, as if measuring his words. She finally nodded. "Okay. I'll call the sheriff."

He pulled her over, settling her on his lap. She draped an arm around his shoulders and ran her finger over his whiskered face. "But why would I need the sheriff when I have you?"

Chapter 7

Patrick glared at the clock for the third time in fifteen minutes.

Where was Lisa?

Just in case his ancient mariner's clock had decided to run afoul, he checked his wristwatch. No, still only six-thirty-five. Any minute now Lisa would return from delivering Bluebell to Grace Richardson, and he could escape The Right Cup. He had nearly stepped on the cat when he found it huddled outside his shop after lunch. Johnny Fair came over shortly thereafter and groused about how the animal had set off two alarms in the last week. Patrick had sent Lisa packing with the cat as soon as they had a lull in business.

But did she need to spend the next decade delivering the feline?

Patrick wiped the counter again, lost in last weekend. He and Justine had spent a glorious Sunday afternoon hiking the Appalachian Trail back to Laurel Falls, a treasure hidden between rhododendrons, sugar maples, and dogwoods. As the spray of water played a romantic symphony in the background, they perched on the rocks and shared a picnic. He'd told her about Carma and her passion for missions; about his brothers, Buchanan, Jasper, Bryce, and Quentin; and about growing up the youngest of the Bells gang. She knew nothing about sibling rivalry, being an only child.

And she, in a moment of breath-stealing vulnerability, revealed her mother's tragic death at the hands of a drunk driver when Justine was at the tender age of eight.

She'd invaded his heart. Increasingly, he'd had to stop and breathe through the swell of emotions that threatened to send him to his knees. He'd stopped short of saying the words, but he knew to the marrow of his bones that he loved Justine Proof, headstrong Yankee and mystery writer.

And wasn't that a hoot? A writer. She'd been plotting the demise of a character. He'd never tell her he'd suspected her of planning a felony.

The bell jangled, and into the coffee shop walked Theona Hayworth and her crony Bethylou Guinn, both dressed for nighttime fun in black, boot-cut jeans and sequined shirts. He wondered briefly if they were lost, until he remembered Theona dated Ford "Newt" Newton, local deputy. Obviously the man was having a sobering effect on her. The two sauntered up to the bar and slid onto stools. "Two lattes?"

"How about a shot of raspberry flavoring in those?" Patrick asked, grabbing a couple mugs. He glanced at the clock.

"Yum." Theona nodded. "Something new?"

"Yep. A Northern thing, I think, but it's tasty."

Bethylou eyed him with a smirk. "You've met our new anchorwoman, haven't you? Other than that awful accent, she's a cutie. I adore her clothes."

He shrugged and Theona laughed. "Wild Pat found a woman!"

"I would have thought she'd be scared away from the job after hearing how Harley Miller bought it." Theona took the latte Patrick set before her.

Patrick fixed Bethylou's latte. "He went over the Boone Bridge, didn't he? Drunk driving?"

Silence. He shot the ladies a glance and felt as if he'd been punched in the chest. Theona had gone white, quite a feat for a woman who took full advantage of the "Fancy Hair" tanning bed. "What?"

"Ford said that the autopsy revealed not a hint of alcohol," Theona said slowly. "When they hauled the car out of the river, they discovered the cotter pin gone and his brake lines severed."

※

Justine had gone plumb loco. Lost her loose change. Dropped her bricks.

She should be at The Right Cup, enjoying Patrick's smile, letting her heart run away with her.

Instead, she had her nose pushed up to her window while the local heat sat in an unmarked brown Ford in front of the Richardson home, waiting for nothing to happen.

Nearly five days without a mishap. If Patrick hadn't forced the telephone into her hand, she might never have called the sheriff's department.

She moved away from the window, dislodging Maizey, who sprawled at her feet. Patrick would be closing up soon, and she hurt at the thought of not seeing him.

Dixie had won. She knew the second Patrick had cupped

her face and kissed her that she loved him with every ounce of her Yankee heart. His kindred ache to be accepted touched the darkest corner of her spirit and made her crack open her own painful secrets about her mother.

At her words, his eyes had filled, his hands found hers, and he simply sat in silence, letting the waterfall and the rush of the breeze tend the moment.

It took all her Norwegian unflappability not to leap into his arms.

So why was she sitting here, drinking sweet tea in her darkened living room instead of responding to his note? *Justine, please meet me at ElHannon's place tonight at 9 P.M. I want to show you something. Patrick.* Admittedly, it had been a departure from his other whimsical, nearly poetic notes. The note he'd left in her office on Monday had read, *Friends are one of God's greatest treasures. Thank you for a perfect day yesterday.*

Maybe he wanted her to be present when he resurrected his friendship with ElHannon. She should march out to the deputy's car and tell him to chuck this inane stakeout. Hadn't her overactive imagination created enough trouble? She wanted to crawl under her chair, remembering how she'd run down her list of suspects for the sheriff, including Johnny Fair and Grace Richardson. The sheriff nearly burst in half, laughing.

So why, then, the stakeout across the street? She wondered if it had to do with the deputy who stopped by the sheriff's office. She'd introduced herself, and suddenly, the law was glued to her tail.

She peered out the window again. The moon had slimmed to a thumbnail, lending pitiful light to their efforts. She saw nothing more sinister than the scrape of shadows across the street.

Maizey suddenly stirred. Perked her ears. Stood. Justine patted her, but her pulse thumped. She held her breath and stared into the darkness.

Yes. Her heartbeat hiccupped, then thundered as she saw a figure hustling up the street. He stared for a moment at her house, as if judging her attendance, then disappeared behind her car.

Justine glanced at the deputy. Be awake! She saw light moving under the chassis.

Maizey growled. Justine couldn't agree more. Her paranoia suddenly shot from lunacy to bone-deep truth.

Someone was trying to kill her.

She dug her fingers into Maizey's fur. "Shh." Glancing again at the cop car, she wished she believed in ESP.

The light flickered, the saboteur hard at work, and then—

Hallelujah! The cop moved. His car door eased open, he rose, strode forward, two hands gripped on a weapon. Then as Justine's heartbeat urged him on, he stopped in the middle of the street and yelled.

The stalker's light stilled. He stood, raised his hands. Justine leaped to her feet and had flung open her front door before common sense engaged.

"Stay where you are," the deputy was saying.

Justine froze on the porch. Oh, how she wished Patrick was here, just to hold her up when she faced her killer.

The cop strode forward, turned the creep around, and pushed him against her car. Justine bristled under the man's stare. Darkness shrouded his face, but she shivered at the sensed hatred.

Who was trying to kill her, and why? With a bravado she

didn't feel, she reached out for the porch light. Let him face his victim and know he'd lost.

The glow swept out into the yard, barely denting the shadows on the street.

Still, she plainly recognized her killer. She managed not to howl, but something inside her shattered as she made out Patrick Bells, the renegade who had stolen her heart.

⚜

"Justine, please believe me." Patrick wrestled with the handcuffs. "I was worried about you—"

"So you decided to crawl underneath my car and collect souvenirs?" She gestured to the cotter pin he'd discovered lying on the ground beneath her drive shaft.

"Of course not!"

Ford shook him. "Don't sass the lady, Wild."

Patrick bit back an ugly word and pleaded with his eyes. Tears ran down her cheeks, but she folded her arms over her sweatshirt and gave him a smoldering look.

"I heard Theona talking about Harley Miller," Patrick said. "He was killed."

"Who?"

"The guy who had your job before you."

She looked pointedly at Deputy Newton.

Patrick had no doubt Newt was enjoying every minute of this, perhaps remembering the time Patrick and ElHannon had shaved him bald in tenth grade.

"It's true," Newt said, and Pat could have hugged him. But his joy died when the deputy added, "So I guess we'll have to figure out how Wild knew Miller, huh?"

What—?

Patrick died a little when Justine just nodded. Then she dug into her jean pocket and pulled out a piece of paper. "He gave me this today. It's an invitation to join him at ElHannon's place."

Newt read it in the dim light. "Hmm. A drive up Murphy Mountain with a missing steering pin. Sounds like the makings for an 'accidental' death." He gave Patrick a stun-gun glare and yanked him toward his car. "I think you'll be safe now, Miss Justine. Thank you for your cooperation."

Patrick climbed wordlessly into the vehicle, feeling as if he'd left his heart on the street for her to trample. As if to give it a final kick, she turned away from the cruiser as it drove away. He couldn't ignore the wretched shaking of her shoulders as she ran back to the house. . .nor the very definite outline of a shape— not of a cat—huddled in her rhododendron.

Chapter 8

Patrick hung his head in his hands, his backside digging into the cold contour of the metal bench in the Carter County jail. They'd updated the place since his last visit, an attendance arranged by his father after a particularly wild homecoming. The field trip made an impression strong enough to give him a distaste for bars, public commodes, and the feeling of despair that embedded the cement walls.

He'd lost Justine. Even if he did manage to convince her of his innocence—and that seemed about as likely as finding a snowball in Hawaii—she'd never trust him again. The betrayed expression in her eyes felt like a knife between his ribs.

Even so, she was in danger. Her steering would have failed on her first serious drive. Up Murphy Mountain. Contrary to the evidence logged against him, he hadn't written that note. Why would he want to face ElHannon, the friend he'd betrayed? ElHannon was just as likely to wallop him as he was to forgive him.

A decade-old ache throbbed in the recesses of his soul. He should apologize. But ElHannon wasn't about to give him a second chance. And after tonight, he'd be lucky if he wasn't tarred and feathered and run out of town on a rail.

Oh, God, how did I get into this mess? Patrick scrubbed his hands over his face. He had only been trying to be a gentleman, tell Justine he loved her. How had he ended up in a chilly cell with Tanked Hank snoring in the next slot?

"Bells, you have a visitor." Newt stood in the doorway, a glower on his face that could chill Jack the Ripper.

Patrick looked up, hope flaring. Justine?

ElHannon Murphy stood in the gap to the free world. "Hiya, Pat."

For a moment, Patrick felt a boyhood thrill rushing through him. Then reality smacked him upside the head, and he huffed in disbelief. "What are you doing here?"

ElHannon leaned against the opposite wall, his hands in his leather jacket pockets. "I figured you might need a friend."

Patrick winced, his chest tightening. "I guess I'm a bit short on those right now."

"Um hum." ElHannon moved closer to the cell. "What's up with you and Justine? She came to my house a few weeks ago, hunting information. And from the tenor of our conversation, I don't think it had anything to do with wanting to print it in the paper. Does she fancy you, Wild?"

Patrick shook his head. Wasn't this poetic justice? "Just get out of here, Han. I don't need your ridicule."

ElHannon shook his head. "I want to help."

"Right. I'll bet you're just itching to hike over to Justine's and make her forget she hooked up with the town bad boy."

ElHannon let out a real Tennessee bellow that sounded like an echo from the past.

"She's a looker, but nope, she's got too much sass for me.

245

Wild Pat is the only one who can handle that Yankee."

Patrick frowned at him. ElHannon sobered and shook his head, his ponytail shifting like a golden retriever's tail. "You're still wearing that chip, huh?"

"What?"

"Pat, you gotta get over it." ElHannon's expression gave the slightest hint of sadness. "Hey, you did me a favor twenty years ago. You saved me from a lifetime of betrayal from a girl who didn't love me. Sequa had been itching to break up for weeks before she hooked you. It just took me awhile to figure that out." He smiled wryly. "Forgive me, Man. I should have never let a girl between us. And I'm sure not going to horn in on your woman, Wild."

Patrick blinked at him, wordless. ElHannon reached through the bars and held out his hand. Patrick stared, and then, with a grin that started in the center of his chest, he shook ElHannon's hand. "I'm sorry too, Han. I should've behaved myself."

"Oh yeah, teen boys are known for their sanity, especially when they have a drunk cheerleader breathing in their ear."

"Still, I earned a sorry reputation in this town. And by the looks of things, I haven't shaken it." He nodded toward Newt, still propped in the doorway.

"When are you going to stop wearing your sins and realize that not everyone thinks you're the local black sheep?" ElHannon asked quietly.

"I guess never after tonight."

"You gotta stop living in the past, Wild." ElHannon leaned close. "I had a heart-to-heart with Lisa down at the Cup, and she updated me on your recent turnabout. I'm proud of you. You're not the only one who got right with God in the last twenty years, and I think it's time we earned ourselves a new rep in this town."

"Fat chance. My reputation is etched in stone."

"You know, I figure if Paul can step foot back in Jerusalem after persecuting the Christians and still be used by God, you and I can take back these Blue Ridge Mountain foothills. That's why I returned. To start over. Find a nice girl and raise a family in the old home. It doesn't really matter what people think. It's only who you are inside. Paul knew that."

ElHannon dug into his coat pocket and pulled out a. . . Bible? *Since when did he stop carrying a bowie knife?* The guy had transformed into some sort of preacher, and Pat stared at him, completely undone.

ElHannon flipped through the Bible. "Paul said in 1 Corinthians 1, 'Christ Jesus, who has become for us wisdom from God—that is, our righteousness, holiness and redemption. Therefore, as it is written: "Let him who boasts boast in the Lord." ' " He closed the book and impaled Pat with a look that spoke of divine authority. "God has done a great work in you. Be that man, and don't let anyone tell you you're not."

"Justine thinks I'm a stalker."

"Well," ElHannon said, smiling. "You sorta are."

Patrick gripped the bars. "No, listen! Someone is after her. Someone besides me."

"You're serious."

"Spring me, Han, because I have this sick feeling my Yankee gal is up to her neck in trouble."

"Please, don't close the—"

The root cellar door slammed shut with a very definite, very final thump, leaving only dust, pitch darkness, and Justine's frantic heartbeat to fill the silence. She heard footsteps edge away.

She was alone. Justine swallowed hard, refusing to let tears muddy her already grimy face. Her kidnapper had a fight getting her down here, and she tasted blood on her lip where he'd slapped her. She felt a spurt of satisfaction that she'd bullseyed a kick into his shin, although she might have broken her toe in the exchange. Her throat tightened as she thought of Patrick, sitting in the county jail.

Innocent.

She didn't deserve Patrick. She'd looked him full in the face, ignored the pain in his eyes, and accused him of betrayal, despite the fact that every fiber in her heart wanted to believe he couldn't, wouldn't hurt her.

Barely ten minutes after she'd sent Patrick to jail, the real stalker had arrived. Someone banged on her back door, and like the town idiot, she'd opened it, dreaming up Neighbor Richardson.

A second later, Tall, Thin, and Masked had grabbed her by her hair, bound her hands, and dragged her through her backyard to his waiting pickup. After securing her in the cab of his truck—what kind of lunacy was it to clamp her seatbelt around her if he meant to kill her?—the kidnapper had driven her out of town and into the hills. Parking in a tangle of pine, maple, and rhododendron, he'd hauled her out of the car and propelled her, not gently, toward a milky gray dent in the forest wall. They'd emerged onto an overgrown meadow. The long weeds whipped her arms as she stumbled under the silver moon.

Ice needled her veins when she spotted the barn. "ElHannon?"

The man laughed, a deep, ugly croak, and suddenly Justine knew exactly who had her. "Toad!" Then her stupidity hit her. He'd worn a mask, and if she'd kept her mouth shut, she just might have lived through this. "Why are you doing this?"

She added a touch of Northern sass to her voice. Fury seemed to be the only thing keeping her glued at the moment.

Only when he pushed open the barn door, and she betrayed her undulating terror with a gasp, did she hear an answer.

"Maybe this lesson will take." The voice was high, sweet, and very, very Southern. Missy Scalf. Justine tripped and earned a yank on her hair.

Missy stayed shrouded in shadow, but she directed Toad toward a gap in the barn floor, the one that had "buried alive" written all over it. Justine hit full-scale panic. Kicking, biting, and twisting, she nearly had the thug licked when he slapped her with a chops-ringing blow and muscled her down the steps.

. . .where he secured her, tightly, to a foundation pole.

"Sorry, Honey," Missy said from the gray-black opening. "But down here in Dixie, we take no prisoners, and we've had about enough from you."

"But what did I do?" No hiding her fear now. It lay bare and raw in her voice.

"You took my job and stayed. Couldn't figure out that you'd invaded hostile territory. Even after we stole your radio and ran you down the mountain."

"You sabotaged my car?"

"Sure enough. Any Southern-bred gal worth her salt can

turn a wrench. I have to admit, Yank, you're made of grit. I never thought you'd last this long. Too bad no one is going to miss you."

Then she slammed the door, leaving the moles, the roaches, and Justine's guilt to keep her company.

Justine's hands ached with chill, and when she sat, a nail arrowed square into her tailbone. Hunger clawed at her, and she fought her imaginings of what could be peering at her in the dark.

At least she wasn't alone. The thought sent her to the edge of hysteria, and out of her rattled a guttural laugh that didn't sound anything like humor. Alone? There wasn't one chance in a bazillion that anyone would find her. In a hundred years, when they finally decided to excavate the old Murphy place, they'd find her skeletal remains tied to the foundation.

Her eyes burned again, and she let the tears run. After all, who was she trying to impress?

The thought hit her hard. Exactly. Who was she trying to impress? Her father? KMPR? Joe Bob? How about Patrick? Oh, she had them all just standing at attention, saluting. She drew her knees up to her chest, feeling wrung out, hollow, and utterly unimpressive. She'd never be a mystery writer, she'd never fit into Stoney Creek, and she'd never be able to trust someone enough to find true love.

Except, had she even tried? Had she paused to let Patrick explain? She should have pushed past her suspicions and trusted him. Isn't that what love did, trusted in the face of betrayal? But what if she did trust him, did hand him her heart. . .and he dropped it? She'd be right back where she started.

Alone.

In the silence, she allowed herself to grieve for what could have been. She ached for Patrick's smile, his eagerness to help her, his arms around her when she'd needed more than words. She'd found a real friend. . .and kicked him in the teeth.

Oh, Lord, what have I done? The request for answers seemed unearned. Still, the desperate place inside her reached through memory to her spiritual underpinnings. To her mother holding her as she prayed at night, to her father tucking her in his lap and singing hymns. Suddenly she remembered the song Lisa had been humming, the one that tugged at the back of her brain. With a nearly audible *whoosh!* it flooded back to her. "What a Friend We Have in Jesus." Justine didn't so much remember the words as felt them. "What a friend we have in Jesus, all our sins and griefs to bear. What a privilege to carry everything to God in prayer."

Justine hung her head. She hadn't prayed in years. Since her mother's death. She heard her mother's voice, sweet and full, singing words, fragments from the same hymn. "Have we trials and temptations? Is there trouble anywhere? We should never be discouraged, take it to the Lord in prayer. Can we find a friend so faithful, who will all our sorrows share? In His arms He'll take and shield thee, thou wilt find a solace there."

Sorrow shook her as truth sank in. She'd forsaken God's friendship. Not deliberately but slowly. She'd filled her life with others—her father, now in Minnesota. Here and there friends who betrayed her simply because they were human. No wonder she felt so bereft. Without God to cling to, she was utterly, eternally alone.

She wiped her cheeks on her knees. So that could be changed. She didn't have to wait for daylight to call on God.

She needed solace. In His arms. Now.

Pressing her forehead to her knees, she shuddered and began to pray. Her voice shook, but the whispers grew stronger until finally, as she confessed her sin and declared her need, her voice filled the room and reverberated the wooden poles. And then, in a voice she knew wasn't hers, she sang.

Oh, what a friend she had in Jesus.

And deep in her soul, she knew she wasn't alone.

Justine was gone. As Patrick stood in the open back doorway, staring at the scattering of cans and boxes from the back pantry, something inside him snapped.

If he didn't find Justine alive, he might just lie down and die.

ElHannon followed him as they searched the house, then the yard. Bobcat to the core, she'd fought her assailant and left a telltale gap through the back hedge leading to the dry cleaners.

From there, the trail vanished.

Patrick had stood in the moonlit-strewn lot only a moment when memory clicked. "The note. It told her to meet me at your place."

ElHannon frowned. "My place? Why?"

"I thought it was because of the roads. . . ."

Han sprinted back through her yard and had his SUV in drive when Patrick dove in. Maizey chased them down the street, barking.

Patrick braced one hand on the ceiling, the other on the dash as they careened down gravel roads toward Murphy Mountain. The moon ducked behind a wad of black clouds as they curved toward the house. Patrick jumped out of the car before it stopped moving. "Justine! Where are you?"

Nothing but the swish of the wind in the grass. *Oh please, God, give me a break here. I know I'm not worthy of her, but please, help me be the man she needs right now. Help me find her!*

Patrick ran through the thigh-high weeds toward the house. He vaulted the stairs and landed on the porch. It shuddered. "Justine!"

The house greeted him like a tomb. "Justine!" Nothing but the creak of old boards and the groan of the wind.

"She's not here," he yelled to ElHannon, who stood at the bottom of the steps.

"You sure? It's a big house." ElHannon took the stairs two at a time. "I'll check inside. You check the barn."

Patrick leaped to the ground, his breath hot in his lungs as he ran down the rutted drive. A shadowed bulk against the blue-black of the sky, the barn moaned as the wind lashed it, appearing like it could tumble to the ground with one good push. Patrick raced inside. "Justine!"

His heartbeat filled his ears. The barn smelled of age—rotting boards and old straw—and the expanse loomed above like a guillotine waiting to plunge. Then he heard. . .music. No, singing. A hymn. He inhaled slowly, listening, not wanting to fracture the sound with breath.

The music sounded muffled, as if sung from a cupped mouth. Or. . .under the barn? He stalked the ground in huge, earth-eating strides, willing his eyes to adjust. The song grew louder, and when his foot scraped against wood, it stopped.

"Help!"

"Justine!" Patrick dropped to his knees, ran his hands over a rough-hewn door, earning splinters. He found the latch and heaved it open. "Justine?"

"Down here!"

He took the ladder in three large leaps, and then, in the recesses of the pit, he detected movement. Dropping to a crouch, he brailled his way toward her, finding her leg and then her face. It was wet. "Justine, it's okay. You're safe."

"Patrick?"

"It's me, Yankee. You're safe now." He reached behind her, feeling her fear in the way she trembled, and found the rope binding her hands. ElHannon might carry a Bible now, but his bowie had been in his glove compartment, ready for Patrick to add to his boot. Patrick freed her.

Her arms flew around him, and he scooped her to his chest, his breath rasping in gusts of relief. "I was so worried."

She clung to him, tighter than anyone ever had, and it scared him a little. "Forgive me, Patrick," she said, hiccuping back sobs, her voice muffled in his shirt. "Please. I should have trusted you. I should have believed that you wouldn't hurt me."

He ran his hands into her hair and gently pulled back from her. "Of course." He couldn't see her eyes but imagined them to be full of tears and deliciously sweet. "I love you, Yankee. I should have told you that. Maybe that would have convinced you that I would never hurt you—"

She kissed him. How she found his face in the darkness, he didn't know, but suddenly she was kissing him with a ferocity that nearly made him forget that she'd been hurt, bound, and shoved into a hole. Nearly. Catching her face, he eased back. "Are you okay?"

He felt her nod and was fighting the urge to let her continue this new nonverbal method of communication when she settled for the old-fashioned, "I love you too, Patrick. I fell for you the day you stalked out of the hills and into my life. I should have known then that a good ole boy would steal my heart." He heard the smile in her words. "And, you're going to think this is crazy, but I've found the perfect 'escape from death' ending to my mystery."

He pulled her close, inhaling her sweet fragrance, joy nearly exploding his already swelling heart. "What's that?"

She kissed the soft spot under his eyes. "The rapscallion hero finds the lonely, stubborn heroine, and she promises to trust him until the end of time."

"Aw, shucks," he said. "That's about as predictable as Elvis rising again."

She laughed, and he found sweet pleasure in silencing her with a kiss.

"Welcome to the South, Yankee," he whispered.

"Glad to be here," she said, and this time he knew she meant it.

SUSAN MAY WARREN

Susan and her family recently returned home after eight years of living in Khabarovsk, Russia, as missionaries with SEND International. Now writing full-time while her husband manages a lodge in northern Minnesota, this born and bred Yankee draws her stories from the rich well of experiences in her life—from traveling overseas to living in Tennessee, where she left a huge chunk of her heart behind. Find out more about Susan and her books at www.susanmaywarren.com.

'Til Death Do Us Part

by Diann Hunt

Dedication

To my sister, Shelia Dawson,
and my brothers, Jess and Fred Walker,
for their love and encouragement.

The Makings of a Great Mystery
by Drake Axelrod

Chapter Four
End with Happily Ever Afters

Rule: Thou shalt capture the villain, tie up all the loose ends, and leave the reader with a feeling of victory.

Exercise: Write a climactic death scene with a confessing villain.

Chapter 1

I said 'til death do us part," the killer hissed between clenched teeth. "Remember?"

Like the sharp tip of an icicle, his wild eyes pierced through her. Fear wedged frantic screams in her chest. Pain slashed through her temples.

With the little strength that remained, she gouged his ankles with her boots. Her body twisted to break free while her fingernails punctured deep into his flesh like poisoned thorns.

She thrashed about until her fight was gone. She saw the knowing in his eyes.

He had won.

A light from a window caused her engagement ring to flash. In the flicker of that moment, she knew she and Colby would never marry.

" 'Til death do us part, Babe." His laugh, sick and demented, faded into the darkness.

⚜

Cassie Jordan glanced at her assignment once more. "How am I supposed to get to a happy ending after all that?" Frustrated, she thumped her purple notebook shut. Cassie glanced around the empty coffee shop. What had she been thinking when she agreed to write a mystery novella? Though crime occasionally polluted her midsized Indiana town, she knew it didn't compare to the big cities.

What did she know about murder and mayhem? Enough to know she didn't want to write about it. Being a court reporter made her shy away from writing mystery or suspense stories.

She was, after all, a romance writer. How did she let her three writer friends, aka "Sleuth Sisters" for purposes of their mystery book, talk her into writing a mystery novella for an anthology proposal?

In spite of herself, Cassie allowed a reluctant smile when she remembered sitting with them in the airport coffee shop after the writer's conference. Tina Frank had wiggled her fingers at Cassie while Raine Wells and Justine Proof crooned the theme song to *The Twilight Zone*. They told her what fun they would have creating mysterious tales where good would triumph over evil. She believed them.

They lied.

She was not having fun.

Cassie stretched her legs and let out a yawn. Okay, so she was not one to allow obstacles to get in her way. Somehow, she'd rise to the challenge. Maybe she would talk to her friend Aaron James. After all, detectives knew about that kind of stuff, didn't they? Maybe she'd ask him if she could tag along on a case and see how to solve a mystery firsthand.

A spark of excitement lit through her. She might be able to pull this off.

Cassie took a deep breath and pulled in the rich coffee

aroma wafting around the room. She wanted to linger there but decided instead to go to the bookstore two doors down and browse through the mystery section. Maybe she could learn the trade through osmosis. With one last sip, she drained the mocha from her cup, tossed it into a trash dispenser, and headed out the door.

Cassie pushed through the bookstore entrance. Reader's Refuge smelled of crisp pages and new books. Walking through a few aisles, she noted the bright covers and catchy titles.

"Ms. Jordan?"

Cassie turned toward the masculine voice that almost made her fall off her shoes. Whatever possessed her to buy those clogs anyway?

"Yes?"

"Hi. I'm Ethan Hamil." He extended a firm handshake, for which she was thankful. It was the only thing holding her up.

The pure blue of his eyes made her gulp. *Hang on, Cassie,* she told herself. She could feel herself slipping into the writer mode. Another perfect hero.

No, don't go there. Her thoughts warred. *Listen to what he has to say.*

At last, she conceded to taking one last look to absorb the necessary details. She made a few mental notes. Six foot two, thick, soft hair—*wonder if he'd let me touch it*—the color of an expensive camel-haired suit, um, slightly darker. A strong dimple rutted deep in his chin. And a crooked smile. She could almost feel herself typing the description. She stared at him, speechless. Why, he represented the sum total of every hero she'd ever dreamed up.

"Ms. Jordan?"

Cassie's eyes refocused. She realized her mouth gaped and promptly clamped it shut. Would she ever stop daydreaming of characters and plots?

"I'm the new owner of the bookstore."

"Oh, yes, Mr. Hamil, mice to neet you." She hiccupped loud enough to draw the glances of several nearby customers.

Now his mouth gaped.

Mice to neet you? Did I say that out loud? Her hand quickly covered her mouth. "Excuse me." Inside she grimaced. True to form, when she was nervous, her words scattered about like mixed-up letters in a word game, followed by a punctuating hiccup.

She would consider it a blessing if the floor opened and pulled her into oblivion. Better still, why not fall into a vat of melted chocolate and die happy?

Thoughts of chocolate improved her disposition considerably. Not one to linger in self-pity, Cassie mentally shrugged the matter aside and cleared her throat. "Yes, Mr. Hamil, how may I help you?"

His mouth tipped into a slight grin. "One of our clerks recognized you as the author of some of our romance books." He waved his hands in a great sweep toward wooden shelves filled with assorted books lined up like soldiers at attention, several bearing her name. "I was wondering if you would consider doing a writer's workshop for us?"

Cassie felt herself relax. When she talked about writing, especially romance, she felt very comfortable. "Oh, I would be happy to."

"Good. Could I give you a call and set up a date?"

Excitement shot through her.

"I mean, for the workshop?" He shuffled his feet. A slight flush tinged the tips of his ears as he corrected himself.

"Sure. Let me give you my card." Gripping the notebook under her arm, Cassie rooted through her purse. "I'm sorry, could you hold these?" She handed Ethan three pens, all of them purple, her special pen adorned with purple feathers, two highlighters, three paperclips, and a rubber band. She shrugged. "My business equipment. I can't leave home without them." Before he could respond, she continued to pick through the debris. The notebook slipped and she readjusted it. "Oh, here they are." With a happy wave, she produced her cards and extended one to him.

He returned her business equipment. A cursory glance at the card seemed to tell him what he needed to know. "Okay, then, I'll call you this week."

"Great." She feared her voice sounded positively giddy. Ethan threw her a wide grin before walking in the opposite direction. Cassie looked after him, feeling as though she could walk on air. Anything to do with writing always excited her.

Especially when it involved a handsome hero.

The next afternoon, Cassie carried lunch to the computer desk in her bedroom. Though not a big area, a montage of deep purple, lavender, and beige splashed the room with color. The Victorian decor filled her with inspiration when she wrote romance novels. Fluffy pillows perched on her bed, thick with comforters. A wooden desk held her computer and essentials, along with plenty of purple accessories, pens, stationery, and the like.

Cassie muttered a prayer of thanks, bit into the wheat

bread and turkey, chomped her way through a baby carrot, then clicked into the E-mail account. Just as she suspected, a couple of E-mails addressed to "Sleuth Sisters" awaited her. She tapped into the cyber-correspondence with the eagerness of a child at Christmas.

A blaze of warm sunshine spilled upon her shoulders from a nearby window. Cassie reached for her cola and took a sip while reading the words that popped onto her screen. A quick review told her what she needed to know. She then responded.

Once finished with her E-mails, Cassie clicked off her online connection and consumed the rest of her sandwich, though she didn't take notice of the flavor. The mystery novel occupied her thoughts.

She glanced over at her golden-haired spaniel curled up on a tattered rug on the floor. "Well, Sparky, looks like they've already begun to spin their tales. Oh, sorry, a different kind of tale, ole boy." Although she knew her fifteen-year-old cocker spaniel couldn't hear a sound, let alone understand what she said, Cassie still shared her inmost secrets with her stubby-tailed friend. After all, Cassie had been doing that since she was ten years old and wasn't about to stop now.

She bent down and waved her hand. Sparky looked at her with dark, melting eyes. His tongue lapped the tip of his nose, and he pulled himself up from the floor with as much gusto as his tired bones would allow. Ambling over to Cassie, he nudged her leg with a soggy nose. Cassie laughed and rewarded her aging friend with a scratch behind his ear. His arthritic leg thumped happily against the carpet, sending muffled taps through the room.

Rising, Cassie gathered her dishes and walked into the

kitchen. She flipped on her favorite Christian radio station while loading the dishwasher. Spilling the liquid gel into the washer cups, she quickly snapped the door closed. The machine settled into its familiar whir, drowning out the radio.

Cassie walked over and turned up the volume just as the news anchor gave an account of a murder in the area. A young woman on the west side. . .the police had no suspects or motives. . .listeners would be updated as the story unfolded.

A touch of fear settled in her chest. Visions of the police swarming about her neighbor's house down the road only last night flashed through her mind. The hour was late when she arrived home, so no neighbors stood outside for her to inquire as to what had happened. It could be coincidence. Just because she lived on the west side didn't mean that was where the murder had occurred. She lived in the country. Crimes usually occurred in the city, didn't they?

She took a deep breath and wiped her hands on a dish towel. Writing a mystery made her a bit edgy, no question about it. She wouldn't borrow trouble. She'd find out soon enough. Until then, she'd go about her business. Cassie shook her head. "What a world we live in," she said to no one in particular. Unless, of course, Sparky counted, but he was too busy scratching his backside to pay much attention to Cassie's worldviews, even if he could hear.

Once the kitchen sparkled, Cassie turned off the radio and grabbed a chocolate bar from the hidden stash in the cupboard. She shrugged. Everyone had a weakness. Chocolate was hers. She walked into the living room, settled into her favorite recliner, pulled up the footrest, and bit into her candy. Closing her eyes, she took a moment to enjoy the sweet flavor.

Breaking through her reverie, thoughts of the murder crept upon Cassie like a stalking black cat. Beside her, the phone screamed, causing her to jump. Her feet thumped hard against the footrest. It slammed back into place. Her heart raced, and she took a moment to calm down. She coughed. Someone once told her a deep cough could calm an erratic heartbeat. She reached for the receiver. "Hello?"

Ethan Hamil's voice did little to slow her pulse. He invited her to meet him in the coffee shop a week from Saturday. They needed to go over the final details for her upcoming workshop. Once the appointment was set, their conversation ended. Cassie's heart zoomed like an Indy 500 race car.

She coughed again.

Chapter 2

The bell above the entrance jangled when Cassie entered the coffee shop. She waved at her best friend, Penelope Hansen, who already waited at a nearby table with drink in hand.

Once Cassie received her mocha, she joined Penelope. "Morning, Nell."

"Hi." Nell took a sip of her latte. "Isn't it a beautiful Saturday? I love days like this, sun shining, just the right fall temperature."

Cassie swallowed some mocha. "You've obviously had more coffee than I've had this morning."

Nell lifted an eyebrow. "Feeling grumpy, are we?"

"No, not grumpy, just got a lot on my mind."

"Want to talk about it?"

Cassie explained about the mystery novella and then about meeting Ethan Hamil.

"Sounds to me like you just might be interested in this guy." Nell adjusted her bracelet, causing gold charms to rattle and clank. Distracted for a moment, Cassie thought of the four cats and three dogs on Nell's farm, now symbolized in the gold pieces that dangled from her wrist.

"Oh, Nell, it's nothing like that, and you know it. I see the perfect hero for my stories. That's all. And stop grinning." Though somewhat irritated at her best friend, Cassie couldn't help rolling her eyes and granting a reluctant smile.

"Well, time will tell." Nell pushed the matter aside. "Hey, do you know any more about that murder on your road?"

Cassie almost choked. "That was by me?" She wiped the mocha from her chin. "I wondered about that."

"Duh. Where have you been?"

For once, Cassie was totally speechless. Her mind raced in all directions.

"Didn't you see the police or anything?"

"Yeah, but I didn't know what it was about."

"Did you know her?"

"Only enough to wave when I jogged by her house. She'd just moved in a couple of months ago. I've seen her a few times. Didn't even know her name." Remorse washed over Cassie that she hadn't taken the time to get to know her new neighbor.

"You better watch yourself."

"Do you think it's a neighborhood thing?" Cassie could feel the fear rising.

"You take too many depositions. They'll probably find it's drug-related. Usually is." Nell took a bite from her cinnamon roll and another slurp of latte.

Cassie decided Nell was probably right. "Someone once told me life is hard, but God is good." She shook her head and looked back at Nell. "I have to remind myself of that all the time when I hear so many sad testimonies in pretrial depositions."

"Yeah, I feel that way too when I learn the background of

some of my second graders." Nell wiped her mouth with a napkin, leaving a crumb of roll behind. "It breaks your heart."

Cassie reached up and brushed away the crumb.

"Thanks. Hey, have you talked with Aaron lately?"

"Yeah." Cassie smiled, thinking of their childhood friend. "A couple of days ago. Why?"

Nell picked up her drink and shrugged as if only casually interested, though Cassie knew better. Ever the matchmaker, Nell was digging for clues. No doubt about it.

"Are you sure you don't like him?"

"I love him," Cassie quickly asserted, triggering Nell's bracelet to rattle and nearly causing her to spit out her coffee. Cassie covered a smile behind her cup. She knew she should be ashamed at the pure pleasure rushing through her.

Nell's eyes grew wide in a flash. Cassie's conscience pricked. She reluctantly added, "But not in the way you think."

Nell's nose wrinkled; her shoulders slumped. She stuffed her napkin into the empty latte cup. "You're absolutely no fun at all."

"I know."

Cassie caught Nell's glance, and they both laughed. Cassie looked at her watch. "Hey, you'd better get home to Ralph."

"Yeah, I guess you're right. I need to go grocery shopping first." Nell pulled her slightly pudgy body up from the chair. With some effort, she shrugged on her jacket. "Ralph. Good old Ralph." She stopped and looked straight at Cassie. "Why did his mom name him that?" Before Cassie could answer, a starry glaze fell over Nell's blue eyes. She looked upward and said rather dramatically, "He looks like he should be named Rock, Cary, or. . ." She paused, looked back at Cassie, and gestured with a brush of her hand. "Well, you get the idea." Nell smiled, and her eyes shone bright with love.

Cassie finished pulling on her jacket, grabbed her purse, and smiled back, though she felt quite sure Ralph's name fit him to a T.

✤

Cassie barely had time to get her jacket off, when Aaron pulled into the driveway and walked up to her door.

"Hi, Cassie. Want to go to lunch?"

She made a face. "I just got back home from coffee with Nell." Her words held apology and a definite not-this-time sound to it.

"Oh, come on," he urged. "I finally have a day off, and I don't want to clean the garage. I need an excuse. Please?" Although Aaron stood before her looking as tall and strong as a California redwood, Cassie could only visualize him as her freckle-faced childhood friend with dirty fingernails. She remembered how she and Nell used to trick him into eating mud pies and drinking pretend tea of water sprinkled with salt and pepper. Heavy on the pepper. She felt herself go soft. Would she forever spend her days trying to make up for the tea and mud pies?

He wiggled his dark bushy eyebrows, a gesture that always made her laugh and give in to his pleas. Once again, she reluctantly agreed. Although she had plenty of writing to do, she decided friends were more important. This might be a good time to talk about tagging along with him while she worked on her mystery. She pulled on her jacket once more, grabbed her purse, and followed Aaron to his car.

They had barely received their meals before Aaron whispered a quick prayer and bit into his burger like a starving lion.

"You doing okay?"

He wiped his mouth and took a drink of pop before answering. "You know how eating helps me solve cases?"

Cassie smiled, remembering his countless claims to solving crimes between bites of hamburgers and fries. She nodded.

"Well, I'm working on a big case." He guzzled some more of his drink, then leaned toward her. "You know about the murder down the road from you?"

Cassie nodded again.

Aaron slid back and took another bite of his sandwich.

Cassie waited. She could almost hear his brain clicking with every chomp.

"It's a big deal. I can't give you details just yet. Can't let word leak out till we get a handle on things." His face turned serious as his hand reached across the table and covered hers. "You be careful, you hear me?"

Cassie felt a nervous twitch in her stomach. "Do I have something to worry about?"

"We don't know who's safe and who isn't at this point," he said, returning his attention to the sandwich. "Just be careful."

Cassie coughed. "Well, that brings up a matter I've been meaning to talk to you about."

Aaron nodded but kept working on his hamburger.

"I'm writing a mystery, and, uh, well, you know how I like to experience things firsthand, and I was wondering—"

Aaron stopped chewing and swallowed hard. He looked at her and rolled his eyes. "Uh-oh, I smell trouble."

"Come on, Aaron, I just need to learn about solving cases, and—"

"Cassie, it won't work. Every time I let you talk me into

one of your harebrained ideas, I get into trouble. Like eating mud pies."

She grimaced. "Oh, here we go with the feel-sorry-for-me-I-ate-mud-pies speech."

"Okay, so maybe you've done enough penance for that, but I'm not so sure."

"Aaron, I really need to do this. I'm just at a standstill on this story. I have no idea how to pull together a mystery."

He started eating again. "So don't do it."

"I have to. I'm committed. Please?"

He swallowed, took a drink, and let out a sigh. "I'd have to clear it with my supervisor."

Cassie clapped her hands together.

"But that doesn't mean he'll say yes," he added quickly before she could plunge full swing into a victory celebration.

"I know." She reached over and squeezed his hand. "You're the best!"

"Yeah, whatever. I know I will live to regret this." He called the waitress and ordered another burger.

Chapter 3

T he Monday alarm intruded earlier than usual into Cassie's dreams. She groaned when she saw the 4:30 display on the clock. With a reluctant sigh, she rolled out of bed. If she hurried, she could glance over the story outline and e-mail it to the Sleuth Sisters before her eight o'clock deposition.

Across the room, she slipped into the chair in front of her computer. In hopes to jump-start her creativity, Cassie picked over the dried flower bouquet she had purchased from the florist the day before. She laid the arrangement down and worked with a vengeance on her outline. Once satisfied, she clicked the sketch of her story into cyberspace.

Rain pelted against her window as thunder growled overhead. She glanced once more at the bouquet and shivered slightly. She could hardly wait to get back to romance writing. Mysteries, she decided, gave her the creeps.

Cassie pulled on her slippers and made her way to the kitchen for coffee. She clicked on the radio.

"Bonita Lutz, the west-side murder victim will be buried today. The family has offered a reward for anyone who has information leading to the killer's arrest."

After making a note of the preservice viewing hours, Cassie turned off the radio. Grabbing her coffee, she went back to her bedroom, showered, and dressed for work. She knew this would not be an easy day.

Later, Cassie went to the viewing, noting a sparse crowd. Evidently, the victim hadn't lived in the area long enough to develop strong friendships. A young woman with a long future ahead of her cut off in her prime by an inhuman act of evil. The crime and the grief it left behind sickened Cassie. She prayed for the family, then left for her afternoon deposition.

The rest of the week passed in a blur of depositions, transcription, and writing. Although Cassie had managed to get a lot of work done, there was still much to do. She knew she should be home working, but wild horses couldn't have kept her from meeting with the handsome bookstore owner, if for no other reason than to get his appearance and mannerisms down on paper—or so she told herself.

Leaving the dusky night behind, Cassie followed Ethan into the coffee shop near his bookstore. The grinding of coffee beans sounded from behind the counter as they placed their orders. Once the coffees were ready, they picked up their cups and carried them to a round table.

They settled into wooden chairs and took sips of coffee. "So tell me how you got into writing," Ethan began.

Cassie shrugged. "I've always loved to read and write. I went through a hard time when my mom died five years ago and found myself at the computer writing my thoughts. Next thing I knew, I was writing inspirational romance." She smiled and glanced at a young woman studying at a nearby table.

"Why inspirational romance?" Ethan's eyebrows lifted, causing faint wrinkles to crease his forehead. Cassie made a mental note to jot down the physical characteristic.

"God wrote the greatest love story of all when He sent His only Son to redeem a lost world from sin. I want to share that message through my books. It's all about love."

Ethan nodded and looked at Cassie a little too long for her comfort. No doubt she had talked too much. An uncomfortable silence fell between them. She squirmed in her seat like a child waiting for the recess bell to ring. How many sips of coffee she took, she didn't know. One thing she did know, she couldn't hold the cup to her lips much longer.

Her cell phone rang, saving the day. She picked it up and looked at Ethan. "Sorry."

"No problem." He took another drink from his cup.

"Hello?"

"How's my girl?"

"Hi, Dad. I'm fine."

"Do you have practice after church tomorrow?"

"No. We can head straight for the restaurant."

"Great. So what are you up to?"

Cassie could almost hear her dad settling in for a lengthy conversation. "Well, uh, I'm having coffee with a friend right now. Can we talk tomorrow?"

"Sure thing. Sorry to interrupt."

"No problem. I'll see you then." Cassie clicked off her phone and put it in her purse.

"My dad's moving to Ohio. He's taking a teaching position with a university. We're spending the day together tomorrow, before he leaves on Monday."

"Sounds like you're close to your dad."

"Very. Since Mom died, we make it a point to get together. I mean, we're not guaranteed a tomorrow, so we've learned to make the most of the time we have."

Ethan nodded, pausing for a moment.

She laughed a little. "Goodness, enough heavy conversation." She waved her hand and took a drink.

"So you're writing a mystery this time?" Ethan finally asked.

"Yes."

"We'll look forward to ordering that."

Cassie sighed. "Well, I have to finish it first."

"Oh? You haven't finished it?"

She explained how she was working with three other authors, each doing their own novella to add to the collection. She made him take a vow of secrecy before sharing with him some of the outline she had sketched out. "The hero's fiancée is killed by a murderer who leaves behind a dried bridal bouquet on each of his victims. The hero helps solve the case, justice is served, and he learns the value of forgiveness."

He cocked an eyebrow. "Oh, sounds interesting."

She shrugged. "A little sordid, but I think I'm getting the hang of it."

He grinned. When his blue eyes searched hers, warmth ran through her like a hot drink on a cold night.

"You're a pretty unique gal," Ethan finally said, breaking the spell of the moment. He fingered the jacket on his coffee cup, but his eyes never left hers.

"Unique as in weird?"

His fingers stopped in place. "Oh, no, not weird. Unique.

Special. Unlike any other." His mouth spread into a lopsided grin.

Cassie hiccupped, crossed her right leg, and bumped the table, causing their coffee to slosh upon the wooden center. "Oh, I'm sorry." She snatched a handful of napkins from her purse. She had learned at an early age, one could never have too many napkins on hand, and she mentally praised herself for being prepared.

Ethan helped her mop up the mess. When they finished, he reached over to take the soiled napkins from her. Cupping his large hands over hers, he slowly pulled the napkins from her grip. Could he see her goose bumps? He looked at her, their eyes locked for a heartbeat. Cassie felt like she had stepped into the scene of a romance novel. Feeling awkward, yet not knowing what else to do, she took a remaining napkin and scrubbed furiously at an invisible stain.

Ethan walked over to toss the napkins in the trash. Cassie's mouth suddenly went dry. She tipped her cup and looked at the empty bottom. Oh, dear, the last time her mouth got this dry, her lips stuck to the top of her gums. Before Ethan could return, she ran her tongue over her teeth and swallowed hard.

When he came back to the table, Cassie lifted an expression of apology. "Like they say, 'Please be patient, God isn't finished with me yet.' " She shrugged her shoulders.

Ethan laughed. A pleasant laugh, she thought. She could almost imagine this hero sitting on a sofa, her heroine wrapped in his warm embrace in front of a fireplace snapping with burning logs. Something clever and witty would come from the heroine's mouth, causing him to laugh in just such a manner.

"Cassie?"

She jerked herself to attention. "Oh, I–I—" Warmth climbed her cheeks.

"Checked out for a moment, eh?" His teasing grin told her he didn't mind.

With a shake of her head and an impish smile, she tried to explain. "My mind is always off on a story line. Sorry."

He eyed her carefully. "Well, it occurs to me I ought to be offended or flattered."

"Why is that?"

"Either I'm boring you to death or you're placing me in a scene of your next book?" His eyes pinned her.

She let out a nervous laugh and hiccup.

A pleasing spark lit his eyes, a faint smile played over his lips.

Cassie glanced around the room, then looked at him. "So, tell me about you. Do you have family nearby?"

"My sister, Megan, lives in town. Mom and Dad live in Florida full-time now. My—" He stopped.

"What's that? Were you about to say something else?"

Ethan shifted in his chair. He studied his fingers for a moment. "I have a brother. Kyle." The words seemed to struggle out of him.

"Does he live around here?"

"I–I'm not sure."

The comment left Cassie searching for what to say next.

"We don't talk anymore. Haven't talked in about five years."

"Oh, I'm sorry." An uncomfortable silence followed. Cassie purposely glanced at her watch. "You know, I really need to get going."

Ethan cleared his throat and nodded.

She reached for her bag. "I'll be at the bookstore Monday

night at seven sharp," she said as she lifted the handle onto her shoulder.

Ethan pushed back his chair and rose. "Again, a pleasure, Cassie." He grabbed her hand and held it firm within his grasp.

Nerves clogged her throat, making it hard for her to speak. Her thoughts skidded to a halt. "Nonday might then." Cassie groaned and looked at him to see if he had noticed her twisted words.

He had.

"Nonday might," Ethan said with a grin and a wink before turning away.

Her legs felt like cooked spaghetti but at least she wasn't wearing clogs.

❀

When Cassie arrived home later that evening, she hung her coat in the closet, checked the front and back doors to make sure they were locked, then went to her bedroom to prepare for bed. Sparky sauntered into the room after her, standing only a few inches away. Cassie scrunched down, and the old spaniel warmed to the routine. He nudged against her leg, his stubby tail wagging furiously. His cold, wet tongue lapped happily at her hands. She giggled and rubbed the side of her face against Sparky's soft fur. Cassie rewarded her faithful friend with comforting scratches until the two finally settled into their various bedtime rituals.

Cassie performed her nightly exercises, cooled down by drinking some cold water, and finally washed her face. After her evening prayer, she slipped in between the bed sheets, allowing the softness of the featherbed to ease the day's tension. She reached for her Bible and read the Scripture allotted to the day. Though life could get hectic, Cassie always tried to read her Bible. She felt with all the evil in the world, she couldn't afford to skip her time of reading God's Word. How else could she know the God of the Bible without reading about Him?

When she finished reading, Cassie jotted some notes in her journal. She placed the Bible in the basket beside her bed and stared at the ceiling, her thoughts focused on Ethan. Why wouldn't he talk to his brother? Five years. Such a long time. She whispered another prayer, this one for Ethan and his brother. Two brothers whom Cassie felt sure would never know peace without first finding a way to heal their relationship.

She clicked off the lamp beside her bed and snuggled into her pillow. Believing in the power of prayer, Cassie finally drifted into a deep sleep with a prayer for Ethan and his brother on her lips.

Chapter 4

On Monday afternoon, Cassie's deposition lasted longer than expected, throwing her into a flurry of activity to reach her workshop on time. Despite her awkward start, she was grateful that the twenty eager participants made the class a breeze.

Ethan didn't show. One of his assistants had helped Cassie set the table display and get her ready for the class. Cassie couldn't ignore her disappointment, but she refused to examine the reasons for it.

After the crowd had thinned to only a few, Cassie decided to pack up and go home.

"Excuse me, would you sign this, please?"

Cassie turned just in time to face a thin young woman with shoulder-length red hair and green eyes. The voice had startled Cassie. She took a step back. "Oh, hello."

The woman held up Cassie's latest romance novel. Cassie lowered her bag and reached into her purse for a pen.

"Here, use this." The woman offered a black pen. "Make it out to Mara Gray."

Cassie wanted to use purple ink. It had been her trademark

from day one. On the other hand, since it was only one book, and she didn't want to rummage through her purse, she gave in. "Thanks." She scribbled her name and a Bible verse and returned the book.

Mara glanced at the words but said nothing. Cassie tried to fill the awkward moment. "Did you enjoy the class?"

"Yes, very much." Her eyes lit up. "I want to learn more about writing mysteries, though. I'd like to write suspense stories, you know, about murders and stuff like that."

Cassie nodded. "Depending on the results of the sign-up sheet, we may have future classes. Although I won't teach specifically on a certain genre, I'll teach about writing in general. Point of view, plotting, that sort of thing."

Mara nodded.

"Give me your name and address, and I'll let you know if we start meeting on a regular basis."

"I'm kind of hard to reach. Why don't you give me your number, and I can check back with you?"

Cassie stumbled a moment. She wasn't in the habit of giving complete strangers her unlisted number. Being a writer, she liked her privacy. Before she could answer, Ethan walked up behind her and nudged her elbow.

"Hello!" Cassie said as she turned to face him. Realizing she had said her greeting with a little too much enthusiasm, she added quietly, "Good to see you."

"Sorry I wasn't here for your workshop. I was caught in a meeting and couldn't make it in time."

Cassie thought he looked genuinely sorry. "No problem."

"I'd like to make it up to you. How about some pie and coffee?"

Cassie turned to say her farewell to Mara and discovered the woman had gone. Turning back to Ethan, she answered with a shrug, "Why not?"

"Great!"

Amid the clanging of silverware and quiet chatter from nearby tables, Cassie slid into her side of the vinyl-covered booth while Ethan scooted across from her. She breathed in his cologne. It smelled of fresh sea air, reminding her of summer vacations in Florida when her mother was still alive.

The soft glow of lamplight flickered between them. Cassie pulled off her lavender jacket, then reached for the pie menu. With choices made and orders given, she began the conversation.

"So how was your meeting?"

"Well, I guess it wasn't a meeting exactly."

Cassie raised an eyebrow. "Oh?"

Ethan lifted his palm. "Remember, innocent until proven guilty."

"I'm listening," she said with a smile.

"Okay, it's like this. I work with the city school corporation in a literacy program."

Cassie's estimation of him kept growing. This guy was a wonder. Good looks and a soft heart for kids. What could be more charming?

"One of the kids was faltering, and I met him for a soda. These kids are middle school age."

"Sounds like an important meeting to me," Cassie teased. "That's pretty neat."

Ethan shifted his weight in his chair. "No big deal. I want to get the message out to kids that it's cool to read."

Something flickered across his eyes. What she had seen there, she couldn't tell. It disappeared in an instant.

With the waitress quickly approaching, Cassie's imagination had little time to explore the matter. Instead, she placed her napkin on her lap. "Well, speaking as an author, I, for one, am glad you encourage reading," she stated matter-of-factly.

The waitress spread their pie plates and coffee on the table. Once the woman left, Ethan picked up his fork. Before he could delve into the spicy pumpkin, Cassie bowed her head. "Father, we thank You for this food we're about to eat. Thank You for this time we have together, and I pray You will be with the kids Ethan is mentoring in the reading program. Especially this one who is faltering. Reading opens futures, unlocks doors, offers hope. You are the Father of hope. Rescue them, Lord. In Jesus' name.

"Tell me about the literacy program." Cassie reached for her fork and plunged it into the chocolate cream pie.

"Where do you go to church?" he interjected.

"The little white church just down the road."

He nodded.

"How about you, where do you attend?"

Ethan cleared his throat and took a sip of water. After what seemed a lengthy pause, he finally answered. "I attend that big church on the southwest side of town."

"The one that presents the beautiful Easter cantata each year?" Cassie thought he looked uncomfortable, like he was struggling to breathe. She thought he was going to cough. Maybe his heart was racing too, though she couldn't imagine why.

He did cough. "Yeah, that's the one," he managed, his raspy words choked to a whisper. He took another drink of water.

Cassie waited a moment for him to get his voice back. "Are you a part of that?"

"What? Oh, never have the time with work and everything."

"That's too bad. You were going to tell me about this literacy thing."

As they made their way through dessert, he shared different aspects of the program.

"You developed it?"

"I guess I did," he answered as if he hadn't thought about it before.

"What made you think of starting such a program?"

"I'm tired of kids feeling like they're second-rate citizens because they like to read. What's up with this world, anyway? Kids who read are called nerds, bookworms, whatever. Yet these kids grow up to be scientists, doctors, teachers. They run the world, you know?" He stabbed a piece of pie and ate it as if it were a chore.

Something bothered him, and she knew it. They hadn't known each other long enough for her to pry. She decided if he wanted to talk about it, he would.

Being a little more bold than usual, Cassie reached over and laid her hand on his left arm. "Hey, thanks for caring about the kids and about reading."

Ethan stopped and looked at her. The spark in his eyes subsided. "I'm sorry. I guess I'm a little opinionated about the matter."

Cassie pulled her hand away and smiled at him. "Hey, I'm an author, remember? We share the same opinion."

He smiled and nodded.

"Ethan. . ." She had never called him by his name before—it

seemed almost too intimate—yet at the same time, she liked saying it. "I'm glad you made the effort to show up tonight."

He wiped his mouth on the napkin. "I'm glad you came out for pie. Maybe we can do it again sometime?" He made the comment almost as if he couldn't imagine her entertaining such an idea.

"I'd like that." There. The words were out of her mouth before she had time to think about them. Of course, that was nothing unusual. She said many things without giving them thought first. She honestly felt embarrassed, though she wasn't at all sure why. Friends. They were becoming friends.

Still, she felt her cheeks flame as her imagination led her to cozy dinners around a warm hearth. . . .

Chapter 5

First, dessert after the workshop last Monday, now a Saturday night dinner, huh? Things seem to be moving right along." Nell browsed through the sale rack at the department store.

Cassie smiled, offering no more information.

Nell turned to Cassie. "Okay, I'll let it go for now, but I want every detail after tomorrow night."

Cassie laughed and shook her head.

"So how's your story coming along?" Nell rummaged through more clothes.

Cassie pulled out a black dress, held it up to herself in front of a mirror. "It's coming. I've finally decided how I'm going to commit the murder." She looked through the mirror in time to see an old woman behind her gasp for breath and scurry away.

"Don't tell me. Let me guess." Nell held her hand up and bit her lower lip. "Um, let's see, the baker beat the victim with a rubber spatula in the kitchen."

"You're a genius," Cassie said with amusement.

Nell glanced at her watch. "Hey, I've got to scoot. Ralph will be home soon."

"Yeah, I need to get home too." Cassie followed Nell, who stopped abruptly at the men's fragrance counter.

"Don't tell me Ralph's out of the cologne you bought him for his birthday already?"

Nell shook her head. "Checking for new scents. I like variety."

Cassie picked up a bottle and took a whiff. "Ethan wears a nice fragrance, but I don't know what it is."

Nell's eyebrows rose. "What does it smell like?"

"The sea. Fresh, clean." Cassie continued to pull off caps and breathe deeply. She finally glanced over at Nell and found her staring. "What?"

"You remember his cologne, do you?" Nell was like a hound dog sniffing out a trail.

"You need a life, Nell." Cassie put the bottle down, and they both laughed as they left the store.

🪬

The next morning Cassie had just pulled on her jogging shoes when the phone rang. "Hello?"

"Good morning, Cassie."

"Hi, Dad!" Cassie couldn't hide her excitement upon hearing her father's voice.

"Just wanted to see how my favorite girl is doing."

"I'm doing great. Are you getting settled into your new job at the university?"

"Yes, I am. The only thing I don't like is how far away I am from you."

"Yeah, but now it gives us both a reason to travel." She heard him chuckle on the other end.

"I miss you."

"I miss you too, Dad." She waited a minute. "You doing

okay?" He had suffered with depression after her mother died, and Cassie hoped his new position would help him move on with his life.

"I'm doing great. What are you up to this morning?"

"Oh, just getting ready for my morning jog." Uh-oh, she forgot how he felt about that. Silence on the other end reminded her. "I'll be fine, Dad. I'm very alert." Cassie knew he was trying to find the right words without sounding like a controlling parent.

"Just be careful. I don't want to lose my girl."

They talked a little longer, then finally said their good-byes. Cassie pulled on her jacket and headed out the door.

The sun burned away the morning dew as Cassie broke into a steady pace. Her thoughts skipped from plotting, to her father, to Ethan, and back to her story again.

Approaching the last block of her journey home, she noticed that a gold Camry had slowed down behind her, making her uncomfortable. Not knowing how to handle the situation, Cassie prayed for guidance. At just about the same time, the person drove off. The driver might have been reading a map or something. He was probably lost. Country roads could be confusing.

※

Cassie opened her front door. Aaron's tightened face spoke of bad news. He stepped inside.

"I can't tag along with you, is that it?"

Aaron shook his head. "No. My supervisor said you could participate in the interviews, but that's it."

"Wonderful! Thank you, Aaron." She started to ramble on, but another look at his face stopped her. "What's wrong?"

"There was a second murder today." He said the words like

a protective big brother.

She felt a lecture coming on and wondered what any of it had to do with her. "What's going on, Aaron?"

He shook his head. "You'll find out soon enough when you start working with me. You have to sign some papers to relieve us of liability and swear to confidentiality. And—listen carefully to this—I am responsible for you, so you have to follow my instructions. Such as, you can't touch anything at a crime scene. So don't let me catch you picking anything up and analyzing it. In fact, you're only in on some of the interviews, so you must not enter a crime scene. Deal?"

"Deal." Though somewhat disappointed, she decided it was better than nothing.

"This is a dangerous business, Cassie. I hope you know what you're doing."

"I know," she said with the seriousness of an old schoolmarm, though she struggled to see her childhood friend in a professional role. She couldn't get past the vision of him eating mud pies. "Where did it happen this time?"

"An apartment on the southwest side near Oakhurst Community Church."

"Oh, that's Ethan's church."

Aaron's gaze fixed on her face.

"What else?"

"Nothing." He looked at her dress. "You going somewhere?"

"Yeah, Ethan is taking me to dinner."

His brows furrowed. "How well do you know this guy?"

"Okay, calm down, big brother. I think he's harmless." She almost laughed at his protectiveness, but the look on his face stopped her.

"Everyone is a suspect till we get to the truth," he said, his voice firm.

Ethan's car pulled into the driveway. Aaron turned around, glanced out the door, then looked back at Cassie. "Well, I'd better go. Be at the department by eight tomorrow morning. We'll have coffee, look over some paperwork, and hopefully start with some interviews." He shot her a look of warning. "But remember what I said."

Just then Ethan knocked on the door, and Aaron stepped out of the way. The two men looked at each other.

"Ethan, this is my best friend from elementary days, Aaron James." Cassie couldn't help noticing Aaron's chest puff up like a rooster. "Aaron, Ethan Hamil. Ethan owns the Reader's Refuge." Aaron eyed him with suspicion.

They exchanged formal handshakes and somewhat awkward greetings. Ethan ran his finger along the collar of his shirt, and Aaron shot Cassie another look of warning.

"Well, I'll just grab my purse."

Aaron said good-bye and left. Ethan and Cassie followed close behind and settled into Ethan's car.

"So he's your best friend?" The worry on his face made her feel good.

"More like a brother." She noticed Ethan seemed to relax. "We actually grew up together. Aaron, Nell, and I have been the best of friends for years."

"Yeah, I've heard you speak of Nell but not Aaron. Where does he work?"

"He's a detective for the police department."

A shadow crossed his face. "Is he involved with that recent murder?"

Though tempted to tell him the latest, Cassie held back for confidentiality purposes and said only, "Yes, he's somewhat involved, but I don't really know to what extent. He doesn't talk a lot about his work." She knew only too well the truth of that statement. She practically had to use a crowbar to pry information from him.

"Is he the more serious type or just suspicious?"

"What do you mean?"

"Oh, I can't quite put my finger on it. I just got the feeling he didn't trust me."

"It's that brother thing."

"Guilty till proven innocent, huh?"

"Yeah, something like that."

"You're sure it's nothing more?" The car stopped at a light. He searched her face.

"Like what?"

"Like maybe his interests are more than that of a brother?"

"It's never been like that between us." Cassie wondered about his concern. After all, she and Ethan had just started to see each other. Why the endless questions?

Maybe he noticed her discomfort. "Well, I don't know about you, but I'm starving."

Cassie nodded, still feeling a little unsettled by their conversation.

❧

On the drive home, Cassie laughed as she listened to Ethan talk about his African Grey parrot, Shakespeare. "Stop, you're making my stomach hurt."

Ethan pulled into her driveway and shut off the car engine. He turned to her. "I'm telling you, it's the truth." He crossed his heart and held up his hand. "Shakespeare's favorite part of the movie is the wedding scene. So I play the movie for him while I'm at work. His phrases have come from that."

"What are his phrases again?"

Ethan looked away for a moment. "Um, let's see. 'I do; here comes the bride.'" He shrugged. "There are more, but I can't remember them right now."

"That is totally amazing. Maybe I'll write him into my mystery."

"That will cost you, dear lady."

"Oh?" She raised her brow in question.

"Another night out for dinner; maybe even a movie?"

"I'd like that."

He leaned gently toward her and she toward him. His left hand reached up to the back of her head. Strong fingers gently stroked through her hair as though exploring the softness of a silken scarf. His lips firm, yet gentle, caressed her own. Her heart raced. She wanted to cough but couldn't break away. White stars danced across her closed eyes. Ethan pulled slightly from her, feathered light kisses up her cheek, then kissed her once more.

He appeared breathless. "I'll call you."

Getting out of the car, Ethan walked over to let her out. Cassie coughed several times, but it didn't help. She felt sure nothing could calm her thumping heart tonight.

❧

The next morning when Cassie arrived at the police station, the officers greeted and teased her with lighthearted banter, making her feel welcome. When Aaron gave the signal, she grabbed her coffee and followed him to his police car.

With her left hand grasped firmly on her cup, she pulled the legal pad onto her lap and clutched the purple pen in her right hand.

"The feathers hardly seem appropriate for the police car," Aaron said dryly.

"What's wrong with the feathers? Kind of lightens the murder thing, don't you think?" She smiled at him.

Aaron shook his head. "Just don't let the guys see it," he quipped before nosing his car into traffic. "We need to interview some of the neighbors of the second victim to see what we can find out, if anything."

"Any evidence found to speak of?" Cassie started writing.

"It gets more bizarre by the minute. Seems the perpetrator leaves behind a dried bridal bouquet on every victim."

"What?" Cassie almost spilled her coffee.

"Whoa. Be careful. I just cleaned the interior." He glanced over at her. "What's wrong?"

"How strange."

"What?"

"The murderer in my mystery leaves the same thing behind."

"You're kidding. Leave it to you." He shook his head again. "Well, you might not want to broadcast that just now."

"Yeah, I guess not."

"Have you told anyone up to now?"

Cassie thought about it a moment. "Just the Sleuth Sisters, my other writing partners."

Aaron shrugged. "Weird coincidence." He pulled up in front of a white house with a missing black shutter on the right-side window. "Don't worry about it."

An eerie feeling settled over her. She wanted to write romance and leave the mysteries to someone else. She consoled herself with the fact that at least no one else knew.

A thought pierced her like the strike from a poisonous snake. She had told someone else.

Ethan Hamil.

The shadowy figure sat in the car far enough away to be hidden, but close enough to watch. Plan. Prepare. It was important to know Cassie's routine: when she was home, when she was gone, her habits. The timing had to be perfect. The slightest mistake would mean she won. That wouldn't happen.

Not this time.

Bony fingers reached into the darkness and picked up a dried bouquet, rearranging the attached bow. "Not yet," the voice whispered into the night air.

"But soon."

Chapter 6

"Hey, Cassie, you want to go to lunch after church? Ralph is watching a game on TV, and I'm so tired of watching sports. Please say yes."

"You know you're just digging for details of my relationship with Ethan."

"Well, that too. It's been forever since we've talked, and you have been seeing him nonstop for the last month. I need an update."

"Nell, have you no shame?"

"None whatsoever."

The two laughed together as they headed down the hall. "I'll meet you after church," Cassie said before ducking into the choir room.

The service passed too quickly for Cassie. She wanted to linger in the Lord's presence. Confusion muddled her mind, and she longed for wisdom. Though she and Ethan got along great and were growing close, she still stumbled with her feelings each time she thought of the dried flowers thing. She mentally shook herself. What had gotten into her? It wasn't like he was a killer or anything. So what if he knew about it?

Still, the nagging thought persisted. Maybe she needed to do a little off-duty sleuthing to ease her mind.

After church, Nell and Cassie ordered their burgers and fries, walked over to a table, and sat down.

Nell offered the prayer and pulled the paper napkin on her lap. "You want to talk about it?"

"Me and Ethan?"

Nell shook her head. "About what's bothering you."

Cassie shrugged and squirted some ketchup on the inside of the burger wrapper. She dipped two fries in the sauce and ate them. "I shouldn't tell you this since it's confidential police work, but I'm beside myself with worry." With a sigh, she made Nell take a vow of secrecy, and then Cassie explained the dried bouquet.

"And so you're worried about. . ." Nell interrupted herself to carefully situate her food in front of her.

"Well, don't you think it's a little weird that a bridal bouquet is left on the victim and that's also in my story?" Cassie wiped her mouth with a napkin.

Nell looked up for a moment. "Are you trying to tell me you're the killer?" She turned her attention back to the sandwich as if the idea wouldn't bother her in the least.

"Yes!" Cassie pulled her fists into claws and pretended to strike at Nell.

Undaunted, Nell slurped on her soda. "Call me dense, but I don't get it." She picked up her sandwich.

Cassie hiccupped.

"Uh-oh, you're nervous." Nell put her sandwich down.

Cassie waited a moment, trying to gather the nerve to say the words. "Ethan knew about the bouquet."

Nell's features relaxed. "Cassie, surely you don't think—"

"I don't know what to think."

Nell scrunched her face in disbelief. "You can't be serious. You've known this man long enough to know he's not a murderer! He's a bookstore owner, for crying out loud. He likes kids and books. Does that sound like a killer to you?"

Cassie leaned back in her chair. Listening to the conversation made her realize how ridiculous it all sounded. "Oh, I don't know what's wrong with me. Aaron's got me all stirred up."

Nell laughed. "Aaron's always been protective of you."

"Yeah, I guess you're right."

They continued talking their way through the meal. Once finished, they walked out the door.

"I still can't believe you would even consider Ethan a possible suspect," Nell said as they headed for their cars.

"Oh, I don't know what I was thinking." Cassie opened her door and looked over the roof of her car. "See you tonight at church."

Nell waved, and they both pulled out of the lot.

Cassie put on her sunglasses. After she traveled a mile down the road, she glanced in her rearview mirror. Fear tightened her chest. A gold Camry had pulled in behind her.

✤

Okay, so he hadn't been lost in the country. Who was this guy and what did he want from her? Cassie couldn't believe the things going on in her life. She felt trapped in her own mystery.

Would he follow her home this time? Where could she go? Maybe Ethan was home. His church service would be over, and he would have had time to eat lunch. She'd drive by and see if he was there. If not, she'd keep driving somewhere, anywhere.

The Camry continued on her trail. If only she could pull in behind it and get the license plate number. Like a perpetrator clutching his victim, panic seized her. Stubborn determination pulled her free. Her jaw clenched. She refused to live in fear. Her foot stepped harder on the accelerator as she held the steering wheel in a death grip.

After spotting Ethan's car, Cassie pulled into his driveway and watched in disbelief as the car sped on down the road. Blinding tears blurred her vision, leaving her helpless to read the license plate.

She rolled the window down for a moment and took great gulps of air.

"Are you all right?" Ethan poked his head just inside the car window.

Cassie jumped.

"Cassie, what is it?" He opened the car door and helped her out. Her body shook as he pulled her next to him. She melted into his strong, protective arms. When she had calmed down, he placed one arm firmly around her and helped her inside the house. He walked her over to a chair in his living room. "I'll be right back. I've got to get Shakespeare back in his cage. Will you be okay?"

She nodded. When he left the room, Cassie absently placed her sunglasses beside her on the chair. A parched throat compelled her to look for a drink. Stepping around the corner, she searched for the kitchen. Once she found it, she walked over to get a glass of water and stopped cold.

On the table laid a dried flower arrangement.

Cassie couldn't get home fast enough. Fortunately, Ethan bought her story about the migraine, though it took some convincing for him to let her drive home alone. She should have asked him about the flowers, but the thought never occurred to her. All she wanted was to get out of his house.

Once she got home, Cassie locked all the doors. This whole business made her plumb crazy. She hiccupped. Grabbing a glass of tea, she went into her bedroom and clicked on the computer. She wrote a note to the Sleuth Sisters and told them everything. Maybe they could help her. After she sent the note, she went over to her bed to lie down.

She prayed about the matter and finally settled into a restless sleep of dreams filled with policemen, criminals, and dried flowers.

When she awoke, her throat still felt dry and scratchy. She glanced at the clock. She'd overslept for evening church. A slight swallow made her wince. Uh-oh, she could feel a sore throat coming on. She decided to go to the store and buy some cold medicine.

Cassie brushed her hair, put on some fresh clothes, and headed for the store. Once there, she glanced through the health-and-beauty aids aisle in search of a quick cure.

"Hi, Cassie."

Cassie turned around to see Mara Gray. "Hi, how are you?"

"I'm fine."

Cassie didn't really feel like chatting, but neither did she want to be rude. "Did you find out there's enough interest for a continuing writer's workshop?"

"Yes, I called the bookstore. I'll be at the next one. It's in two weeks, right?"

"Right." Cassie hoped her nerves would calm down by then.

"You don't look like you feel well."

"I really don't. Came in to pick up some cold medicine. I should get home."

Mara shrugged. "Hope you get feeling better."

"Thank you. See you, Mara."

⚜

By Monday evening, Cassie was feeling much better and even a little more adventurous. She decided to go to Ethan's house and look around. After all, she needed to pick up her sunglasses. She knew he would be at the bookstore.

With no neighbors stirring around, Cassie went up to Ethan's door just to make sure he wasn't home. She rang the doorbell. Nothing. Her hand jiggled the knob. Locked. Maybe if she looked around the house, she'd find something.

Carefully stepping around the bushes bordering the house, she tried to maneuver the windows. They didn't budge. She scoured the ground for clues, though the moonlight did little to assist her. The growing darkness between the houses made her edgy.

"Yoo-hoo."

Without turning around, Cassie recognized the voice of Mrs. Butler, Ethan's neighbor. The older woman prided herself in knowing the neighborhood goings-on. Cassie forced herself to swallow the needless fear in her throat and face the woman with a smile. Mrs. Butler's back screen door slammed behind her as she rushed toward Cassie, happily waving a key on a ring.

"You need to get into Mr. Hamil's house?" the pudgy woman asked, quite out of breath with excitement.

"Well, uh, yes. I left my sunglasses last night, and the sun's glare gives me a headache," Cassie said, reasoning that was the truth.

Mrs. Butler all but salivated with power. Her chin lifted ever so slightly while her mouth pinched into a thin line. "Mr. Hamil gave me a key for emergency situations such as this."

She pushed the key in the lock and shoved open the door. "Mind you, had I not seen you with him before, I wouldn't have let you in." Her expression said she took her position seriously.

"I appreciate it," Cassie said when she spotted her sunglasses on the floor beside the chair. "Would you mind waiting just a moment while I go to the rest room?" She tossed the neighbor a look of discomfort.

"Oh, sure." Mrs. Butler waved her hand, acting like a Realtor showing a home.

Cassie followed Shakespeare's squawks, knowing the parrot stayed in the TV room. She glanced around for what looked like a video cabinet. Bingo. Tiptoeing over to the cabinet, she scrunched down and fingered through the videos, one by one, never coming upon the wedding video Ethan had talked about.

"I do," Shakespeare squawked from his cage. "Marry me." Squawk.

Cassie felt like a traitor rummaging through Ethan's things, but she had to know what was going on. Her search proved futile. She closed the cabinet and rose to her feet.

For good measure, Cassie stopped in the rest room to check her makeup before heading back to Mrs. Butler.

The old woman greeted her with a smile and closed the door behind them as they stepped outside. "If you don't mind, Mrs. Butler, would you keep this visit just between you and me? I feel a little embarrassed at my forgetfulness." Cassie smiled and winked.

The neighbor seemed to enjoy being on the inside of a secret, so she quickly agreed. "Sure. After all, you merely took what belonged to you."

They said their good-byes, and Cassie turned toward home. She only hoped Ethan hadn't noticed her glasses.

Chapter 7

H ow's your dad?"

"He's fine." Cassie placed a bowl of popcorn between her and Ethan on the couch. Glasses of iced tea sat on the coffee table. "He called just last night. He likes his new job, and it seems Ohio really agrees with him. He misses me, though." She grinned.

"I'm sure he does. You doing okay?"

"Yeah, I miss him a lot, but I'm all right. You're really lucky to have a sister and bro—" She stopped herself.

He looked at her. "It's okay. We never really have gotten back around to talking about Kyle, have we?"

She shook her head.

"Where do I start? Um, let's see, Kyle is the muscle-bound type. Always worked out in the gym. He made fun of me for loving books. I got tired of it. One night we had a big fight. It was the night before he left to join the marines. I haven't seen or heard from him since." He took a drink of iced tea.

"I'm sorry, Ethan."

He shrugged. "I think what started out as a pride issue for both of us just kind of swelled into something neither of us knows what to do to fix. To be honest, I never really cared until recently. Watching your close relationship with your dad makes me see things differently."

"Do you want to talk to Kyle?"

"I don't know. I wouldn't know what to say."

"I'll pray for you, Ethan. God will give you the words."

Ethan stirred on the couch and grabbed another handful of popcorn. "So, you ready to take me on in Scrabble?"

"Remember, I'm a writer."

"Remember, I own a room full of books."

She chuckled as she lifted the game from the bottom shelf of her coffee table. "I've been meaning to ask you if you knew the girl who was killed the other night. She lived down by your church."

Ethan cleared his throat. "No, I didn't recognize the name."

"It's all rather frightening." Cassie eyed him closely. She knew she shouldn't talk about confidential police matters, but she had to know if Ethan was involved. "Can you believe the killer leaves a dried flower arrangement on each victim?"

Ethan stopped throwing the popcorn in his mouth for a moment. "He does? I didn't know that."

"Weird, huh?"

"Yeah, just like your story. Are you the killer?" He quirked his brows with suspicion.

"No. I thought maybe you were." She tried to make her comment lighthearted, though her heart thumped louder than popping corn.

"Me? What would make you think that?" Just then, the light bulb seemed to go on in his head. "Ah, the dried flowers my sister left at my house."

"Your sister?"

"Yeah, Megan. She likes to dry flowers and make arrangements out of them. She's trying to make one for me. Don't ask me why. I'm not into it myself. Hey, maybe my sister is the killer." He let out an evil laugh before shoving a handful of popcorn into his mouth.

Cassie giggled. "I'm kind of in the mood to watch a sappy movie these days. Do you think Shakespeare would mind if I borrowed his video?" Cassie continued to chew on the popcorn with nonchalance, though her pulse raced to her throat while she watched Ethan for any signs that might give him away.

He frowned. "Oh, sorry. The tape broke last week. Pulled apart. I think I played it too much." He continued to chomp his way through the popcorn. "Had to throw it away."

She studied him. He did seem to be telling the truth. Didn't he?

"We can rent something, if you'd like."

Cassie waved the matter aside. "No big deal. Just thought I'd see why Shakespeare liked it so much."

Ethan made no comment.

Around eleven o'clock, Cassie kissed Ethan good-bye and opened the door for him. The porch light went on just in time to catch the gold Camry cruising down the street. Cassie gasped.

"What is it?"

"That car." Her voice trembled as she pointed.

Ethan pushed her farther into the house. He closed the door and locked it. He turned and placed his hands on her arms. "What's going on?"

She pulled in a nervous breath. "I don't know. I think that

man is stalking me."

"How long has that been going on?"

"A couple of weeks, maybe longer."

"What does he look like?"

"I've only seen him close enough to know it's a man, dark hair. That's all I know."

"Did you get his plates?"

"No."

Ethan pushed his fingers through his hair and started to pace. "Have you told Aaron about this?"

"No. He worries too much as it is."

"You keep your doors locked, do you hear me? I'm going to drive up and down your road. I'll call you from my cell phone. Don't you open these doors for anyone. Promise me, Cassie."

"I promise. Why would anyone be after me? It makes no sense."

"People are crazy. It's probably nothing, but it doesn't hurt to be careful."

She nodded.

He kissed her cheek. "I'll call you." He opened the door, turned the lock, and pulled it shut. "You need to get a dead-bolt lock," he called through the door.

"Okay." Once she heard his footsteps fade down the walk, Cassie ran up to her room. Sparky slowly hobbled up the stairs behind her.

Quickly putting on her nightgown, Cassie slipped into bed and pulled the covers just under her chin. She felt like a little girl again. She wished her dad were there.

She shook when the phone rang. "Hello?"

"It's me. The coast is clear. Whoever he is, he's gone now.

I've been up and down this road several times."

"Thanks, Ethan."

"Keep my cell phone number by your bed."

"I know it by heart."

"I know, but when people are in a panic, they forget things."

"Okay."

"I'll call you tomorrow."

"All right, bye."

"Cassie?"

"Yes?"

"Um, listen." He paused a moment. "I care about you, okay?"

She coughed.

❦

Somehow just hearing those words had chased away Cassie's fear. Ethan cared about her. The destroyed video proved nothing, and she believed him about the flowers. He was not the killer, and he would protect her from whoever was tracking her.

Cassie attached the next chapter of her novella to an E-mail for the Sleuth Sisters and sent it on its way. The story was growing a little more gruesome than she had planned, and she needed their input before proceeding with the next chapter.

They had written her with encouragement and advice on her recent events and each revealed they seemed caught up in real-life mysteries of their own.

She walked into the living room to straighten things from the night before. Dragging out the vacuum sweeper, she swept around the couch where bits of popcorn littered the carpet. Sparky tried to get to the pieces first, but cataracts slowed him down.

Once the task was finished, Cassie put the vacuum away

and walked over to plump the pillows. When she lifted the pillow that had been on Ethan's side of the couch, a slip of paper fell to the carpet. She bent down to pick it up. A barely legible number was scrawled on it. She recognized it. The number was to her church.

How odd. Why would Ethan have the number for her church? Not that it was a big deal. Just made her curious. She laughed. She was beginning to think like a mystery writer. She eyed everything with suspicion.

Cassie's phone rang. "Hello?"

"Hi, Girl!"

"Nell, how are you?"

"Fine, Kiddo. I just wanted to tell you I was over at the church this morning and who do you think I saw walking out of the pastor's office?"

"I'm sure I haven't a clue."

"Lover boy, that's who."

"Ethan?"

"You got it."

"Why would Ethan be talking to our pastor?"

"I thought you might know. I was afraid you were planning a wedding and hadn't bothered to tell your best friend about it. . . . Cassie, you still there?"

"I'm here. I'm just confused, that's all."

"Oh, well, probably working out some kind of book deal for the library or something."

"Yeah, maybe."

"Well, I'll let you go. I just wanted to call you and see what was going on, but since you don't know, I might as well hang up."

"Thanks a lot."

Nell laughed. "I'll call you later. Ralph is waiting on me to go to the store with him."

Cassie barely heard her friend hang up. Ethan Hamil grew more mysterious by the minute.

❦

Cassie finished cleaning up around the house, then worked on reediting the first part of her mystery. She checked her E-mail to see if anyone had responded to her last chapter. Nothing yet.

Her body ached from lingering too long at the desk. She decided to take a break. Cassie did some stretches and walked down the stairs. Sparky lazily followed.

She grabbed a glass of iced tea in the kitchen and started to make her way back up the stairs when a knock sounded at the door.

She peeked through the peephole and saw Aaron dressed in his police uniform.

"Hi, Aaron, come on in."

"I can't stay long. I just wanted to let you know there's been another murder on the north side."

She gasped. "When?"

"Around one o'clock this morning."

"Another bridal bouquet?"

He nodded.

"You want me to come with you?"

"No, you can join me tomorrow." He pulled off his hat and toyed with it in his hands. "Look, Cassie, I'm just a little, uh, concerned. This woman ran a used bookstore in town."

"For crying out loud, Aaron, would you quit trying to implicate Ethan?"

"Listen—"

"No, I won't! If he's under suspicion, why haven't you arrested him by now?"

"We need proof."

"Okay, you don't have any, so quit trying to upset me. You're a good friend, Aaron, but you're not my dad, okay? So please, stop trying to act like him."

"Cassie, just hear me out. Victim number two attended Ethan's church. Victim number one applied for work at Reader's Refuge."

"I don't see the correlation." She tapped her foot nervously on the floor.

He blew out a sigh. "I'm not sure I do, either. It just scares me. I mean you haven't known this guy long. And, well, there's one more thing."

"What's that?"

"The victims. All women, mid-twenties, short brown hair, brown eyes." He paused, then looked at her. "Just like you."

Chapter 8

By Monday afternoon, Cassie was frazzled. She couldn't imagine where she had laid her driver's license. If the cashier hadn't requested to see her license when Cassie wrote a check for gas, she might not have known it was missing. She had more important things to do, but since she couldn't drive without a license, she decided she'd better get a new one.

She prayed all the way to the license bureau that she wouldn't get pulled over by a policeman. Once inside the bureau, she took a number and sat down by a gray-haired woman who looked friendly enough.

"Don't you hate waiting in here? I'm taking time from work that I don't have," the woman said.

Cassie smiled. "I know what you mean."

"Oh, well, I guess that's life."

"Where do you work?"

"Oh, I'm a secretary at Oakhurst Community Church."

"The big church that gives the Easter programs?"

The woman fairly glowed. "That's the one."

"My boy, um, my friend goes there."

"Oh, really? What's your friend's name? I'm sure I would

know him. I know everyone." She sat up taller in her chair. "I've served as secretary for thirty years now."

"His name is Ethan Hamil. He owns Reader's Refuge."

"Oh, yes, I'm quite familiar with the bookstore. Go there a lot myself. I've met the owner. Very nice young man."

Cassie smiled, feeling somewhat relieved the woman knew him.

"Can't say he goes to the church, though." She thought a moment, then shook her head. "No, I'm sure I would know if he went there. Maybe he's visited during the program."

Cassie didn't know whether to rejoice or be sad. After all, that cleared him from knowing victim number two, well, at least through the church, but it still meant he had lied. She stammered. "Oh, yes, maybe that's it. I must be mistaken." Cassie barely heard the rest of the woman's comments. Why would Ethan lie? Things didn't add up. The dried flowers, a parrot that talked in wedding phrases, and now a lie. She had no clue what was going on, but she intended to find out.

❧

When Cassie got home, she worked on her mystery until it was polished to her satisfaction. Too tired for dinner, Cassie grabbed some popcorn and iced tea and sat on her couch. What was the matter with her? Why couldn't she shake Ethan free from her suspicions? He explained away the dried flowers and the damaged tape, but the lie still stood between them.

Her head ached from thinking. All she wanted to do was climb into bed, leaving her mystery and the twisted world behind. Cassie finished the last of her popcorn, gathered the dirty dishes, rinsed them, and placed them in the dishwasher.

She climbed the stairs to prepare for bed. After reading her Bible and writing in her journal, Cassie knelt beside her bed once again and asked the Lord for wisdom and strength for the days ahead. Once she sensed His peace, she crawled beneath the covers, knowing she'd sleep well.

Her thoughts scrambled with the recent events. The guy in the gold Camry. The victims that looked like her. But didn't she look like a million other girls her age? Why the concern?

Aaron suspected Ethan. She resented Aaron for putting that thought in her head. On the other hand, what if he were right? Aaron was a policeman, after all. He looked at things from a different point of view.

Ethan's integrity hung by a thread. Cassie felt her heart trapped somewhere between love and fear.

She hoped love would triumph.

☙

The week passed all too quickly. A good group showed up at the workshop. She was getting to know some of the regulars.

"How's your story coming along, Mara?" Cassie stuffed her things in her bag as people cleared from the area.

Mara turned to her. "Oh, I haven't started it yet. Just gleaning information for now."

"I see. You like mysteries, did you say?"

"Murder mysteries. Stories thick with crime and suspense."

Cassie laughed. "Well, there seems to be a market out there for that, though I can't say I'd be very good at it. I get enough of that at work."

"Oh, that's right, you're a court reporter during the day?"

"Right, and a writer by night. Kind of makes me sound like Clark Kent, doesn't it? A reporter by day, Superman by night?"

Cassie laughed at herself but stopped when she noticed Mara wasn't laughing.

"I've gotta go," Mara said.

Mara sometimes reminded Cassie of a nervous bird. Aaron approached them. "Aaron, what's up?" Despite how frustrated she was with him, she had to admit she liked how safe she felt when he walked up in uniform.

"I was in the area, and I remembered you were having your workshop tonight. Thought I'd stop in to apologize for, well, how I've been acting lately. I don't mean to upset you."

She smiled. "It's all right, Aaron. You're a great friend, or you wouldn't care."

"So, Aaron, we meet again." Ethan walked up beside them.

Cassie noticed Aaron's smile tightened. Still, she had to credit him for trying.

"What brings you here?"

"Just cruising the area and thought I'd stop in and say hi to Cassie."

Ethan nodded.

Cassie felt a little uncomfortable. "You guys want to go over to the coffee shop?"

"Afraid I'll have to pass. I've got to get back to work." Aaron turned to go, and Cassie caught him by the arm.

"Thanks, Aaron."

He smiled. "No problem. You be careful." He turned toward Ethan. His gaze rested on him a moment, then he walked out the door.

Ethan let out a low whistle. "I'm telling you that guy doesn't like me."

"Oh, stop." She pulled on his arm. "Let's go for coffee."

"I've got a few things to finish up here. Why don't you go on down. I'll join you in a few minutes."

"Okay." She grabbed her things and walked two doors over. After waiting awhile for Ethan, she decided to go ahead and order. Evidently, he had some interruptions, and she had to go soon. Once she ordered her drink, she sat back down. The bell on the door jangled, causing her to look up just in time to see Ethan walk in with a pretty, slender woman of average height and shoulder-length brown hair.

Cassie felt a twinge of jealousy. No wonder it took him so long. Guess he had been preoccupied. Well, it's not like she and Ethan had ties or anything. They weren't high school kids anymore and certainly had the freedom to see whom they chose. She just kind of thought they had an understanding. Obviously, the understanding was only on her part.

Ethan waved toward her, and they headed her way. Cassie noticed he guided the woman with his hand in her back. They arrived at her table and the woman stood smiling beside him.

"Hi." Cassie threw a weak smile toward the woman, not wanting to be rude, but feeling rejected nevertheless.

"Sorry I'm late, Cassie. Okay if we both join you?"

"Uh. . ." She thought he was already planning to join her. Alone.

Before Cassie could answer, he turned to the woman. "You want a latte?"

She nodded. "Before you go, Ethan, don't you think it would be nice if you introduced us?"

He hit himself in the forehead. "Duh, sorry. Cassie, this is my sister, Megan. Megan, Cassie. The woman I've told you about."

Megan gave Cassie a warm smile. Shame rushed all the way down to Cassie's toes. Relief made her smile back. They shook hands. Megan sat down while Ethan went for the drinks.

"It's so nice to finally get to meet you," Megan said while taking off her coat.

"You too. I've heard a lot about you."

"Well, you can only believe half of it. My brother likes to exaggerate."

Cassie smiled.

"You know, he talks about nothing else but you." She pulled her fingers through her hair to smooth out any strays lifted by the wind. "Seems you've got his attention, and believe me, that takes some doing."

Cassie's hand absently touched her warming face.

"Course, he loves the fact that you're a writer. He's been an avid reader since he learned to read. And now you're writing mysteries, his favorite."

Cassie perked up. He hadn't told her that. Come to think of it, he never really said what he liked to read.

"You look surprised. Didn't you know he was an avid murder mystery fan?"

Cassie smiled and shook her head. "I guess I didn't." She picked up her mocha and took a sip.

"Well, I'm surprised. We always teased him when he was home and said if he had a bent toward evil, he would certainly know how to murder someone."

Cassie choked.

"Oh, my, are you all right?" Megan looked on in horror.

The mocha went down her windpipe. She couldn't breathe. With great effort, she tried to inhale, but her breath struggled to break free. A Darth Vader–type sound came out in shallow breaths, gaining the attention of everyone in the coffee shop.

"Can I do something?"

Ethan rushed to Cassie's side and hit her on the back a few times. *For crying out loud, it isn't food,* Cassie wanted to say. Her back stung, and she couldn't breathe. Everyone was staring at her, and Ethan could be a murderer.

She held up her hand. "I'll be fine," she barely managed without a respirator. "I've got to go." She grabbed her purse, flashed an apologetic look toward Megan, and headed for home.

All the way home, she cried. She'd messed up her first meeting with Ethan's sister. Not only that, but Ethan loved murder mysteries. Why hadn't he told her that? She felt bone weary. Weary of all the questions. Weary from the fear. Weary from working so hard on her mystery.

Weary of the man in the gold Camry who followed her once again.

Chapter 9

Shaking fingers clutched the steering wheel in a death grip. Country meadows passed in a blur as Cassie pushed forward. On she drove through the cold, dark night. Fear told her not to look, but she was tired of running. With energies spent, she dared to look back. No lights. No cars. Only darkness. When had she lost him? Was she hallucinating? What if he was waiting at her house? He seemed to know her every move.

She called Nell from her cell phone.

"Hello?"

"Nell? Cassie. Would Ralph mind if you spent the night with me? I don't want to be alone. I'm so scared."

"Whoa, Cassie, slow down. What's wrong?"

"Someone is following me. Ethan reads murder mysteries. Another girl was killed. She owned a used bookstore." Cassie was near hysteria.

"Cassie, come to our house."

"I can't. I have to take care of Sparky."

"I'll be there in ten minutes."

"Thanks, Nell."

Cassie tried to stop her crying. Told herself things would

be all right. The truth would come out eventually. For now, she needed to push aside her fears and trust God.

Not wanting to be alone at home, Cassie drove around awhile to give Nell time to get there. When Cassie finally pulled into the drive, Nell sat waiting in her car.

Cassie thanked the Lord for her friend. When they exited their cars, Nell ran up to Cassie and hugged her.

"It's gonna be all right."

"Thank you." They gathered their things and went into the house. "Let me take care of Sparky, we can dress for bed, then I'll tell you everything." Cassie looked carefully around her yard before she chained Sparky at the back door. She filled Sparky's food and water bowl, then went upstairs to put on her pajamas. By the time she had dressed, Sparky barked to come back in, and Nell waited on the couch with a glass of pop in hand.

"Hope you don't mind I helped myself."

"You're family. You can help yourself anytime." Cassie smiled and settled in a chair with her own glass of iced tea. She took a deep breath like it was her first breath of the evening.

Just when they had a chance to talk, the phone rang.

"Hello?"

"Cassie, are you all right?"

"Hi, Ethan." She looked at Nell, who glanced back at her with a look of apprehension. "I'm fine. I'm so sorry I had to leave your sister in such a hurry."

"Don't worry about it. We were just concerned you were okay. You can meet with Megan another time."

"Thanks."

"Cassie, uh, can we go out Saturday night? I'd really like to talk with you."

"Ethan, I'm sorry, but I have to finish my story, and, uh, well, I need some time." Cassie wanted to stop those words. She didn't want to be away from Ethan, but at the same time, she feared him. She felt so confused.

"Oh." He waited a moment. "Guess I've come on a little too fast. Sorry."

"No, it's not that, I—"

"No problem. I understand. Hey, I'll talk to you later."

"Ethan—"

"Bye, Cassie."

The dial tone whined in her ear. Cassie looked over at Nell. "Are you okay?"

Cassie pulled her hands to her face and cried the few tears she had left. Nell rushed over, offering some tissues.

Several wads of tissue later, Nell got up and walked back to the couch. Over the next couple hours, Cassie explained everything that had been happening. The two of them discussed what it could all mean and different options for Cassie. Though they couldn't come up with an answer for the situation, the discussion and prayer made Cassie feel much better.

"I don't know what I'd do without you, Nell."

"Cassie, I know you're frustrated right now, but why don't you let Aaron check up on you from time to time?"

"No! He is making me crazy."

Nell held up her hand. "Okay, okay. Just a suggestion."

"Sorry, guess I'm a little edgy."

They gathered their glasses, put them away, and went to their rooms. "See you in the morning, Nell."

Nell patted Cassie's arm. "Get some sleep and don't worry. The Lord will see you through."

"I know. He always does."

If only she knew how it would all end.

With the workshop over, Cassie packed her things. She had been so busy putting the finishing touches on her story, she had barely noticed the passing of three weeks. No murders. No sign of the gold Camry. Maybe she could have a normal life again.

A normal, lonely life.

She and Ethan hadn't talked since that night on the phone. He avoided her when she went into the bookstore. Had she made a dreadful mistake? Did she give up the only man she had ever truly loved?

Cassie thought she had seen him in traffic a couple of times, but decided it was her imagination.

She could hardly believe she had only one more workshop before Christmas. She had grown accustomed to the weekly gatherings, though it took great effort to enter the bookstore. She missed Ethan and longed to be with him. She hadn't meant to sever the relationship completely, but evidently he wanted things that way.

She lifted her bags and started out the door.

"Hi, Cassie."

A flutter rippled through her. She turned around. "Ethan, hi."

"You doing okay?"

"Yeah. How about you?"

He shrugged. An awkward silence stretched between them. She shifted her bag on her shoulder.

"Well, you've got a load there. Just wanted to say hi."

Her heart screamed for him not to leave. She wanted to drop everything and feel him hold her, kiss her, say everything would be all right. Instead, she smiled weakly, turned, and walked out the door into a dark, lonely night.

While driving home, she thought she saw Ethan's car again. But he wouldn't be out this far in the country. The car turned off. She seemed to be imagining she could see him everywhere.

Once inside her garage, she carried her things in, greeted Sparky, and prepared for bed. She had made a mess of things, and she knew it. "Thanks a lot, Aaron." She threw her clothes on the bed in a huff and plopped down. Grabbing her pillow, she curled it in a ball and clutched it to her stomach. "Oh, God, help me to forget Ethan. I love him so much. Please, help me let him go."

Sparky sat at her feet, looking up at her. She reached down and patted his head. "Okay, okay, I'll let you out."

Cassie finished putting on her nightclothes and headed down the stairs with Sparky. She turned on the back porch light, tied Sparky to a chain, and let him out.

Deciding to go to bed, Cassie walked over to the front window and flipped the blinds closed, but not before she noticed something shiny across the street. She quickly turned out the lights and peeked out the side of the curtain.

"Ethan."

She didn't know whether to be happy or sad. Why was he parked outside of her house?

Sparky barked, and Cassie quickly let him in. She went back to the front window. Ethan was gone. How odd. Why would he be watching her house? Chills coursed through her. "No, I won't go there."

Maybe she would call Aaron. She wasn't sure that was a good idea. Yet, she couldn't deny the nerves jumping around in her stomach.

What if Ethan was the killer? Could she betray him to the police? She loved him. Yet she couldn't let a killer go free. Ethan a killer? It wasn't possible. Was it?

She didn't know anything anymore. An uneasy feeling ran through her like a slow poison. She and Sparky climbed the stairs.

Cassie picked up the phone beside her bed and punched in a number. "Aaron, this is Cassie."

He sounded sleepy. She glanced at the clock. Eleven.

"Yeah, what's up?"

"I'm sorry. I woke you, didn't I?"

"Not a problem. Just got in bed. I worked overtime."

"I'm sorry. I'll call you tomorrow."

"No, it's okay, Cassie. What's going on?"

She explained to him about Ethan following her and how she had quit seeing him. Though she wasn't convinced he was the murderer, she admitted to Aaron she was frightened by everything.

Aaron talked to her and let her know he would keep an eye on things for her, not to worry. They didn't have a suspect on the case yet, but they had some leads. She had been allowed to follow his investigation only so far. That's all he could tell her.

She felt better having talked to him. After they hung up, she rose from her bed and walked over to the bedroom window to see if anyone was there. No one. She took a deep breath, went over, and knelt by her bed. Once she had finished her prayers, Bible reading, and journaling, Cassie switched off the light. Totally exhausted, she surrendered to a deep sleep. When the car door sounded down the road, she barely heard it.

The light scuffling of footsteps up her front walk didn't alarm her, they merely mingled with her dreams. . . .

Chapter 10

I've waited long enough," the voice whispered dark and low into the night. "Tonight is the night. No one can save her this time. The papers won't lie to me. I'll show them. I'll show all of them."

The bony fingers reached for the bridal bouquet. Dried pieces loosened and scattered on the seat and floorboard.

When the killer stepped from the car onto the street, the door squeaked. An eerie ballad hummed through the trees on the bitter winds. An icy palm rubbed along the cold steel of the gun shoved in a right-side pocket. Skillful fingers maneuvered the front door lock. No bolt. It opened easily.

Evil eyes adjusted to the darkness, then glanced at the stairs. The killer had barely slipped into the house when a noise sounded outside.

A look out the curtain revealed someone walking toward the house. Shadows hid the identity.

Holding onto the gun, the killer dashed to the back door. The bouquet dropped to the floor, but there was no time to pick it up. The front door clicked open.

"I know you're in here. It's over. You might as well show yourself." The man's words were whispered. The killer frantically tried to place them.

"Come out and show yourself, you coward." The man seemed to stumble. Something crashed to the floor.

Sudden silence. Then a thump sounded upstairs. She was coming down.

⁂

Cassie woke with a start. She looked over at Sparky, who snored from his rug. "A lot of help you are," she whispered through the darkness. Another sound. This time like something breaking. Someone was definitely in her house.

Her mind scattered over options of what to do. She reached for the phone. No dial tone. She grabbed her cell phone. The batteries were dead. She got up, pulled on her robe, and reached for the baseball bat, all the while praying her softball days would see her through to safety.

She made her way down the stairs despite the fear trying to hold her back. She stopped midway and took a deep breath. The breath caught in her throat. A familiar scent wafted up the stairs, causing fear to crawl across her skin. Ethan's cologne. He was in her house. The man she loved was going to kill her. *Oh, God, please help me.*

Cassie reached the end of the stairs and spotted him. He stood in the living room with his back to her. Her white-knuckled fingers clutched the bat. She stepped away from the stairs into the living room. Her arms lifted in slow motion, shaking with every inch upward. Each step drew her closer, closer to the man she loved. A cough stuck in her throat; she would not allow it passage. Arms extended overhead, she stopped a breath away from him. Just as she started to swing, before she could whack him a good one, her motion stopped midair.

She hiccupped.

He swung around and looked at her with wild eyes; his right hand held a dried bouquet. Cassie backed away. "Go back upstairs." Though the words were whispered, he said them as a command.

"No, I won't. If you're going to kill me, you may as well do it down here." Her mouth quivered. *Father, am I to die like this?*

His mouth opened, his eyes widened. "Cassie, what are you saying?" He stepped closer to her.

"Stay away from me!" She took two steps back. "I trusted you!" Tears streamed down her face. Still holding onto the bat, she jerked the back of her fist across her cheek, annoyed with the evidence of weakness.

He looked at her, then at the flowers in his hand. He threw them on the couch. "It's not what you think." He eased closer.

"No! Stay away from me!" She edged between him and the front door.

"How could you think I would hurt you?" The words pleaded for her trust.

"What are you doing here, sneaking around in my house, if not to hurt me?" She glared at the dried bouquet. "And what about that?"

Someone stepped through the front door. Cassie and Ethan both turned to look. Mara Gray lifted a book. "I wanted to return this, and I heard a commotion. . . ." She stopped when she looked at them.

Cassie backed away to the side so she could keep both of them in view. "Why would you return the book this late, Mara?"

Just then a low guttural growl sounded behind Mara, seeming to catch her off guard. They turned to see Sparky crouching low. His mouth quivered into a snarl, revealing large teeth with a few missing.

During the distraction, Mara stepped away from Sparky. Ethan tried to reach Cassie, and she scooted sideways to maintain her distance.

In the moment of confusion, a gun dropped to the floor in front of Cassie. In one quick swoop, she dropped the bat, grabbed the gun, and clutched it with all her might. Mara and Ethan now stood side by side. Still growling, Sparky stood near Cassie with the stance of a dog on a foxhunt.

Who had dropped the gun?

"Cassie, let me help you." Mara reached out to Cassie, but she backed away. "Give me the gun, and I'll hold it on him while you call the police." Mara's left eye twitched.

Though Cassie didn't trust Ethan, something troubled her about Mara too. Cassie squeezed the gun tight. Her fingers cramped. Her pulse throbbed against the steel.

"Don't listen to her, Cassie. Trust me. Give me the phone, I'll call the police."

"The phone is dead." Her words implied he already knew that. "Where's your cell phone, Ethan?"

"In the car," he said with a thread of defeat.

Cassie couldn't hold them like that all night. She needed to call the police but didn't have a phone. Whom could she trust? Her heart told her God was the Author of Truth. He would guide her. She prayed for direction and added it might be helpful if God would send the answer ASAP.

They stood there for some time while Mara and Ethan each tried to plead their case. Sparky snarled from behind Cassie, then seemed to lose interest and walked over to Ethan, inviting a good scratching.

Knowing Sparky didn't take to people easily, his gesture was exactly the sign she needed. It was as though the old spaniel gave her the freedom to trust what her heart had been saying all along. Ethan was not a man capable of murder. In that moment, Cassie made her decision. "Ethan, you hold the gun, I'll get your cell phone. Is it in the front seat?"

It seemed to take a minute for the impact of her words to hit him. He came over cautiously and took the gun from her hands. She ran out to the car and called the police.

When Cassie stepped back into the house, Mara's words hissed at her. "You can't escape me, Jennifer." Her eyes were clouded and distant. She glanced at Ethan, then back to Cassie. "I knew you wouldn't stay with Randy long."

"Mara, I'm Cassie. What are you talking about?"

"I'm talking about Randy. My fiancé. The one who left me at the altar with you on our wedding day. You. My best friend and maid of honor." Mara's mouth twisted into an evil grin. "What a joke." Her eyes sparked with revenge. "I trusted you. But you lied. Just like the newspapers. I knew you weren't dead. How did you escape before?" Her eye twitched again.

"Look, Mara, it's a mistake. This isn't Jennifer. This is Cassie, the author, remember? You attend her workshops." Ethan tried to make her understand.

"I remember. When did you learn to write, Jennifer? I must say that was a clever cover-up. Just like the other three times you tried to throw me off. Staying down the road from here, then on the south side, then the north. You kept me going. I thought I left you dead. You won't escape this time." Mara sneered and tipped her head as she glared at Cassie.

Stepping closer to Ethan, Cassie squeezed his arm. "I'm so sorry I ever doubted you."

Ethan's gaze never turned from Mara's face. Sweat trickled down the side of his face as they waited for the police. The tension made Cassie nauseous.

All of a sudden, Sparky barked, setting off their frayed nerves. Mara pounced on the opportunity. She jumped at Ethan and wrestled for the gun. Sparky joined the struggle. Cassie looked on in horror. The three were a ball of confusion, a tangled mass of arms, legs, and paws. Cassie screamed just as the gun went off.

For the next moment, Cassie stood trembling. Fear pinned her in place. She dared not breathe, not knowing who would surface. Finally pulling free, Ethan turned to face her, and Sparky strutted over with the confidence of a watchdog in his prime.

Mara lay silent in a pool of blood.

At that moment, the front door swung open, and in rushed Aaron and several policemen. Aaron looked at Ethan, who was still holding the gun. "Put it down, Ethan. The game's over."

Ethan looked at him, then at the gun in his own hand, and placed it on the floor.

Aaron walked over to him with handcuffs. "You're under arrest. You have the right to remain silent. Anything you say can and will be used against you in a court of law—"

"No! He didn't do it!"

"Sorry, Cassie, we have to take him in. You need to come in too. We'll need your statement."

"I'll get you out, Ethan. I promise."

Another policeman bent down beside Mara. He checked her pulse. "She's still alive."

Someone radioed for an ambulance. Cassie ran up the stairs to change clothes. When she came down, the EMS had arrived and were taking Mara out the door on a stretcher. Aaron and Ethan had already gone. Cassie ran to the garage, jumped in her car, and made her way to the police station.

Once Ethan pulled from his pocket the tape recording of Mara's admission to the murders, his name was cleared. Aaron, another officer, Ethan, and Cassie sat around a stark table. The odor of cheap, bitter coffee drifted from the back corner of the room. "Looks as though Mara's distorted upbringing finally caught up with her," Aaron said. "When her fiancé left her at the altar, she snapped. It happens sometimes." Aaron turned to Ethan. "I'm sorry, Ethan. We had the suspects narrowed down to you and Mara. Frankly, when I saw you with the gun, I thought we had the answer."

"I understand. I'm just glad you caught the murderer and Cassie's safe." He reached over and squeezed her hand.

She corrected him. "Actually, Sparky nabbed the murderer."

Ethan smiled. "I guess he did at that."

"I have no clue what made him bark when he did. If he heard Aaron's car pull up, it was an act of God. Sparky hasn't heard a thing in years."

They all laughed.

Aaron glanced at his watch. "Wow, it's four o'clock. Sorry about the early morning hour, but you're free to go."

Cassie drove Ethan back to her house to get his car.

"You get some rest," he said before he closed his car door.

"You too."

"Dinner tomorrow night, my house, okay?"

"Okay."

"Come to my house by six-thirty; we'll plan dinner for seven."

"Sounds good. See you then."

"Cassie?"

"Yes."

"Thanks for giving me another chance."

Chapter 11

The December winds howled as Cassie made her way up Ethan's porch. She snuggled into her jacket and rang the doorbell. Ethan opened the door.

"Hi, Cassie. Come on in."

Cassie followed him. "You know, I don't like that cologne as much as I used to." She explained how she associated it with her fear of him being involved in the murders.

He raised his brows. "Okay, you'll have to come with me and pick something else out."

She nodded and took a deep whiff. "Um, dinner sure smells good."

Ethan helped her off with her coat and hung it in his hall closet. "Steaks, potatoes, carrots, you know, just like Mom used to make."

Cassie laughed. "Not only the brilliant owner of a bookstore but a good cook too. What a catch!" She flashed him a smile.

"In case you haven't noticed, I'm trying to impress."

"It's working. Can I help you in the kitchen?"

He shook his head. "Nope. It's all under control. How about some spiced cider?"

"Great."

Ethan fixed the hot drinks, then joined Cassie in the living room and set the steaming mugs on coasters on the coffee table. "We've got a few minutes before dinner. I know you've got some questions, so shoot."

Cassie groaned. "Did you have to say that?"

"Sorry."

"Okay, what about the missing wedding tape? Doesn't it seem strange that you would have a bird that talks in wedding phrases, yet when I asked about the tape, you said you threw it out?"

Ethan laughed. "I guess it does sound suspicious, but cross my heart, that's the honest truth."

"Okay, and the dried flowers you said belonged to your sister?"

He nodded.

Cassie shook her head. "Boy, Aaron's got a hard job."

"Yeah, he does."

"What about the church thing?"

A shadow crossed his face. "You got me there. I lied, plain and simple. I was afraid if I told you I didn't attend church, you wouldn't see me anymore, and I wanted to get to know you. You seemed to sparkle from the inside out, and it made me long for that kind of a relationship with God."

"So are you attending somewhere now?"

"I'd rather save this discussion for later tonight." He answered her questioning look. "You'll have to trust me on this one."

"Great, here we go again."

He laughed.

Cassie took a sip of her cider. "This is a little lukewarm. I'll just pop it in the microwave," she said as she rose and headed for the kitchen.

"Here, let me do it," he insisted.

"I'm not helpless, Ethan. I'm happy to do it." They walked into the kitchen, and Cassie stopped short when she looked at the dining-room table. It was set for eight.

Ethan followed her gaze. "Now, see, you're spoiling the surprise."

"What surprise? Who's joining us?"

Before Ethan could respond, the doorbell rang. "Say a prayer."

"Ethan, what is going on?" She watched as he paused at the front door, took a deep breath, and opened it.

A man, a woman holding a baby, and two little girls stood at the door, along with two pieces of luggage. They stepped inside with their belongings.

"Kyle!" The excitement in Ethan's voice stopped Cassie in place.

Once the family entered, the two men embraced. Their faces dampened with tears. "I've missed you, Brother," Kyle said.

"I've missed you."

When they finally pulled apart, Kyle laughed. "I'm forgetting myself here. Ethan, this is my wife, Amber, and our three girls, Macy, Micah, and six-week-old Zoe Grace."

Cassie guessed Macy to be a little over three years and Micah not quite two. Both were blond and adorable. Cassie tried to blink away threatening tears.

Ethan hugged Amber. He scrunched down and spoke softly to the girls. Cassie watched him. How could she have thought him to be a killer?

Before Ethan could introduce Cassie, the doorbell rang again. Aaron entered with Ethan's sister, Megan.

After everyone had been introduced, coats were put away, and the luggage was placed in a spare bedroom for Kyle's family visit. Cassie then helped Ethan in the kitchen. "What a great idea to set Aaron and Megan up!" She smiled and patted his arm. "You matchmaker, you!"

He shrugged. "Aaron ran into Megan and me when we were at the store. I could see the sparks fly."

"I'm so happy for you and Kyle, Ethan."

His eyes sparkled. "Yeah, me too." He squeezed her tight, then pulled back to look at her. "You know your pastor made this possible."

"My pastor?"

"Yeah. I went to him." He sighed. "I've got some explaining to do."

She folded her arms in front of her and tapped her foot against the floor. "I'm waiting."

"I told you, watching your relationship with God showed me what's been missing in my life. I decided to talk to your pastor. I met with him several times. He answered my questions and finally led me in a prayer of repentance." His eyes glistened with tears.

Cassie choked back the knot in her throat.

"After that, he offered to help me get things straightened out with Kyle. My sister gave me his number, and I pushed away my fear and called him. To my astonishment, he said they wanted to see me." He smiled. "Well, you know the rest."

"Oh, Ethan, God is so faithful. I'm really happy for you."

"God used you to make it happen," he whispered into her ear, causing her skin to tingle.

He looked into her eyes. His mouth tenderly claimed hers, strong emotion mingling between them.

"I love you, Cassie."

"I love you."

Together they carried the food into the dining room. The next few hours found the group getting acquainted on a new level with the promise of lasting friendships.

Cassie helped Amber get the girls situated in the bedroom Ethan had prepared for them upstairs. With Kyle's family living only two hours away, Cassie hoped they all could keep in touch on a regular basis now that things were settled between the brothers. Once the girls were tucked in bed, Cassie and Amber went back downstairs to join the others. Ethan and Kyle shared stories of their home life. They also talked of the recent murders and all that had happened.

"Hey, I just thought of something," Cassie said, her eyes wide with worry.

Everyone looked at her.

"There's still the matter of the guy in the gold Camry." Apprehension tinged the tip of her nerves.

"George." Aaron whispered the name almost under his breath.

"What, Aaron?" Cassie searched his face.

He coughed and shifted in his seat. "Um, it was George. One of the guys at the station. I asked him to look after you since you wouldn't let me."

Everyone relaxed and smiled. Cassie threw a pillow at him. "You dope! He nearly scared me out of my wits."

Aaron caught the pillow and laughed. "Sorry, Cassie. A guy's gotta do what a guy's gotta do."

They all joked for a bit, then the room grew quiet.

"Have you heard how Mara is doing?" Cassie asked Aaron.

"She's doing fine. It will take her a few weeks to recover from the bullet wound. They'll do some psychological testing to see if she's competent to stand trial, then go from there."

Silence stretched between them. Everyone looked from Ethan to Cassie.

"What's going on?" Cassie asked.

"Now?" Ethan looked around the room.

They all nodded and grinned.

He cleared his throat and knelt down on the floor in front of Cassie. She couldn't imagine what he was doing. It made her nervous being the center of attention. She hiccupped.

He pulled out a black velvet box. She gasped. When he opened it, a beautiful diamond glistened from the center. "Cassie Jordan, will you marry me?"

"You meally rean it?"

Ethan threw his head back and laughed. "Yes, I meally rean it!"

She squealed and wrapped her arms around him. Someone called out, "Is that a yes?"

Cassie lifted her face from Ethan's shoulder. "Yes!"

The room filled with cheering and applause. The group spent the next hour teasing the newly engaged couple, and the women talked of wedding plans. Cassie pointed out to Megan she did not want dried flowers at her wedding.

When it was time to go, Cassie pulled on her coat and said good-bye to everyone.

"Let me drive you home," Ethan suggested.

"No, don't leave your brother. You've just gotten reacquainted. I'll be fine."

"Do you like the ring?"

"It's beautiful, but I like the ring bearer better."

He held her close. His warm breath brushed against her ear. "I love you so much, Cassie Jordan. I can't wait to claim you as my bride."

She looked up at him, wishing with all her heart that the moment could last forever.

He threw her a wicked smile. " 'Til death do us part, Babe."

Cassie tapped him playfully on the shoulder. Wrapped in his warm embrace, she murmured, "God knows how to write a happy ending, don't you agree?" She pulled away to look at him.

His eyes penetrated her heart. "I do, Cassie Jordan. I do."

DIANN HUNT

Diann Hunt resides in Indiana with her husband. They have two grown children, three grandchildren, and one on the way! Feeling God has called her to the ministry of writing, Diann shares stories of lives changed and strengthened by faith in a loving God.

Epilogue

I hate to send you in alone, Rebecca, but this will insure we maintain the element of surprise." Drake Axelrod parked his rented economy car between two minivans in the middle of the bookstore parking lot. From this vantage point, he could see all those who left or entered the Reader's Refuge. "Since the Sleuth Sisters have yet to meet you, your presence won't give me away." He checked his watch—10:00 A.M. on the dot.

Drake grabbed Rebecca's hand. "Ethan Hamil said he'd be watching for you by the writer's reference section. He'll give you a signal to come get me when all the women are in position for their book signing and the coast is clear. They'll pull my books out and set them on a nearby table once I enter." He scratched his head. "I've never seen anyone so hyped as Ethan. He put a lot of work into pulling this surprise together. Why, you would think he'd just planned the perfect mystery!" Drake glanced at the sky. "And by the looks of those gathering clouds, I'd say Mr. Hamil even persuaded the weather to cooperate."

A playful grin touched Rebecca's lips.

His fingers trailed the cheek of his former editor and new

fiancée. "You're a good sport," he said with a smile. "And a beautiful one too."

Rebecca's cheeks fanned a delicate pink. She looked down at her lap and pushed her glasses snug against her face. For a moment, she paused, then took a deep breath before turning to him. "Well, wish me luck."

Drake squeezed the hand of the woman he loved before she stepped from the car and walked across the lot. He found it hard to believe he had corresponded with her for so many years without having met her face-to-face. The day his gaze lit upon Rebecca Rygamen was his lucky day, indeed. They'd been practically inseparable ever since.

He adjusted his bifocals and watched her disappear through the doors. Some might describe her as rather plain, but he found her intriguing. A milky complexion, light brown hair, and graceful stature all added to her mystique. Still, he had to admit it was the depth in her dark eyes that melted his heart.

He absently rubbed his goatee. Though her shy nature caused some to view her as a bit standoffish, he knew otherwise. She was a woman of complexities, with twists and turns about her personality that always surprised and pleased him. A woman of mystery and determination. She'd lost sixty pounds in the year before they met. He admired that kind of discipline. No doubt about it, the perfect heroine had stepped from the pages of his novels and slipped into his heart. His pulse skipped with the mere thought of her. He could hardly wait to introduce her to the Sleuth Sisters.

The Sleuth Sisters.

He sat up straighter in his seat and focused his attention on the window. He didn't know how long his thoughts had lingered on Rebecca, but he'd better quit daydreaming or he'd ruin the surprise.

As if on cue, Rebecca exited the bookstore doors, nodding toward him. He grabbed his keys and got out of the car to join her. She motioned him to the side. "Walk over here, so they can't see us," she whispered.

Though calm by nature, the excitement of a little intrigue always thrilled him. He grabbed both of Rebecca's hands and held them. "Did you see the ladies?"

She smiled. "Yes, I did. They don't suspect a thing."

"How ever did Mr. Hamil manage to keep this from Cassie?"

"He's a clever one, and hyped, just as you said. It seems he had a special bookstore ad announcing the Sleuth Sisters placed in a newspaper just for her. She didn't see the ad that was distributed to the public, announcing a famous guest mystery author." Rebecca lifted her chin as she said the words, making Drake feel she was proud to be with him.

They stood just outside the door's entrance. A distant rumble caused them both to look up. "Perfect," Drake said, feeling as though he'd just downed a pot of coffee. "Simply perfect." He looked at Rebecca and pulled her arm through his. "You ready?"

Her eyes twinkled. She adjusted her glasses and smiled. "Ready."

Together they pushed through the doors. He had barely caught a glimpse of the mystery writers before Raine Rowoski spotted them and squealed, "Professor Axelrod!"

At that, the other three authors looked up and ran to greet him. In one swoop, they descended upon him like adoring fans. Hugs, greetings, and a good deal of chatter followed. When they stopped to catch their breath, Drake turned to Rebecca. "Ladies, I would like to introduce you to my fiancée, Rebecca Rygamen."

As the words sank in, their eyes opened wide, and smiles spread across their faces.

"You're the editor—" Before Tina Villarreal could finish, Rebecca nodded.

Hugs and congratulations were cut short when lightning sliced through the skies, causing the bookstore lights to flicker.

Drake looked over to see Cassie send a worried look to her husband. He shook his head as if there were no need for alarm. Then Ethan glanced at the group. "Looks like the impending storm hasn't discouraged your fans." He turned and pointed toward the chairs where smiling customers sat patiently waiting for the authors to tell their stories. He started to walk away.

"Wait a minute, you," Cassie said, playfully poking Ethan in the side.

"Ouch!"

"How did you pull this off without me knowing?"

"Well, now, that's my little secret!" He laughed and turned, leaving her speechless.

The others laughed as they walked toward their chairs.

"Don't worry, Cassie, we'll tell you all about it later," Drake encouraged.

The Sleuth Sisters settled at the table with their mystery books fanned out in front of them. Drake and Rebecca seated themselves in front of an ample display of his book, *The Mennonite Murders*.

Cassie gave the introductions, followed by each author sharing his or her writing journey and a little about her current book. A question-and-answer period followed. Afterward, the group mingled, helping themselves to coffee and cookies, purchasing books, and obtaining autographs.

Once the crowd disbursed, the band of writers pulled their chairs out of the way, grabbed some coffee and cookies, and settled in for a nice chat.

"We'd better fill Professor Axelrod in on what's been happening with us," Cassie said once she was settled into her seat. "Raine, I never had a chance to ask you what happened to your cousin, Drew."

Raine sighed. "Drew was charged with planning the burglaries and museum heist. After further investigation, the FBI turned up incriminating evidence, and he was found guilty on several counts regarding theft and smuggling."

"I'm sorry," Cassie said.

"Thanks. I'm just praying that while he's in prison, Drew will find the Lord. According to testimonies I've heard, others have."

Cassie and the group nodded.

"Did I tell you my uncle's attorney was also sentenced for conspiracy?" Raine asked, after taking a sip of coffee. "It was quite a shock."

"Oh, no!" Cassie shook her head. "What a mixed-up world."

"I'm praying for him as well—but enough of this," Raine said with a wave of her hand. She brightened considerably. "So, don't you all just love married life?"

The Sleuth Sisters looked at each other, broad smiles on their faces. Beside them, their husbands nodded.

"Yeah? Me too," Raine said with a laugh.

"Were you surprised to see me in this condition, Professor?" Tina asked. A flush crept up her cheeks.

The other women smiled.

"Very." Drake looked at Tina and thought pregnant women really did have a special glow. He made a mental note to put such a character in a future mystery.

"You look adorable, Tina," Justine said. "Remind me, again. When is that sweet little baby due?"

Tina and Miguel beamed. "In one month, two weeks, and three days."

Justine gasped. "Oh, Girl, I can't believe the time has gone by so fast. Don't get yourself too excited here. We don't want to be birthin' any babies at our book signing." A smile lit her face, making her look the perfect Southern belle.

Everyone laughed.

"Ya'll must be thrilled," Justine said. Drake noticed she intertwined her fingers with her husband, Patrick, and wondered if they were working on a family as well.

Tina nodded. "We just have a few finishing touches to add to the nursery, and we'll be all set." She shifted in her chair, no doubt to get more comfortable.

Drake turned to Miguel. "Did I hear someone say you're a sheriff?"

Miguel brushed any possible cookie crumbs from his face and looked up. "Yes. When Tina agreed to marry me, I decided it was high time to settle down and give up my work with the FBI. I took on the maintenance for Tina's rental properties so we could spend as much time together as possible. I'm still working that job, but when the sheriff in Canal

Pass retired, Tina and I both thought I might be the town's best-suited candidate for the office. Never really expected to win the election, though." He shrugged and smiled. "I'm just as busy now as I ever was with the FBI, but at least I'm sticking close to home."

"That's quite a load. Sounds like you have a bigger honey-do list than most." Drake chuckled. He glanced at Rebecca, who sat quietly fidgeting with her hands on her lap. Conversing with people she hardly knew did not come easily for her. He wished he could help her feel more comfortable.

"So have you set a wedding date?" Cassie asked, directing her question to Rebecca.

She glanced up. "In September." Her words were soft. A gentle smile adorned her face. "We'll be sure to send you invitations."

"You'll have a fun, mysterious journey together, that's for sure," Cassie teased, emphasizing the word "mysterious."

The Sleuths ganged up on the professor for a round of good-natured ribbing. He noticed their banter had put Rebecca visibly at ease.

When the laughter died down, Drake was the first to speak. "Raine, tell us about you. How do you like your job with the *Gladney News?*"

"I love it!" Her brown eyes sparkled as she directed a teasing glance Lance's way. "And having a private eye for a husband sure does help when I'm hot on a story and need someone tailed, or any other time I require a detective on the case."

With a crooked grin, Lance took a place behind her chair and squeezed both her shoulders. "Glad to help, Honey. I'll always be there for you—to help you pick up any loose ends." She blushed but turned her head to give him a big smile, which he returned with a wink.

"I knew from the start you had that ace reporter instinct." Drake took a sip of coffee.

Everyone agreed.

Drake turned in his seat. "Justine and Patrick, what's going on with the two of you?"

Justine looked at her husband, a grin on her face. "We're heading out to the Philippines to visit Patrick's sister, Carma. She serves there as a missionary."

"When do you go?" Tina asked.

"In two months. We can hardly wait." She squeezed Patrick's hand.

"You'll have to e-mail us and tell us all about it when you return," Drake suggested.

Justine nodded and took a sip of coffee, then turned to Cassie. "Hey, Patrick should teach you his new specialty." A quirky smile played on her lips. "He's a pro at serving up white chocolate lattes." She winked at her husband, and Drake chuckled at the man's reddened face.

Cassie shrugged. "Yeah, well, we should join forces. You supply the coffee, we'll peddle the books."

"I think that's already been done," Raine said with a laugh.

Cassie joined in the laughter. She crossed her leg, and the toe of a purple sandal peeked out from beneath her grape-colored pantsuit. "I still can't believe the real mysteries we lived through while we were writing our whodunits!"

They turned pensive. "I never want to go through that again," Tina said before biting into a cookie.

"No, thanks. Ya'll can keep that kind of fun to yourselves next time. I'm still jumping every time I see a spider." Justine gave a mock shiver.

Raine looked at them. "Yeah, I plan on confining all my mysteries to paper in the future."

"Well, I want you ladies to know I'm proud of your accomplishments. You took up the mystery challenge and stuck with it through publication." Drake smiled, feeling like a proud teacher.

They each seemed to stretch a little taller in their seats.

Drake looked across the group. "Tell me then, are you considering a sequel?"

Without hesitation, Tina, Cassie, and Justine bellowed in unison, "No!" Their overwhelming response almost made him spill his coffee.

Each one turned to Raine, who said nothing. She merely brought her coffee cup to her lips and slowly covered a smile.

"Not another call to adventure," Cassie complained in a loud tone, as if someone had just told her to grab a bucket and scrub the bookstore floor. All three women looked at a smiling Raine. Tina, Justine, and Cassie winced and let out a unified groan. . . .

A Letter to Our Readers

Dear Readers:

In order that we might better contribute to your reading enjoyment, we would appreciate your taking a few minutes to respond to the following questions. When completed, please return to the following: Fiction Editor, Barbour Publishing, Inc., P.O. Box 719, Uhrichsville, OH 44683.

1. Did you enjoy reading *Novel Crimes?*
   - ❏ Very much—I would like to see more books like this.
   - ❏ Moderately—I would have enjoyed it more if _____
   _____
   _____

2. What influenced your decision to purchase this book?
   (Check those that apply.)
❏ Cover	❏ Back cover copy	❏ Title	❏ Price
❏ Friends	❏ Publicity	❏ Other	

3. Which story was your favorite?
   - ❏ *Love's Pros and Cons*
   - ❏ *Suspect of My Heart*
   - ❏ *Love's Greatest Peril*
   - ❏ *'Til Death Do Us Part*

4. Please check your age range:
❏ Under 18	❏ 18–24	❏ 25–34
❏ 35–45	❏ 46–55	❏ Over 55

5. How many hours per week do you read? _____

Name _____

Occupation _____

Address _____

City _____ State _____ Zip _____

E-mail _____